Snow

JONATHAN LOVEJOY

For every Belinda

There is a mountain in the distant West

That, sun-defying, in its deep ravines

Displays a cross of snow upon its side.

The Cross of Snow

Henry Wadsworth Longfellow

Part One

The time is now. The place—a typical suburban street in a typical town. There may be nothing to a single inch of this familiar space, nor the two legged creatures who inhabit it. They spend their lives in perpetual motion. Endless envy. Unquenchable ambition. And this day, this hour, is no different from any other.

Ms. Annabelle Freeman. My mother Anna, rushes home early from where she spends too many hours every day. A small, plush boutique of nonessentials. Her refuge from poverty. A thriving little fancy, left to her by an enterprising bolt of lightning she was once married to. That same husband whose body was pulled from the snowy wreckage of his luxury car—a few long years ago.

Anna's boots make muffled sounds as she hurries through the bitter cold, seeking shelter from her own thoughts. Not thoughts of her husband, who had died carelessly on these snow lined highways. Anna seeks protection from warm memories. Reflections of a world not covered in white ice every single day of every year.

Mother hurries over this last cold mile, remembering the comfort that waits for her. My sister Amanda, her youngest, whose face takes its plainness from the father, and its sweetness from the beautiful mother. Anna thinks fondly of her fifteen year old, who was a child of nine when these unnatural phenomena began.

She presses on through the glow, glimmering white from the streets. Shimmering gold from immaculate house windows and brass lamp fixtures. Each perfect lawn and property is a hidden, frozen echo of its former self. Not that it matters, because every blade of grass and long dead leaf has been buried since the first snowstorm hit—nearly seven years ago.

A cold wind whistles the powdered snow at her feet. The breeze is as icy as it ever needs to be, but tragically not a winter breeze, because the calendar in her fancy boutique has registered the 21st day of *July*.

This unnatural breath of winter chills her. Taking firm root. Nurtured by a thought as cold as the snow—

Belinda

School is out for the summer. My sister Amanda will be home, waiting for Mother like always. Maybe, I'll be home too.

Snow

Anna steps onto the brick walkway of her property, casting a final, fleeting glance at the brightest part of the gray sky. The powdery snow floats across the shoveled walkway, as she clumps icy boots toward the door that is as white as the frozen landscape around her.

"*Hi,*Mom."

"Hello, Mandy."

Her smiling face is a treasure. A thin, busty girl. Quiet. Plain by standards of beauty.

"Dinner smells wonderful. But you didn't have to."

"I knew you'd be tired today." She takes our mother's coat, and hangs it in the front closet.

"How was business?" A quick hug and kiss.

"I think everybody was at the grocery store today."

"I figured you might be home early."

"You were right this morning. I should have just stayed home."

"The storm won't be here until tomorrow," Amanda says. "I guess you had to try."

They tread lightly through the fog of tensions, trying not to think about so many things. Like the fact that today's trek through the snow had been pathetically stubborn. Or that not a single person had bothered to put a footprint anywhere near her little shop of trinkets. Or that walking through knee high snow has become second nature to everyone in the neighborhood, because cars are useless on these snow covered residential streets.

They tread quietly through affluence, trying not to think about the snow. But the two worlds they know, outside and in, are both oppressively cold, with winds whispering echoes of gray misery night and day. The outside world is poised on the edge of another blizzard. So too, is the world inside our palatial home.

"What should we eat with the ham?"

"Oh, I don't know," sighs Mother, looking around the kitchen. Her red blouse and long gray skirt hug her shapely figure. Waist small. Hips infinite. "Whatever you cook is fine, honey."

"How about candied yams?"

"Sounds great."

Anna Freeman watches her daughter glide timidly over to the cabinet. She thinks of how pretty my sister seems, with her ponytail and girlish bangs. Her bustiness is always covered in a colorful sweatshirt and a pair of jeans.

"They said the earthquakes were in a hundred new places this month," Amanda says.

"You're kidding."

"I saw it on the news last night. Some of them are even stronger than the one we just had. They think this'll be the worst blizzard we've ever seen here."

Anna glances out the window. The first few flurries are falling already.

"Did your sister come home today?"

"She's upstairs."

"Oh."

Sparks of a nervous glance are exchanged. Amanda clamps the opener onto the can, twisting it without thought.

"It's never as bad as we think it'll be," Anna says. "The first few days are always the worst."

"I think it's beautiful."

"I did too. For a while."

They suddenly hear the dreadful, soft calling of angry footsteps, thumping heavily down the stairs. Amanda watches our mother look around tensely.

"I'd better go get changed. I'll be back in a little bit, okay?"

She barely has time to respond, before Mother takes a hasty exit and a quick climb up the back staircase.

Amanda tends to her candied sweet potatoes, while a ravened brunette switches shapely hips into the kitchen.

A head of long black hair, draped around a face that is positively bewitching. Full lips, smooth skin and dark, exotic eyes that are always ready for a contemptuous glare. There is too much ravishing beauty and bosom in one package. Packed into a form fitting white sweater and tight, black jeans.

Seventeen?

I am.

"I thought I heard Mom come in."

Amanda opens the oven, pretending to check the ham.

"Well, where is she?"

Amanda isn't afraid of the brunette inferno—

My sister isn't afraid of me.

"Forget it then, you little *bitch*," I say, almost under my breath. "I know I heard her come in."

I start the hunt, knowing it begins at the bottom of the back stairs. The scent of fresh prey makes my instincts click. The killing awaits, somewhere on the second floor of our fine dwelling.

"She's probably up there already." I murmur the words, moving towards the staircase with purpose.

"Belinda?"

I turn. Burning a frustrated gaze.

"Please don't."

"I'm just gonna talk to her."

"But she's so tired today."

I look judgingly at my younger sister. Even at 15, she is dependable. Sensitive. Protecting. I glance at the rose pink sweatshirt hiding two white melons, and pitiful little bangs covering half of her pale little forehead.

she's so pathetic she makes me sick

The thought registers on my features. Smoldering, they are. But Amanda is jaded by the years of it, and stands her ground.

"She's doing her best, Belinda. And you're not making it any easier."

There is satisfaction. Because my little sister will never know I have just resisted the urge to rush across the kitchen and slap the taste from her mouth.

In bitterness I turn the corner. Clumping up the stairs in slow confidence.

"*M*om?"

There are no harbors. No rest for the weary. Mother looks at her own lovely, distressed features in her bathroom mirror.

"Mom?" A brief, discourteous knock. A fearless entrance.

"I'll be out in a minute, Honey."

She feels modest. Nervous. Like she is about to be interviewed. She is in her white bra and half slip, but may as well be trapped without a stitch of fabric over her shapely form.

Half slips or winter coats. It doesn't matter. I am always able to expose and whip the skin off her, without touching her at all.

Happy face

"Hello, Darling," Anna says, smiling brightly, enthusiastically stepping over to me.

"Hmm." A quick hug and kiss. A long glance at my mother's voluptuous figure. Her waist to hip curve is extraordinary.

"How was work?"

"It was slow today. I'm glad I came home early."

Her voice smiles fake happiness. *Fungalooga,* it's called. She is at the closet now, slipping into a comfortable navy dress.

"I can't believe you even bothered to go."

Deep breath

"Well you know how it is with places like ours," she says, moving towards the mirror. "One day I'm lucky if I see anybody. The next, I can't ring the register fast enough."

She stands at the mirror, about to struggle with the zipper. A bewitching reflection drifts up behind her. Slowly, deliberately I zip her dress all the way up. Staring at her eyes in the mirror.

"Thank you, Linda. You ready to go downstairs?"

Her eyes beg with such pleading, such exhausting cheerfulness, that my angry heart nearly softens.

Nearly.

"This is probably going to be the worse blizzard we've ever had—"

Mother takes a deep breath, and lets civility fade.

"You don't know that."

"Were you paying attention three days ago? Were you here when it happened?"

"Those earthquakes don't always tell how long the storms will—"

"Yes they *do,*" I insist, cringing. "God, you're so stubborn you make me—what are you going to do when the snow finally gets so high we can't open the damned doors without it pouring in on us. We'll be trapped in here for…"

"We've had to stay in for as long as a month before, Belinda, and things always turned out alright. We're still here aren't we?"

Anna suddenly cannot look at me. She is drawn to the window, gazing out at the new falling snow.

Snow

"It's happening more and more. There's hardly an inch of this whole country that hasn't seen at least one of these snowstorms."

"Right. So why keep talking about moving?"

"Because it hasn't happened everywhere. And in some places it hardly happens at all. Two *years* ago I told you we should have moved. We could have sold this icebox and built a house in the country or something."

"Do you know how much we'll lose if we sell this house now?"

"I'm not talking about now, Mom. Who do you think would buy it now, anyway? I'm talking about getting out of here. A lot of people around here are doing it. The Wards are getting out tonight—to the country. They say it hardly happens at all in some isolated places."

"And I'm sure it will stop here soon," Anna says. "This might even be the last one."

"The last one that we live to see."

Mother closes her eyes, breathing a sigh.

"Mom, I'm not staying here to be buried alive in a mountain of snow because you're too scared and stupid to face the *truth.*"

She gives me a sharp look. A mother's look.

"Veronica's family is leaving before it gets here. I already asked them if I could go."

"What did they say?"

"Mr. Ward said he would take me if I had your permission."

Anna nearly laughs. "Well, you can just tell him I said no."

My eyes glisten.

"His father in law's got a big farm out in…"

"I said *no.*"

"You stubborn…" I crave to finish the thought. "If we stay here were all *dead.*"

Mother turns away, staring out the window. My contempt powers my legs, and I nearly lunge towards her, grabbing her arm and spinning her around hard.

"What do you think you're—"

"Why are you being such a stubborn *bitch?*" I hiss the last word, digging my thumb hard into my mother's arm.

"Young lady, I am still your mother!"

"Then why don't you act like it and help us!"

"Take your hands off of me!"

Anna forgets herself briefly. Frustrated, she grabs my fingers, painfully unlocking my grip and shoving my hand away. My own strength, and the look in my eyes tells her this volatility needs quick diffusing.

What she's been dreading for months very nearly happened.

"Belinda honey, this house is all we have. Your fath—"

"Don't say it." I cover my ears and walk away. "You say that every single time. *Your father left us this beautiful house. Your father left us this beautiful house.*" My voice and mouth are twisted into mocking.

"And I'll keep saying it because this house is important to me. To us. God help me, if your father were here you would never…"

"But he isn't here, is he? If he was he wouldn't have been stupid enough to stay here this long."

"I'm not leaving my house," Anna says pitifully, looking out the window again.

"Is that all you care about? This house? You're just like all the rest of 'em aren't you? This snow *really* got you all where you lived, didn't it? I knew you cared more about this damned house, and this disgusting hoity neighborhood more than you *ever* cared about me."

Anna lets the comment slice through.

"Why won't you let me leave?"

"Because I *do* care about you. So many people have jumped up and moved to places they thought were safe, and were found dead in their cars. Rooves caving in, whole families starving to death. They would have been fine if they had just stayed where they were. Belinda, a lot of places that were really bad like ours haven't had a storm in months. And the earthquakes don't always mean that…"

"Mom, cut it out!" I cover my ears again and step away from her. "You *know* we're going to die this time, and you just want me here to die with you."

I regain my composure. Staring quietly.

"What about the trust?"

"Belinda…"

"Mom, I asked you a question."

"He left you that for when you're 21. You already know you're not getting it now. You only asked me that to irritate me."

A long, icy pause.

"They're leaving tonight. I *could* go with them."

"What's that supposed to mean?"

"I'm leaving here. One way or the other I'm leaving. Either you're going to give me my money, so that I can get the Hell out of here when this storm is over...or I'm leaving with Veronica tonight."

"You're *not* getting that money," she hisses, through clenched teeth. "And you'll leave with that Veronica *Ward* over my dead body."

The aroma of good cooking. Dinner calls. Reminding her of how hungry she is.

"Your sister has prepared us a lovely dinner..."

I roll my eyes. Bitterly.

"I think we should pay her the courtesy. We can talk about this later."

I watch my mother straighten herself up by the mirror. The forced cheerfulness reappears on her perfect features. Then she steps calmly, gracefully into the hallway. Cultured civility glides down the carpeted hall, then clip-clops softly down the wooden staircase.

Since the first snowstorm appeared six, nearly seven years ago, I have been trapped in a continuous dread. Somewhere in the world, the snow does not cover the ground in July. Somewhere, the skies are not gray every hour of the year, and earthquakes do not precede blizzards which last for weeks at a time.

Somewhere.

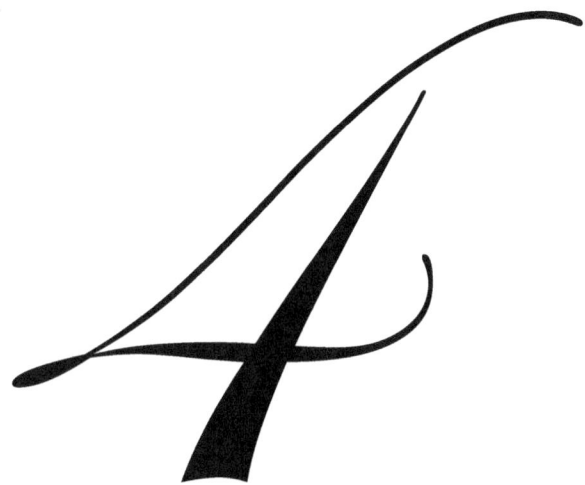

Alonely feast prepared and eaten. A company of two. An exhausted, grieving mother, and her youngest daughter.

"You got it from your grandmother."

"What's that?"

"Your cooking. Every since you were little you loved to cook."

Amanda smiles, while she washes their two plates, placing them in the dishwasher to dry. Mother watches her in quiet appreciation.

"That was the best meal you've ever made, Mandy. It was simple and elegant."

"It was only a ham," she says, clearly embarrassed.

"And it was delicious. Your sister missed a special dinner."

Amanda stops fiddling around the palatial kitchen, and stares out the window. The flakes fall from a gray twilight, illuminated by the glow of the outside lamps. The snow-covered homes rest in odd tranquility. A tragic calm of uneasy acceptance.

"I don't remember what it looks like."

"What's that?"

"The sky," Amanda says. "I can't remember the blue."

No answer. Anna can barely remember it herself.

"I wonder…"

A pause.

"I wonder what God's doing," Amanda says. "Is the world really ending? Are we being punished? Mom, sometimes I just don't know."

Her mother stands up, walking slowly over to her.

"Sometimes I think it's never going to end. That it's barely even the beginning. I feel like we're trapped, Mom. I'm starting to get really scared."

Mother hugs her, gently rubbing her back. Her daughter's breasts are a comfort. Two large, firm pillows of E cushion.

"Sweetheart, there's nothing to be afraid of. It's just a natural phenomenon. I've heard that it might even be an old weather pattern. A cycle, that happens every few thousand years or so. They're finding ancient records of snowfalls in desert climates all over the…"

"It's been happening for six years, Mom. And we haven't seen the ground since."

"Well…"

"Even Hawaii's been under it for seven months. I don't know if it had ever snowed there before. It's everywhere. Mom some places have been buried so deep that they can't—"

"Don't, Amanda. You just have to believe it'll get better."

"But it's getting worse. And the news said they think we're in for the worst storm we've ever had."

"They say that every time. They're just trying to keep us all afraid and glued to that television—you *know* that. I told you, it's just a weather cycle. Something the modern world hasn't seen before. When it goes away, it'll be nothing more than a memory. An interesting little story to tell your children."

"A lot of people are moving out of the cities and suburbs. It seems like it's worse wherever there's a lot of people. That's why I think it's—"

"It'll get better, Amanda," she interrupts. "By next summer, you and me and Belinda will be taking a long, leisurely walk in the park. A warm breeze will be whispering through the trees, and blowing gently through our hair. The air will smell of flowers and fresh cut grass. They'll be birds chirping, and children laughing and playing summer games. And all of the snow will be gone forever…I know it will."

They hold on, hugging each other tight. Ignoring the summer winter whistling outside the window.

"By tomorrow night," Amanda says, "we'll hardly be able to see the houses through the snowfall."

With that, resistance to the icy fear is lost. It envelops them both, until they are chilled to the bone.

Just then, a gust of brunette winter. Thumping down the staircase to the living room. It strikes Anna with revelation.

She's leaving me

She suddenly breaks from Amanda's hug, rushing into the living room.

"Belinda? Belinda where are you going?"

"I've already told them you said I could go. I told them you were too upset to talk about it, and that you wanted me to go before you changed your mind."

Her nervous daughter has two large travel bags, and is carrying her stylish white winter coat.

"I said you weren't leaving with Veronica Ward, to wherever the *Hell* it was you said they were going."

"A big farm, a few hundred miles west of here."

When Anna sees me putting on my coat, a fierce, possessive anger flares. She runs towards me, grabbing the coat with all her might.

"You will *not* leave this house!"

"You can't stop me! I'm sick of this prison! I'm not staying here to be buried alive!"

A violent struggle for the coat. Two beautiful, angry women—both clutching, clawing for dear life, a blood war for tomorrow's hope, and independence from fear and terror.

"Let go! Let go of me!" Teeth clenched. Yelling. Then a final, wrenching pull. Brunette hair flying, a white coat flailing from a mother's desperate grip.

"Nooo!"

A mother's pathetic, angry scream. She grabs the bags and stumbles towards the stairs.

"You come back with my things! I'm leaving here this minute!"

Another struggle ensues. But my own fire cannot overpower my mother's, and I have to let go. When I do, she falls to the floor at the foot of the stairs, her navy dress sliding up to her knees. She just lays there, panting, looking wild-eyed at me.

My anger is a cool, sudden fearfulness.

I have to run

I back up slowly, as if afraid. Mom scuffles to her feet, creeping towards me. Suddenly, I grab my coat from the floor and run towards the front door.

"No! Please, God, no!"

A deep, horrifying cry. Poor, plain-pretty Amanda just stands by, hand over her mouth, watching her mother stumble clumsily towards her sister.

I make it in plenty of time, pressing down the latch, pulling hard. But the deadbolt keeps the door from opening. Mother grabs me and I scream in defiance, and begin to hit her violently about the head and upper body.

"Stop it!" Amanda screams. "*Stop it!*"

Annabelle cowers, covering her face while I pummel her like a wild cat. She grabs my legs, clinging to me like a summer vine.

"Belindaaaa! Belinda please don't leave me! *Pleeeaase!"*

My mother's deep, breathy sobs are terrifying. I push at her face, clawing at her hands so she'll let go. My sister runs over, throwing her arms around me.

"Please don't leave us Belinda!" Amanda pleads. "Belinda don't leave! Please don't!"

I stand still. Teary eyed, chest heaving, while my mother and sister cling to my body. My legs and arms are pinned. They are that way for many seconds. Until Mother stands up and takes us both into her arms.

"I love you," Anna says, her face burdened by sorrow. "And I'll give you the money. I'll give you everything I own if you'll stay. Please swear to God that you'll stay with me."

"Please," Amanda says, tears streaming. "Please don't go."

We stand together. Two crying quietly. One with teary eyes of frustrated defeat.

"I can't do it anymore." My voice is low. Whispery.

"We'll do it together," Mother says, voice trembling. "The three of us will make it together. I promise we will. I swear it."

Outside, the winter winds began to whirl. Swirling the snow in warning to every creature.

"It's only snow," says Mother. "And isn't it the most beautiful thing you ever saw? Isn't the snow beautiful?"

Through tears, Amanda nods. I look on, in anguish. Understanding now that they are more terrified than I have ever been.

"Come to the window, Darlings."

Mother escorts her daughters through the living room to the huge bay window. The window frames for us a twilight of winter white. Pristine houses of icy comfort, with snow drifting down around them.

In renewed understanding, as big as the frozen world around me, I walk away from the house of fear, toward the house of pain. We survived another night of permanent winter, Mother, Sister and I, winds blown from Eden's first snowfall. Although the earthquakes had been the largest I remembered, the snow had blown with so much less fury than a storm, and more of a cold, violent dusting—of a landscape that was already coated in ice and white powder thick enough to kill the proudest ones among us.

"Gone away is the bluebird...here to stay is the newbird..." It plays over and over in my head from Ms. Parton's silken voice. Nature balances itself in beauty when it can. Over the years, the dirty mountains of white, the snowdrifts where we live have settled as a permanent part of us, until the dirt which once colored them has gone. As I walk two cold suburban blocks over, I notice that there only seems to fall whatever gathering of snow we seem to need—to cover our lost hope again in crystal white, and to reassure us that there is no need to want the sight of those black asphalt streets of old, or the beautiful green grasses we once knew. Nature balances itself in the cold. To cover our world with every unanswered prayer, and every broken dream we leave. This dream of freedom, I leave behind—back at the House of Fear.

Freeman, Annabelle. Or *Mother*, I'll think of her now. I've felt the shadows in her spirit grow, until they cannot inhabit the space, but must ebb and flow around her like the icy breeze on my white fur hood. The aura around her now, and not just inside her—is a state of perpetual fear. This is the Fear of Pain, which ultimately is the Fear of Death. Her level of helplessness has risen like the powdered snow on the ground, and I know now that as surely as I am a seventeen year old girl, I am a seventeen year old woman as well, who is now the brackets that hold this family together. Last night, as I watched the snowfall under our dead suburban lights, I saw my mother's dignity disperse as well, and coalesce like crushed diamond crystals at my feet.

*G*one are the colors of the mountains and the trees—the deserts, the canyons, the prairies, the seas…are hardly distinguished from one another with ease. At least, it seems that way to me. Aerial maps don't mean much anymore, when there's nothing to see but white on the real ground, with lines where rivers and highways struggle to live, with vast, spotted plains that used to be dense, green forests, but are now the disappearing remains of green life, with only the tops of the tallest trees still visible in some places. The further south you go, toward the equator, the more patches of green can be seen from high above, from trees that have not yet been buried or killed by the cold.

The same way that a sick person gets used to the pills and the pain, I think I'm used to the ice in my blood, and the endless scenes shown on TV, with reporters driving through desert terrain after a storm, showing the snow covered rock formations and giant cactuses nearly covered under a drift, or in the great barren deserts abroad, where snow dunes ripple in the wind where sand dunes used to be. They are never remiss in their drama— always referring to or displaying what the landscape was before—parched, golden sands or brownish red rocks and clay terrain underneath blue, sunlit skies. Boulders, wildflowers, scattered brush and tumbleweed bushes. Or pictures of the dry, cracked earth of legend, which no one under the age of six has ever seen with the naked eye. In the early days, the snow melted over these death valleys, until the cracks where gone, and the barren countries praised God for the precious water, which fell in giant flakes like manna from the shores of Heaven.

But what blessings are corrupted, when praises are killed and reborn, and spit as curses in the cold desert wind? These skies above us are gray, and many claim not to remember when the sky was blue. They are the lies we tell ourselves as protection from the pain, from the agony of revelation, and the third part of truth, which is cataclysm.

Have I cursed Annabelle, for giving me life? I have. Have I cursed God, for giving me life in the snow?

I have not.

$\mathcal{T}$he houses are bigger on this side of Prosperity. Heather Trace Blvd, in Prosperity Garden Terrace, somewhere in the New England northeast, our place under the snow. Or is it Heather Trace Lane, or Road? I look to the signpost up ahead, just to make sure I have not stepped into another zone of living. I'm not dreaming, I am still alive, and I know where I am. I walk the dawn of yesterday, to the twilight of tomorrow's home. Every day is as hopeless as the last, and as hopeful as the one to come. These at Heather Trace once had hope, perhaps even more than the rest of us here. As I walk the white path from the road to the front door, I know that if a house like this is being abandoned, then there is truly no hope for the future. For the word 'house' is hardly appropriate here, because these are mansions in the purest sense.

A snow flurry whirls an icy breeze on my cheeks. I stop at the mansion door, as fearful as a candle flame might be, looking up into this icy, suburban summer breeze. But thankfully, the flurries I see and feel are blown from the two feet of snow piled up on either side of my path through the snow covered walkway, and not from new crystals thrown and drifted from the gray clouds down to my grave.

Dominique, or Donna Ward is very kind when she opens the door. Forty years old, short blonde hair. A very pretty type that used to be called a 'soccer mom'; all pent up, closed vessels of suburban sexual repression. But when pressure builds up, it has to eventually be released, and it will find its outlet to not be denied. The forms of untapped lust are innumerable, but it is always present on the surface of a woman—if only a certain, knowing glint of the eye, or a twitch of the mouth, or even deeper behind even the nun's expression, until it is hidden from all but only a select few. Sometimes, there are things I think I know that I shouldn't, of how this biology of rage manifests in a private life: in the tightness of a cool white t-shirt that she wears stretched over her breasts, or the gold chain thinly pulled in veiled choking around her neck.

"BeLINdaaahh," she sings with a smile. I know her smile is genuine, as is the smile of any mask fashioned and formed to be so. In the doorway she stands, as steadfast as a rich white woman's black male bodyguard might be, though she is only the rich white woman herself.

28

"Hi, Mrs. Ward. May I come in?"

The first layer of civility fades. Her smile is less genuine.

"Honey I'd love to, but we're so busy it's impossible. You understand. But I'll tell Veronica you came by."

A glance at my body in my white coat, and visions of the punishment she gives. Her earrings are loops of pure gold.

"I know you're busy… I'm sorry I bothered you. But I really would like to see Veronica, if you don't mind. Just for a minute."

The second layer of civility fades partially, when her smile is covered by pretty lips, still trying to uphold a pleasant look.

"Belinda?" I hear it from somewhere in the big house behind Dominique. The voice of her civility's demise.

"Mr. Ward?"

"Hey, Belinda!" His kind smile is too a mask, but hiding a soul of sorrow, rather than bitterness. As he opens the door wider, I watch him use all his strength to do it against his wife's own, as she tries as hard as she can to hold the door half shut. Her body nearly jerks an unintended motion, which I know embarrasses her raw, as I watch the third layer of civility shatter like a glass tabletop on a concrete driveway—leaving a pained, humiliated expression on her—hard pressed to prevent an outright frown.

"Jeff we're too busy for company, I already told her that."

"It's our last days here Honey… Veronica could use the company."

Her face is suddenly older, but somehow more beautiful still. More sensual. Her look is venom. She glances at me one last time—raises her eyebrows and sighs, shaking her head as she turns to walk toward the gigantic kitchen. Do I feel her turn the corner seething, leaning over the sink like an untransformed she-hulk, breathing quiet curses in her mind?

What kind of bruises does she imagine, administered to what severity? Where on my body does she see the harm she intends?

Mr. Ward looks at me with such a quiet, knowing smile that I lose my composure and snicker. Since I was 16 years old, 5 years after the grass was gone, he has disarmed me with a look like we both know, but find unnecessary to explore.

"Changed your mind?"

"You know I wish I could go, but…"

"She could have really used your company down there…Veronica, I mean."

"Can I go up and see her?"

"You better wait a minute. Her mother's probably up there now."

"She's in the kitchen, right?"

"She went *through* the kitchen. Trust me. Have a seat."

Dominique opens her daughter's door. A spark of fear. She walks in unannounced, to interrupt her daughter's IPOD music, without apology.

"Turn that thing off," she says. Her lovely face is a frown. 'What do you want?' is at the tip of Veronica's tongue.

At the foot of the bed, the lovely woman beckons her daughter without a word. Veronica gets up—

"Put that thing down," her mother says of the Ipod. Her nearly 18 year old daughter puts it down and brushes the brown hair from her face. She walks over in refined repose appropriate—the posture learned by the years of knowledge and experience. She stands in front of her mother at the foot of the bed, head down, hardly breathing.

"Sit down."

Dominique sits on the bed beside her daughter. She slides very close, staring her in the eyes. Veronica looks away.

"I told you what would happen if I had to hear that sass, didn't I? Didn't I?"

Her daughter nods her head.

"That fat breasted friend of yours is here. And don't think that I don't know she wants to shove one of 'em in your daddy's mouth."

Pure shock twists Veronica's expression to tears. Her mouth is open.

"That's right. And if you hadn't been running your damned mouth, nobody would have even known we were getting out of here, especially her. But as usual you disobeyed me. And she was *this* close to tagging along with us permanently. Your father's got it so bad for that little bitch it's disgusting."

A pause. The mother's look is deep thought. Contemplation.

"I want you to go in that bathroom and cover those bruises."

It is the last hammer blow. Veronica's reservoir cracks—and the tears drip from her eyes like a faucet left untightened, though her expression is calm.

"If I find out that you told her, I swear to God I'm going to give you worse than what I gave you last night. Do you understand?"

The daughter takes a deep breath in quiet defiance. Her mother grabs the back of her neck and pulls her head down, muscle strength from Vanity's Gym. Her cool white T-shirt is stretched tight. Her daughter is draped by a button down, sky blue blouse and jeans.

"Do you *hear* me?" With both hands, she shakes her daughter's head on the 'hear.' The tears that fall fire dark forces, that inspire no compassion. "Get up."

The two of them stand as mother and daughter. Dominique watches Veronica walk slowly in front of her to the bathroom, to the makeup at the huge vanity. In the mirror, Veronica perceives the reflection. Standing close behind her own.

$\mathcal{T}$heir mansion is as warm as the Ralph Lauren comforter on my bed. I'm tempted to remove my white coat, but for some reason, I cannot deal with his stare today, which would lock on my breasts for memorization. It is the curse I have had for a year now, that they seem grown in proportion to my misery.

"How do you know it's a good idea to leave anyway? It's just as bad where you're going, isn't it?"

"It gets better, the further south you go. I want us to get settled before it gets any worse. People are starting to settle in wherever they are. They say if it keeps snowing, we won't be able to drive long distances anymore. It could be a month. It could be a year, but I don't think it's a good idea for anyone to stay in this part of the country. Canada's done already."

"That's what my sister said. She can't stop keeping up with it."

"How is your Mom and your sister?"

My mind lifts to last twilight, high into the drifting snow. Vapor crystallizes around me, until I cannot stay aloft, and I fall with the billions of other flakes. The wind carries me to Tulip Garden Road, to the roof of my dead father's home. I fall abruptly through the roof snow, a spirit above my own body, clutched in the arms of my terrified mother and sister.

"They're okay, I guess."

"A lot of people aren't as lucky as we are," he says. "We have the means to get what we need. To go anywhere. Do anything."

"There's nowhere *to* go. There's nothing left to do."

"They say it's starting to really warm up in Florida and South Texas. Mexico."

"Mexico? Things are bad enough in *this* country. Even with all this snow, there's still wars everywhere. Crime is actually up in some places."

"I wonder what it's going to take, before we really learn our lesson," he says. "There's no end to the greed. The violence. People have already started killing each other in the streets like it's the end of the world."

"My sister says it is. The end of the world, I mean."

"You believe that?"

"I don't know. Sometimes it just feels like…snow. And one day the sun'll come back out and melt it all away."

He smiles a bit, in recognition of a memory.

I remember before Tom and Dwayne died. You could at least tell where in the sky the sun was."

"You still can sometimes. Not today though."

When Jeff Ward mentions his son's name, I gaze as though transfixed by the theater of his mind, seeing the young Hispanic men stroll into the fraternity unmasked, heads covered by the hoods that shielded them from the cold—black Timberlands white with melting ice and snow, spitting bullets through the air from the metal in their hands, killing nine young white men and women. Not for drug money unpaid, but for the months of money paid by disrespect, being late over and over again and delivered by a smart assed, superior, Ivy League attitude, and a blonde beauty's affection rejection. The campus massacre was a promise kept, to send a message to no one but themselves, that life is too short, and the world is too close to the end to be disrespected by *'these rich white fools'*—over and over again. Knowing only one young man, and two young women present, bullets tore through the hearts, heads and hands of Tom and Dwayne Ward. What innocence could be drawn from their recreational sniff or smoke, of the white powder or black weed? What death did the Ward brothers deserve—among the seven others that fell?

"You were only about 11, so you never saw Tom play. Tom Ward. Coach said he'd never seen a white quarterback so good on the run. Would've been the best Ivy League quarterback of all time, they said. 'Course, they say that about somebody else every year."

"Last year was it for outdoor games up here, right?"

He looks at me, echoes of that same, pleasant grin.

"Their funeral," he says, "is the last time I saw the sun. I always figured it was sign of how special Tom was. That the sun would shine at his funeral. I think I stopped looking for it after that."

"I never stop. I've looked for it so much I can tell where it is behind those clouds. I'm probably just imagining I know half the time."

Looking somewhere past the high ceiling, I try to feel the light climb toward the cold noon day.

"This house is her, you know."

"I figured."

"Her father left her 10 million dollars when he died."

"Wow."

"The wow is that the other 140 million he left to charity. I've never understood that. More charity for the rest of the world than his own child. Donna fought for years to get the rest of that money. That's just one of the things…"

"What?"

A pause…

"We spend so much time focused on money and houses. I wonder how much time we spend caring about things that just don't matter. But I think every day, it's all becoming less and less important. These earthquakes, the snowstorms. We're going to have to forget about hurting and killing each other, and work on building a new earth…"

I listen to the jock lawyer drift philosophical in lost grief. From his death muse, I gather that even with all this snow, it cannot hide the blackness of who we are. That the earth itself is tired of being poisoned by humanity, and is fighting back with all the subtlety and restraint of a God. The snow might be the most beautiful thing the earth can manufacture. And with it, we are being buried alive.

These words are cold. To join my heart—one already iced cold in fear.

"If you don't mind me saying so, Honey, I think you and Ms. Freeman are crazy for staying here."

"I know. But Mom can't leave. And I can't leave her."

His look softens. From lust to longing.

"I wanted a big family," he says. "I was an only child. Always running all over the neighborhood to people's houses. Looking for something I didn't have at home. I didn't want Veronica to grow up lonely like I did."

"Why didn't you have another child?"

He smiles a little, and looks towards the kitchen. "Do you have to ask?"

"Oh."

"It's not too late to change your mind. Donna doesn't realize it now, but you'd be a great help to our family. Especially Veronica." *Especially me*

"Well, I—"

A sound like thunder booms from outside, rippling through our feet and legs and the rest of our bodies, reminding us of ripples on the surface of a lake. Our minds perceive the rumbling as the shaking of the entire earth, and the room before our eyes. The rumbling moves past us, and we follow the sound wave past the walls of the mansion, across the vast, snowy landscape around us.

*O*n the cushion of air waves I find, rumbled from less than one minute behind me, I am adrift to the top of these stairs bricked in gold, to the golden carpet one floor above. The plush ivory carpet from the stairs leads this path to my best friend's room, each footstep as gray as the skies above my snowbound journey had been. I walk the gray carpet to

Veronica's room, standing at the door to high class youth, so much higher than my own. When I knock on the door and call Veronica's name, I feel the barrier (which is Dominique) stiffen to the crackle and shattering of my voice like glass, falling like the diamond crystals I know to the bathroom floor at their feet. Dominique—*Donna* Ward composes herself and steps away from her daughter, over where the shattered diamond words lay vanished, out into the grand white walled bedroom. In the slow motion dream of my life, she steps in front of me with the grin of a shark in pretty human disguise.

"Hey," she sings. Smiling. Worry pressed down like a vacuum sealed bed cushion. "I told her you were here. But we really are busy, so I'll have to cut it short, okay?"

"Okay."

I find myself having to push past her into Veronica's bedroom. In her forced courtesy, beneath cultured civility, I sense the clawing of a beast.

Veronica comes out of the bathroom, not as dark brunette as me, and not as dangerously curved. We hug as though we've not seen each other for months, though it's only been the turn of a day.

What energy builds from a hug? What thoughts are exchanged? What words speak through a fervent embrace, on the eve of eschatology?

"Bee," she calls me. Eyes closed in the hug.

"What's the matter? Hey, what happened to your lip?"

"Playing catch with Dad. The football."

"Oh."

"I only play because he's so pathetic," she says. I can see the other bruises covered in makeup, but I turn my attention elsewhere. It seems that the big closet and dressers were robbed by spirits. Suitcases and bags are everywhere, packed full.

"I'm really sorry I can't go," I say, sitting on the bed beside her. She lowers her head, unable to hide the regret and the fear, coming from a pained and bruised spirit.

"I begged them to let me stay here with you," she says. "But she wouldn't let me. She got so mad—she said Hell would freeze like Hotford, Illinois before she'd let me go."

"Let you go where?"

"Anywhere."

The comment makes me glance again at the cut on her lip. Her jaw is so swollen it seems painful to the touch, though the bruise is hidden by Estee Lauder.

What is the third part of the Truth?

"This last snowfall wasn't as bad as they said. They said it would be the worse one we ever had but it was gone before I woke up this morning."

"You wanted to get outta here more than anybody," she says. "Last night you were hysterical on the phone."

"I guess fear is relative. I thought I knew what it was to be afraid. Until last night."

"What happened?"

"Just me and my Mom. I was gonna run away to your house so I could leave with you. The look in her eyes…it was like temporary insanity or something. It triggered something in me, I don't know. We can't get her to leave, so…"

"Your Mom's really sweet. And so pretty. Like a flower in the spring."

"There are no more flowers in the spring. I was just talking to your Dad, about how screwed up the world is. People, I mean. Your Dad's a great guy. He's really smart."

"He mentions you every now and then. I think he likes you a lot. I can tell."

"What would you say if I told you that…I wanted to cowgirl your Dad like a rodeo whore?"

"What?"

With carnal, comic flair, I close my eyes and wrinkle my brow in mock plateau, shaking my head saying *'Don't hurt me Daddy, don't hurt me Daddy'* in a deep, rough voice—throwing my head back with eyes rolled up, with the first part of a mock siren in my voice. Veronica laughs loudly—pushing me hard enough to wake me out of my fiery slumber.

"You really *are* a slut…oh my God…"

"I know. I can't help it…"

My bouncing and bellowing begins, and continues just enough, even reaching out for her tiny rose bosom, until I hear her laughter cease. I open my eyes delighted, but seeing her holding her mouth near the swollen cut.

"I'm sorry, I shouldn't've made you laugh."

"It's okay."

She gets up and glides quickly to the bathroom. Bewildered, but in knowing, I follow her just as quickly. In the bathroom, I see her at the huge vanity mirror gazing in—head turned, hair brushed behind her ear, looking at the cut on her lip, touching the swollen place where a bruise should probably be. Frustrated, I take a tissue from the counter and dampen it. I begin to wipe the concealer off her face.

"I'm alright…what are you doing…"

Without a response, I begin to wipe hard, to scrub her face.

"Ow, stop it…"

"No." I jerk her arm when I say it, staring her in the eye, to burn an angry expression.

"Please…"

"I said no. Now, wipe off that makeup, or I'm gonna do it myself."

Inexplicably to me, I see the sorrow of defeat in my best friend's eyes. She takes the tissue from me. She begins to wipe the area around her right eye, wincing, but determined to push through the pain. I don't notice my own expression in the mirror, as I see the gigantic, dark bruise come to life.

"My God, Veronica. What happened?"

I watch her wince once again, as she wipes the concealer from her jaw, as close to the cut on her lip as possible. Explanations of balls, walls or falls are pointless, as her face bears not just the marks of a girl who was hit, but who was beaten.

I feel the spirit of fear come to life in my heart, then spread to the rest of my body.

"You have to tell your Mom. Just tell me how it happened and I'll help you tell your Mother. When did he do it? Why?"

The question evokes such a rare look. The one that is conjured by ignorance so epic as to be unfathomable. It is a look that defies description of emotion. Embodying both laughter and tears—at once both joy and sorrow. Twinged by a controlled rage and fury. All at once in the questioning, pleading expression, hidden by the heightened intellect and control, catalyzed by the audacious audacity of my ignorant assumption.

"Please, just tell me when your Dad did this so we can—"

"It wasn't him."

I stare Veronica in the eyes, still amazed by the bruises, and resistant to the third part of the truth.

The fog I'm in is a cloud of disbelief. It keeps me from breathing

free as I touch the finished wood railing (or is it marble?) on my way down

the stairs. My mind shows me two faces, to coincide with the voices I hear.

The deeper voice is the voice of reason and compassion, the voice of a

handsome man 41 years young enough to hold my fantasies captive. The

voice of the abused girl's father, whom she asked of me before I left her room: *"That joke you made about my father…you didn't really mean that, did you?"* *"Oh, God no,"* I had said… *"how could you think that?"* I had chimed, even as the scene of me straddling his body nude with his hand at my throat choking me had flashed in my mind. At this moment, my breasts tingle at the thought, in the vibration of his voice mingled with another— the smooth, velvet tone of deep, feminine lust and power, the craving of a mother's grief gone mad, to ease the pain she feels through hand and fist beatings of her daughter, belt whippings, and a punishment so profoundly private as to have once left the mother's body near a place she must deny in her memory—where the two of them were stripped naked with the mother behind her, twisting her daughter's breasts black and blue, as also testified of the old bruises on the daughter's wrists and ankles, her back and buttocks, and every inch of skin around her bosom. Their voices, their faces in my mind and spirit, all swirl to make me dizzy, and to make me wish again that I had never been born.

I have to get out of here.

"You're not leaving us are you, Bee?" he says, "you just got here."

I open my mouth, but there are no words.

"You alright? You and Vee have a fight or something?"

I glance at Dominique, seeing her bite her bottom lip, with her pretty brow wrinkled in thought. She turns and walks back to the kitchen. Through the kitchen.

"I'm… I'm fine, I just have to get back… in case it starts snowing…"

He escorts me to the door, not resisting putting his arm around my shoulder. We step outside into the blinding white. Our breath fades as fog in the air.

While the beauty of the cold tries to capture our hearts again, we cannot see the beautiful middle aged woman take her cue like a leopard in the woods crouched in a tree, watching a small deer walk the forest floor. While we speak of July snows and Summer's Winter, Dominique, *Donna Ward* glides down the hallway to the upper room in easy step, imagining how best to get in. She knows her prey will have to be coaxed—spoken softly to. Donna arrives at the door of the white rock cave, where she knows warm blood waits for her inside. She stands at the door in full frown, arms folded. Thinking.

In the snowy daydream of my departure, we do not see Donna Ward knock on her daughter's door, saying *"It's me honey, I just came up to see how you were doing. You mind if I come in?* Her daughter answers, *"I'm okay, I'll be out later, alright?" "I want you to come to the door"*, her mother says gently. Firmly.

"Where's Dad?"

"He'll be up in just a second, he's saying goodbye to your friend."

Timidly, foolishly, her daughter opens the door, wide enough to let whatever spirits in. The mother touches the door, to the edges of pushing it forward. Her daughter pushes it back, nearly closing it in her mother's face. In the lightning, a burst of instinct unfolds through her arms like a rattlesnake, and she bursts through the door violently into Veronica's room, chasing her daughter toward the bathroom, hissing *"you told her didn't you. You told her..."* She grabs her, spinning her around saying *"you little bitch..."* and backhands her hard on the word. Veronica spins and falls short of her destination, the safety of the bathroom. Her mother pulls her up and slaps her hard again across the face, reopening the cut on her daughter's lip, knocking her towards the bed. The slap brings a deep scream from Veronica's gut, through her throat into the giant cave of a bedroom—screaming *"Daddy!!!"* at the top of her lungs. Screaming loud enough to reawaken those entombed by the old snow, buried so deeply across the world beneath our feet. In betwixt, above and under the screams, we hear another voice of rage and fury, deep of a woman's pent up madness unleashed. As we run back to the stairs inside, we hear the voice around the daughter's loud, rough screams, yelling words we cannot decipher, meant for her daughter's ears alone, hearing parts of *"now that little whore's gonna tell her Momma what you did... what you made me do to you."* She continues to beat her daughter on her face with big, brutal slaps, knocking her to the floor against the wall opposite the foot of the bed—*"I should've buried you when they killed my boys bitch... always cryin' and pullin' and needin' somethin' from me. I'm gon' give ya what you need right now you f*cking slut..."*—hitting her again on the word, eliciting the howling screams of a daughter's dark destiny—knocking her to the floor between the back wall and the bed.

We burst through the closed door into the room, seeing the beautiful woman's head and teeth bared as she kneels behind the bed looking down—seeing her raise a fist and bring it down to her daughter's eye again. I make it around the bed just in time to see the handsome man grab and pull his lovely, raging wife off of his daughter, her hands having been grabbed and pulled from around the girl's bruised neck. He grabs and holds Donna Ward, and she reacts in writhing, grimacing screams with eyes closed, saying … *"I had to kill that bastard he put in you, you f*cking whore, you want your mother, bitch you've got your mother!!..."*

Jeff Ward holds his wife while she writhes a tiger's rage in his arms, finally pulling her away from the scene out of the room. In a haze, I turn to see Veronica on the floor in the corner, cowering like Fear itself. While her mother is pulled violently down the hall, I touch my friend on the arm— she recoils and screams in post trauma, wide-eyed and angry with fear, backing up fully into the corner. I pull away, mouth open in something greater than shock, watching her tremble and hide her face, while my hands burn from the blue and black fire I've seen.

*A*dvocates of global warming were made the biggest fools of all, as the snows began to slowly fall without ceasing. In the early days of the snow, the world cackled and giggled with collected delight, the requisite pictures and snowmen and snowdays done without much worry. *The end of the world*, some claimed half heartedly; it is a sign of the times we're in. Children laughed and played in chorus with the smiles of their parents while the new snows fell in June and July. Big, wet snowflakes drifted lightly in the cool summer winds, piling loose, fluffy white clumps everywhere, like tufts of cotton fibers grown. Across the cities, the farmlands, suburbs and small towns, parents and children all ran and gathered snow in thanksgiving, some with cameras raised in disbelief that such a thing were possible, to record the fluttering in the breeze that swept through their lives like the fluttering in the pits of their stomachs. Even when the date was June 21st, and the snow began to fall on Hotford, Illinois—the tiny farming town that first abandoned hope—having recorded the coldest temperature in the country's history at -82 F that first winter, but warming significantly every season since, it was all calmly addressed and even more calmly dismissed. The five Great Lakes have never seen another time completely unfrozen since before the snows fell. Across the frozen landscape of Lake Eerie, Lake Huron, Lake Ontario, Lake Superior and Lake Michigan is an alien sea, known as the Great Lake Plains, as the ice is covered every year with another two feet of permafrost. But there is hardly a mood left to skate or even walk upon the Lakes, the prairies of pure ice and snow, frozen so deep beneath the surface as to be called a glacial freeze, which has slowly devoured the land from east to west, redefining every coastline already from North to South America, and parts of every island and continent.

The early days brought tears of revelation, when a National emergency was finally declared, with slow and steady talk of what possibilities there are in a 'snow economy.' The snow alone might have been enough to fuel Eschatology, but in the first year, when the mysterious, arctic summer winds mixed with the warm winds over the south and Midwest, and thousands of people were killed in whirling black, white and gray from the clouds—monsters without eyes came roaring their screaming voices over hundreds of miles, killing thousands of people at a time—the tallest, or widest, or blackest, or fastest moving twisters the world has ever known—with many appearances over tropical waters, where whole ships of people were seen on camera lifted and whirled into the clouds. Even so, there was still hope in those early days, when the grasses would begin to reappear at the end of every summer. But hope soon became as fleeting as the grasslands in winter, as each year the snow line rose slightly higher and higher, and summertime temperatures were lower. The summer thaws were less important each passing year, until they no longer held the promise of hope. Here, in the seventh season, there is the need for heating year round, with the warmest days still in the summer, when temperatures can still rise ten degrees above freezing in August. Even so, people have slowly conceded the arrival of God's unbroken promise, that the world would never again be covered by a global flood, but slowly blanketed by the white of winter ice.

The oceans themselves have reluctantly passed denial and anger, bargaining no longer with God and man, resting in the depression that precedes acceptance. Two generations, they believe, or perhaps even three and there would be no more azure sea, with giant icebergs floating about, but one of pure, pristine ice and crystalline white. But them who believed in the so-called warming still reveled in those days, when the arctic air overtook the last warm spring and summer, killing 44,000 in the deadliest weather outbreak in human history, striking countries all over the world. Hurricanes of a size and intensity unknown to modern man came ashore in the cooling of that final autumn (Last Autumn, it is called), washing entire towns from the map overnight, causing those who refused to run to curse the Almighty, then bow down to him before they died. Churches and hospitals were not spared the pain of new birth, as the earth groaned in the agony of its calling. Medical centers and worship centers around the country, around the world were disassembled in the Summer and Fall tornadoes, brick by brick, many washed away in freezing autumn rains and buried in ice, covered and entombed in the first dusting of the Last Autumn Snow. By the end of the first winter, small roads everywhere where made impassable, major highways were dangerous to travel on. Many canceled flights were never flown again. Large northern rivers and streams carried massive blocks of ice, while many migrating birds knew never to return north again.

Those who had loved global warming felt abandoned and betrayed by the Great Lie they had brought to life, when they watched it freeze in the gathering gray clouds, and begin to fall from the air around them. By the end of the second summer, people stubbornly clung to the beaches in fading numbers, even on the sands that bordered snowy coastlines and water too cool to swim in. Only the tropical beaches remained true to their calling, warm winds keeping arctic breezes away until the third summer, when the beaches on the equator began to receive their first flakes of new winter. The cold air made bikini beach play implausible, with t-shirts and shorts where skimpy cloth had been, until the sandy shores in the tropics bordered water on one side and snow covered sands on the other. Warning flew the winds at the Tropic of Cancer down to the Tropic of Capricorn, encircling the world warming zone into a cooling region, where prolonged, protracted rainstorms began to fall—where typhoons and tropical storms of unearthly duration flooded some islands from the map briefly, until the shores reappeared under colder skies no longer blue, but gray with discontent.

By the 4th summer, every beach on earth had been touched, with every non equatorial lake and shoreline abandoned by necessity. That summer saw nationwide school closings, many indefinitely, except for those accessible by the busiest main roads and highways. Home schooling had already become a way of life for some, especially students from private schools, as their beloved campuses where too burdened by mountains of snow. The world economy slowly ground to a halt overnight; Man's perseverance keeping some interstate roads cleared, truer in this country than anywhere else in the world. Flights abroad were practically nonexistent, that idea maturing by the 5th summer, when international runways were declared impassable, becoming obsolete in the snowfall.

Here, in the 7th year, domestic infrastructure bears the growing marks of battle fatigue, as more and more roads around the country disappear under mountains of snow. People are wiping the cold tears away, and thanking God for the heat and access to what food they have—save a few brave souls who drive the frozen highways south to open farmlands, where the snowfall is the lightest of all places, and the landscape still bears brief hope for the future. Among the network of roads still seen, the grandest interstate remains clear, from Cape Hatteras winding west to the Pacific Ocean, now serving as the unofficial border between the hopeful and the condemned—as the land above it blows winds of a North Country, while south of it remains southern as what is possible, their streets and buildings and forests not as close to being gone.

This was established two years ago by the 5th summer, when parks and outdoor stadiums were declared unusable and too expensive to maintain. Pro football conceded that outdoor play was unfeasible, moving games into every available dome around the country, until roofs could be built over some outdoor fields—the southern orange and aquamarine being the first to comply. In keeping with the strangeness of this latter day, only 1/3 of the farmlands have been lost, as the snowfall disperses evenly around the Great Plains, and all of the largest southern and lower Midwest farming regions. Summers are gentlest over the fields of life, and even in the face of impending doom; talk of eschatology and repentance has died, even when the ground blizzards bury millions in their homes until half of them are dead. Even when thunder rolls from the snow capped Rockies to the plains, or when the snow twisters move ghostly across the white summer prairie.

*W*hen enclosed pressure is added to any space or object in the universe, it creates energy. The more pressure that is applied, the greater the buildup of energy. Even the Almighty understands this, from the Garden of Antiquity, to the Garden of Gethsemane, to every garden in between, as the pressure of His Passion exploded through him to cry *"My God, My God! Why hast thou forsaken me?"* He understands this, when the pressure explodes through Adam—to clamp his mouth upon the fruit in allegiance to the Woman, and disobedience to God, to gain knowledge of good and evil. He understands this, when the lowly preacher gives his heart away to him, then to have the Gates of Hell rise up to destroy every blessing, when the weakness of the flesh brings a curse from the poor preacher's lips to blaspheme the Lord and Savior—then to have him buried in the torment of regret for seven days after, while the nightmare of the burning Cross agonizes the flesh and wires of his mind. Even God understands that the pressure He creates in us must build, until it manifests in our walk with Him.

All over the world, the Cross burns a bright orange and yellow flame in the theatre of our lives, against the backdrop of every new fallen snow. I see the Flaming Cross lit by the pressure of the Ward calling, the explosion of violence and the blood of sin. I walk slower this time, unable to believe what I have seen, the release of built up energy in the Ward family life. While the snow's late arrival begins in earnest around me, I gaze at every grand house along the way—doll houses covered in icicles and old snow, wondering how the pressure of living has exploded—what pattern it has created along the fabric of their lives and times.

What colors and shades are the bloodlines of our neighbors? There are none that are not common to man, I suppose, as is the alcoholism of Mrs. Merrilyn in this beautiful home passing by, made worse by the ice and snow. What of the cigarette burns in the back of little Rosetta Robinson, and the black bruise lines from the extension chord? Is it the snow that raises Tracy Robinson's hands in such violent defeat when her husband is out of town or not, to burn the little girl's skin? What of Hubert Wallace's lovely home, built years ago by a heating and plumbing fortune? What does it matter, really, that his lovely wife engages in adultery with such regularity as to be normal in their lives? What of Terry Harrington's bruises hidden in makeup, and the screams caused by her husband Ben? What of the burning blue and black fire, agonizing the bowels of 15 year old Rhonda Johnson, burned not by the father, but by the artificial member of legend—passed through the motherline of Mrs. Johnson—maiden name Helen Riggs, from her mother Mary Ann Riggs—who still visits Helen as though nothing hath transpired from her youth?

To what pressures have we succumbed by His mighty hand? What manifestations are they? I raise my eyes to the snow, to feel the ice burn them closed—to help me cleanse my mind—my spirit, from the ghosts that move through me, crossing back into the walls of every doll house around me.

Like every prophecy, even those about the weather are bound to come true in some way or another. The heaviest snowfall in 4 years was supposed to have begun last night, but all we saw was the same dusting of flakes seen at least once a week, which is fine for the forecasters, as it keeps them from never being truly wrong. But this time, the mark they missed was measured not in feet, but hours. Twelve hours past midnight, in the dark gray twilight of noon, there begins a steady rain of snowflakes heavy enough to resemble a blizzard—only without the accompanying wind madness. But small, strong gusts still whirl the blowing snow dangerously in my face, trying to cause fear or trepidation. But I am used to the ice and the cold, and my walk through the approaching storm is a leisure, leisurely stroll. When the winds are calm, and the snow is allowed to drift, it is still Nature's Beauty—profound enough to renew itself at every viewing. I listen to the sound of the snowfall, as the flakes fall to the snow all around me, every flake whispering a message, while they connect to those already fallen. It is a tiny crackling noise, like tiny soap bubbles dying in suds, but magnified across a thousand miles of earth.

*A*manda awakens from her snowy daydream in the upper room. She burns a gaze through the falling snow. She hears my footsteps on the staircase, but does not look away from the window.

"Hey."

When she turns and looks at me, I see the pain in her eyes. Or is it fear? She gets up from the chair and hurries over to me. She hugs me tight.

"I thought you weren't coming back. You were gone so long."

"I told you I was coming back. Where's Mom? She didn't go to that boutique did she?"

"She went to the store."

"Why didn't you go with her?"

"She told me to stay here, in case you came back. I could call her."

"Why?"

"To tell her we'll meet her there."

"We'll just wait. By the time we get there—"

"I'll call Mom," she says, flipping her cell phone.

"And tell her what?"

"She told me to call you if—Hello, Mom? Yeah, she just got in…"

The deep breath I take is as involuntary as ever.

"Mom wants to speak to you."

"I'll talk to her when she gets home." I say it on a turn and a drift, as my sister beeps Mother's voice away.

In my mind's eye, I see Mother at the Supermarket Warehouse, piling food and supplies into the cart as though it were mandatory to escape death. Resisting the urge to run through the aisles to the checkout—her and the breastier, older, less beautiful Cheryl Ezman, the only one in the neighborhood lucky enough to have laid claim to my mother's hand—as a so-called best friend and companion in the snow. But Ms. Ezman's loneliness is by choice, overseeing her husband's body in divorce court rather than the cemetery. Cheryl and Annabelle are close enough to hold hands and whisper in private; my mother's sweetness the elixir. And her beauty—food for Cheryl Ezman's soul.

Upon what winter winds come desire! In what whirling clouds do they blow!

One sided longing. Tolerated sweetly by Annabelle—moaning kisses on the cheek, tight arm in arm strolls through the indoor gardens, a firm whack and jiggle to my mother's backside in the kitchen, when her tight skirt reveals what is hidden. "I'll see you in a pair of jeans and a bra if it kills me," she'll say. Even seven years ago, one year before my father's funeral, there was a knowing twinkle in Cheryl's then 33 year old eye, at the mature, sensual beauty in the then 28 year old future widow woman.

I was eleven when we buried my father in the snow. My sister was nine, seven years removed from this summer's sweet sixteen—and my hidden, eighteenth Forest Moon.

These are the things I know in my mind, from the secrets bestowed in my dreams. The private devastations of man and woman—when the doors are shut and locked, and there are no eyes upon them but my own.

In the heart of memory, there is Li Hsu Hahn. Linda Hsu Hahn. Sue Hahn. My fifth grade teacher seven years ago. I see Linda Hsu stand painfully up as if her hips burn with arthritis, though it is not the fire she earns. She cruises our fourth grade aisles to look over the shoulders of every one of us, not really caring at all what every pencil mark means, all of them a blur in eyes that threaten to mist as she remembers, and contemplates the nature of God and Man. It was only yesterday that her fears were confirmed, when she was called into Ms. Ivy James' office and told the news, that little Shaun Gesler's broken arm on the playground most certainly *was* her problem, and that Dr. and Mrs. Gesler wanted her "Asian ass" fired before the end of the week. Mrs. James tells Linda Hsu "I don't know if I have the power to protect you. We're getting hit from all sides. I know you're a good teacher but the fact is, Ms. Hahn—"

Linda Hsu listens to the way the words form in Ivy James' throat and rise into her mouth—the way they flow into the air like rose petals dipped in poison. Words of such skill and mastery over sincerity, as to almost make Linda Hsu believe she truly cares for her future whereabouts and well being. In Ms. James' office she listens, trying to learn her fate in the new storm.

"…but first, Linda, I'm going to need to know how badly you want to keep this job."

"These children are my life, Ms. James. I love this school, this community. I've fallen in love with every student I have…"

"We don't have time to get into it right now—but I'd like to talk about this some more. Here's my card Mrs. Hahn—I need you at my house at seven o'clock sharp—we'll talk over dinner." Linda did not think it too odd of a request, being that her life was on the line. Even when Mrs. James requested that she wear blue jeans because she likes to keep things "casual away from this campus." Dinner was the least she could submit to with the lonely principal, right ? After all, it's keep her job and prove herself worthy for this upscale nightmare of a community, or be fired and sued for child endangerment and neglect.

Linda Hsu walks the 5th grade aisles. Remembering the principal's grand home of brick housed, Martha Stewart living at 110 Baux Mountain Road, with every kind and color of book as decoration. She shakes her head in something close to disbelief from the itching pain that burns—at the behind closed door character of the privileged, and the reckless moral abandon they live. In her flowered spring skirt she walks with arms folded over a flat bosom and white blouse, underneath eyes hailed from the Chinese village of her immigrant mother and father. The trauma poisoning Linda Hsu's spirit draws her mind from her students—to the patio of the blonde haired, forty something year old Ivy James, single and driven in her life, if only to exact her will at this moment on the young Asian teacher in the white St. John's Bay tee and form fitting blue denim jeans.

"I have the power to put a stop to this," Ms. James says, "but only if I know it's worth the risk I'm going to have to take—I'll have to put my reputation on the line for you and it could mean my job—"

Linda Hsu remembers every second of the conversation about little Shaun's upside down hanging from the top of the swing, talking to her friend who was swinging normally. *How did she get up there*, Linda remembers thinking, telling herself to stay calm and just walk over to the little girl without startling her. In the same instant she became distracted by two boys wrestling, then the plink of an aluminum softball bat from a fifth grade class on the big field nearby, and then the sound of a high pitched squeal from the fallen tomboy. She was as devastated as anyone has ever been, at the sight of the lump under the little girl's skin, and the trembling, awkward way she held her arm. Mrs. James spoke to confirm, that yes it was pure negligence, and "we're going to have to color this a bit to make it right. The truth is, I think you've been punished *almost* enough"—

The look on Linda Hsu Hahn's face, the pleading bewilderment was priceless; as unintentionally beautiful as a nighttime spark on a highway, like when someone tosses a lit cigarette out the window and it explodes fiery orange upon impact. Linda Hsu walks away from her students and their exams, drawn to the sudden loss of late spring sunlight at the window. Her mind carries her beyond the glass to the green, grassy field, where she would like to walk alone to the Great Flowering Tree. Her mind is pulled like a phantom through a dimensional tear, back to the night before, when her principal—a 48 year old white woman with a Masters Degree in Liberal Arts from North Carolina Wesleyan College—tells her "I'm going to do for you what my mother and father did for me. And what I did for both of my daughters. My parents taught me that real punishment comes in parts, Ms. Hahn, and each part should be swift and final."

I have read that the types of fear are many. And uniquely distinguished.

"When real punishment is endured, Ms. Hahn, it teaches us to be better people than we ever thought we could be, to learn to absorb the suffering that others put on us, and to cry for the pain that others feel. Real punishment teaches us compassion and perseverance. It teaches us the true purpose of charity: which is to ease the pain in others. It teaches us to have a reverence for achievement, and a fear of failure. To be absolutely afraid to fail, in our mission to make the world around us better. Real punishment is Heavenly Correction, Ms. Hahn, and we have a solemn duty to ourselves, and to society to *'withhold not correction: for if thou beatest with the rod, they shall not die... thou shalt beat with the rod, and shalt deliver their soul from Hell."*

Ivy James tucks her lips and tilts her head. Raising her eyebrows, wondering if Linda understands at all what must happen. That she has waited, wanted, and wished for 20 years to be in this position.

"Some would say that your life is already over. But I believe in second chances. I need to understand that you're willing to dedicate your soul to this school. We're a good school, Ms. Hahn. Trying to become one of the best. And your position here is as far away from being a right as, well... east is from west. To teach here? It is a privilege."

Linda Hsu Hahn watches the light hearted pretense fade, as light from the sky in the evening day. Behind the somber mood on Ivy James' face is a suppressed frown.

"We're a private institution, Ms. Hahn, and our standards are extremely high, as I'm sure you understand when you cash your paycheck. I need teachers who can achieve the highest levels of dedication. Do you understand what I'm saying?"

"I think so," Ms. Hahn says ignorantly, but willing nonetheless. What affections required to resume forgiveness in her life would be welcome. In demurity, Linda lowers her head, and then looks up at the forty something year old Ms. Ivy James, to wait for her proposition.

"My daughters got straight A's, with only the occasional B, Ms. Hahn, as did I. Because we understood the consequences of poor performance in work. In life."

They leave the patio, Ms. James with her immolation arm in arm Through the big, cozy living room. Up the straight staircase to the second floor bedroom.

"I don't want you to be nervous at all, Linda. You still don't really have to do this—"

"But I do. I do want to do this. I have to do it."

In the bedroom, Ivy goes to the closet and pulls a large, wooden paddle. Not smiling. Not delighted by Ms. Hsu Hahn's open mouthed shock.

"If I'm going to put my life on the line for you Linda, I'm going to have to have your loyalty."

The sound of a door slamming down the 5th grade hall makes Ms. Hahn jump. She looks out the door, and sees another teacher clip clop toward the rest room. The bruises on her skin burn and tingle, as she remembers the cloth tied in her mouth to muffle the screams. She remembers the bizarre feel of the paddling wood through her blue jeans, then the burning of it across her underwear. She had been made to first remove her top, until the blows over her jeans sent her to the edge of tears, until she could not speak without choking up, and then her bra was removed. Red faced, brow wrinkled in shock, through deep breaths and watery vision, she imagined how privileged she must be, the power of her calling, and how bright her future must be, to have to endure such exclusive, such unheard of rights of passage. As she removed her underwear, she felt only shame and fear, not perceiving the contrast that lit the heart of her punisher, a lightning flash of exhilaration that made Ivy James have to close her eyes once and breathe a deep sigh.

Every blow had rippled a flame into the teacher's skin, to rip a scream from her throat until she had to call the name of God and Christ, as she held onto the back of the chair for dear life, in the middle of Ms. James' rather largish bedroom. This was the first death scream, prompting her hostess to drop the pretense and gag her with a white cloth, then unbutton her own white blouse and remove it, then take off her white tank top underneath. When it was over, her buttocks were black and purple, with bloody spots where tiny chips of skin were missing, and the paddle was stained with blood.

Ms. Hahn remembers being hardly able to walk when it was over. This morning, one day removed—her legs were blackened from her buttocks down the backs of her thighs, where the bruising had spread enough to shiver her to the bone when she saw it. Her legs and buttocks had ached on the drive here, and she had actually checked the seat of her car for blood and then the back of her skirt. There was none.

Linda Hsu Hahn lets the tears form in her eyes as she looks out the window, too shocked to truly care if she is seen crying. In the watery haze, in the cooling winds of early May, she wonders what the puffed pieces of white are that have begun to fall outside. *A snowfall in May*, she thinks, as the tear falls from her eyes at the window.

Amanda was nine years old that day, still in the 3rd grade, when Linda Hsu Hahn began to cry in my 5th grade class, though it went unnoticed, as the late May skies drew every one of us to the window, to see the beginning of the end fall like flakes of cotton fiber to the ground. Amanda was nine that day, when my teacher excused herself to the bathroom to hide in a stall and shake, while the tears poured down her face. Amanda was nine when the scandal exploded in the new fallen snow, when she and the entire world became aware of Ashley Long Elementary School, and what Ivy James had done to Linda Hsu Hahn. My sister was nine when I saw the Asian teacher walk into the classroom in a bright red dress of Asian cloth, and take out her father's .45 automatic pistol, and put it to her temple and pull the trigger. My sister was nine when I refused to scream, while every other girl around me either shrieked or ran in terror while Ms. Hsu Hahn lay on the floor—when the investigation had already begun even before it happened, when Ivy James was arrested and sent to prison because of the pictures Ms. Hsu Hahn had let another teacher take and give to the police, who then gave the pictures to a higher authority. The evidence displayed on TV screens across the country, among the new snowfalls in May and June, of the crusted bruises that were on the woman's buttocks and legs before she died.

My sister was nine, when the teacher cried.

The gray world spins a click and a chime, until six have passed beyond the noon hour. Amanda and I are in the kitchen, perhaps glad for one another's company today. Mother sits in her burgundy dress on the sofa, legs crossed, biting her thumb, gazing at the nightly news as though... as though it were the end of the world.

"We wish we could tell you we're headed out of the frying pan and into the fire, at least then we'd get some heat. But as it were, perhaps it's out of the ice tray and into the freezer, as the North Eastern part of the country braces for what they're calling "Ice and Fire," or the worst snow and lightning storm we have seen in this country for about six years, although it arrives a day late across much of the region. What was supposed to have begun yesterday at twilight sent us a false alarm, but still a grave warning of what is to come. An expected 10 feet of snow is coming over the next few days with strong wind gusts of up to 30 miles per hour, along with the rare snow lightning and thunder. It is recommended that you have at least a 2 month supply of food ready for you and your family, as the entire north east from Pennsylvania and Ohio up into Maine and Nova Scotia Canada can expect to be buried in snow for at least six weeks..."

My mother closes her eyes to absorb the blow, taking a deep breath. She gets up and walks to the stairs, too exhausted to be polite, ignoring us as she climbs the staircase to second floor luxury. Amanda starts to get up from the table from our game of Mastermind, until I touch her arm.

"I'll go."

The door is open to the upper room. Inside, the beautiful chaste woman sits in her comfortable chair by the window.

"You were right," she says. "It's going to be bad."

"They don't know what they're talking about. I wouldn't worry too much. You bought enough food for a year anyway. Tomorrow we'll get the plow and clear the walkway. It'll be fun."

"Did you hear what they just said?"

"Yeah, I heard it. So what?"

She glances down, as if forgetting what to say. "Did…is Veronica's family gone?"

"They left today. You think *you've* got problems."

She looks away from the window, to see if there can be solace in what I have to say. Mother refuses to say a word. Or to look away.

"Veronica was hiding a set of monster bruises on her face. And I got angry with her father, wondering when he hit her and how he could have done such a thing."

Mother tucks her lips, but can offer no fake words of caring.

"Veronica said it wasn't her father. It was Dominique."

"Who's Dominique?"

"Her real name is Dominique. But everybody calls her *Donna*."

"Oh…"

The appropriate shock transforms her features. Mouth open. Wide-eyed. It seems that every expression she makes only enhances her beauty. Her sensuality.

"Donna Ward hits Veronica?"

"She beats the *Hell* out of Veronica, Mom. It's bad enough for her to get arrested for it."

"Arrested?" She looks again out the window. "By who?"

The question drives the wave of cynicism. To mock the very idea of policemen navigating these white streets to arrest anything.

"You're gonna be alright Mom. We all are."

"I know," she says. Smiling. Blinking.

Smiling.

The three of them drift as flakes of snow, on wheels turned through hope frozen in time. Urgency is the wind driving them through the cold, under gray skies not yet darkened by the evening flow. The husband, the mother and her daughter on the road south, in an attempt to escape the coming north wind, and the icy breezes that blow. In their ice chariot, the Princess gains confidence from the King's compassion, able to speak freely to the Queen's cruelty, until tensions inside succumb to pressure. A burst of energy drives the Queen's arm over the back seat, the hair of her Princess pulling. Screaming bloody murder. The King joins in the volatility, but not fully, so as not to slip on the slushy, snowy road ahead. A deep, masculine voice among the feminine screams, unable to summon a calming spirit among them.

In the aftermath of war, beneath the hidden sun, the Mother grumbles her displeasure—*the next time I get my hands on you I swear to God*—the father yells *shut up, Dominique shut <u>up</u>!* at the very top of his lungs, to ring the ears of the angry Mother. She breathes to calm her nerves, and exhales the words *you shut up* to the man. Turning to look at her Daughter, to see the pleased, delighted sparkle above the despair, the creation of satisfaction in her daughter's eyes.

The four winds conspire in the gray twilight, on the edge of the fall of night. We listen to the howling of the conspiracy—the gathering of the North, South, East and West Wind, to take deep inhales across the hours, then exhale time and again. The breathing of this winter earth, reminding us of our hopeless condition, in the northeastern dead of night. The storm we all dreaded, which has driven thousands from their homes across many states—this storm arrives in ice and fire, until we can only see the snow itself, illuminated by the street lamps outside our window. It appears to be raining snowflakes to me, like any summer storm, accompanied by the dim flashes of blue lightning, and the occasional growl of distant, treble thunder. From any second floor window, I can already see the danger lurking through the white haze, of a ground that does not seem as far away as it did 2 hours ago, already high enough to be hard to walk through, foreshadowing a time where it would be impossible. I know this is what I have warned my mother about for months, this premature burial we were all afraid of, that will bury us alive this time, in a mountain of ice and snow.

'Intrepid fervor' is the summer night, while we imagine our burial in the cold.

> *Tears of a snowy mountain cold*
> *Dreams of dying in the sun*
> *Along the gray eastern seaboard*
> *There is nowhere for us to run*
>
> *The snow will bury us alive*
> *Carry me away in fright*
> *We pray the Lord our souls to take—*
> *So one of us can die tonight*

In my mind's eye, the sea of clouds is parted, and the beauty of the second heaven shows herself to me though the gray. In my mind's eye, through the haze of this night dream, the clouds of my tomb have parted, and I am alive again. The field I stand upon is white from horizon to horizon, but above me is the blackest sky that can be seen from earth, where twinkles many thousands of the stars of heaven.

For reasons unknown, I cannot find the dipper of my childhood memory, but I see a tiny replica of it turned on its side, so that the handle is downward. What constellation, what cluster is this, which is the shape of a question mark, which begs the question of my existence in this space in time (?) The seven stars are the Pleaides, of which I have heard so much of from the beginning of my life, which is the beginning of learning. Though the calendar is July where I live and breathe, in my heart, and in my spirit there is no more summer, and I must join with the rest of Creation to concede the arrival of perpetual winter. I know that the seven sisters are the companion of the mighty Orion, the great hunter, on his journey across the winter sky. I look for the North Star, but being unable to find it in the mix of clusters and constellations, though I can feel its presence somewhere north of where I stand. In my heart, I cry out independently of myself, asking Him to show me the North Star, and I am suddenly aware of it, as the very tip of the Little Bear's tail. Around it circles every other star in Heaven, including those of my spirit's warmest dream, those of the big dipper! It shines in my mind with the stars of Orion's Belt, which are really three gigantic, eternally bright lanterns of blazing blue white energy, to light our way through the ignorance of who we are, and our ultimate purpose for being. With these three, are the stars that bear the number of completion, the Seven Sisters, my guide and comfort under this winter sky.

Above these gray clouds of my inadequacy, my inability to love Him in purity, I see the Stars of Heaven, and then, my hope coalesces into a haze, and the blackness of the giant sky begins to fade to a paler shade, until the whiteness of every star is diminished. The mist thickens before my eyes, until even the memory of the three stars of Orion threaten to fade. But in my mind's eye, I still feel the three stars of the great hunter, when I saw them for what they were, and I perceive the eons of space and time between them. From here, I beg for the purity of the God I can see, but to no avail. My soul is as the mist that forms, as the clouds tumble back in on one another, coming together again as a mountain veil, fixed in the gulf between Earth and Heaven.

The power of my sleep is deepened, until my dreaming is no longer such, but unclouds into a vision of reality. I am awake somewhere in the universe, through my body lies asleep in bed. This vision carries me suddenly away from the clouds of night, to a place of blue skies and light. The sun is bright in the blue sky, to illuminate the fluffy white clouds of this new summer. The warm wind has a cooling effect as it blows through my hair. There is the laughter of children somewhere nearby on this path I walk, and the summer wind gives voice to the leaves of every tree. I listen to the breeze as it whistles by, to hear what message of renewal this is, and by what miracle there is that no snow is on the green grass at my feet. I step off the paved path to walk the field of green grass, and to listen to the wind blow through the summer trees that sway.

"Mom? Mom, is that you?"

A beautiful woman runs toward me in her favorite navy dress (or is it black?), hugs me tight and takes my hand. She tells me, "It didn't end like they thought it would."

"The snow, you mean?"

She escorts me happily to our park bench isolated, beneath a big summer shade tree. Children joyfully play in this affluent park, watched over by a chosen few.

"The earth is under a curse," she says. "These are the last days."

I look at her enigmatically. In her beautiful eyes, I see the peace of joy and knowledge, and nothing of the fear that crystallizes in the snow.

"The evening day is deep twilight," she says, "nearby the edge of night."

"Where'd you get that from?"

"It's the truth. The world is turning fast toward the evening day. And these are signs of the times. Mankind is evil, Honey. You're going to have to be careful."

"About what? What are you talking about?"

"The only salvation is at the Cross. Don't ever let anybody tell you different. Heaven on earth is just a dream."

Our attention is suddenly drawn to the beautiful blonde mother holding her white Pomeranian close to her face, cooing at it lovingly. The woman notices her daughter nearby, with a small but dark grass stain on her white dress.

"I thought I told you to be careful," the mother yells sharply, face contorted with an irritation just below anger, as though she were in pain to resist the rage within. She puts the Pomeranian down gently and grabs the little girl by the arms and pulls her close. "When I get you home I'm going to beat your little ass black and blue. Now I've got to take you home and change before we go to your father's. Why do you think I told you not to go running in this dress!? Do you see what you did? Huh? Answer me!"

As she shakes her crying daughter for an answer where none exists, I look at my mother in the same knowledge as she. She looks anguished at me, as the wind picks up suddenly, blowing her beautiful, long dark hair back from her face. She turns to look at the sky in the distance. I look directly above us, above the mother and daughter, above the nearby trees, and I see the fluffy clouds grown thin and wispy as the sky suddenly begins to phase to a darker blue. Is it more beautiful or less—this I do not know. The wispy clouds begin to change shape before my eyes, and they go spinning around the sky fast enough for us to see. The earth turns rapidly toward the evening day, as the sky darkens to twilight. The mother and daughter join the rest of the people in screaming as lightning sparks, crashing from the blue sky to the park grass nearby. Thick, jagged rivers of blue white appear from the clear sky, which seems to be spinning, while the wind is rising, and the big tree swishes and sways a warning to every man, woman and child.

I am suddenly aware of my vision, that it is simply that, and terror begs me to open my eyes from this nightmare. I do it, and I feel the scratching of ice crystals in my eyes, and the flutter of my eyelashes against the snow I am buried in.

I am unable to panic, disoriented, not understanding fully that I cannot move, or why I can see perfectly the snow over my face. It is like a fluffy blanket from my head to my feet. Unknown to my will, beyond my ability comes the breath of life, where I can suddenly breathe. The breath gives life to my arms, twitching. In the next moment, my arms claw through my snow tomb, and I raise my face up into the cold, gray air, which is at once the air of my bedroom. I am sitting upright, having wiped the phantom snow off my face and hair, amazed that I can still feel the prickling of ice crystals on my skin.

$\mathcal{I}$ open my eyes again with trepidation, after spending the rest of the night in determined slumber, fighting in my sleep to hold the nightmare spirits at bay. The snow was again over my face like a soft blanket. It seemed to be true for most of the night, which woke me up time and again with a start, until I grew accustomed. When I opened my eyes under the snow just now, I didn't jerk myself awake like before, but I allowed my mind to come alive as it saw fit, secure in the knowledge that it was only a ghostly snow blanket that would soon vanish away.

In the warm security of our home, my sister's breakfast calls out to my hunger. It is bacon on the stove. Reminding me that I am still alive, and as well as I can expect to be. Life, it seems, has been frozen to a standstill. I cannot imagine another trip to Mom's boutique or the mall without my best friend, or especially to places as far away as school this fall. I wonder how far along Jeff, Donna and Veronica have gone, and if their snowy paradise will be what they expect.

Do we carry Hell or Heaven everywhere we go?

I'll save my trip to the window for later. We can all take our lonely walk to the lovely bay window later this morning, every morning (every evening), and see whether or not our icy tomb has grown. I'm always amazed that no matter how bad the storm, our lights never go out. Probably a lucky benefit from where we live, for luck has no morality, as some areas in the country may never again see their power restored.

In the bathroom, I stare at what figure God has given me. I'm not exactly sure why (yes, I am), but I love to look at my topless body in the mirror. My breasts are high and rounded, well supported for their double D-cupness, so that my time in a bra is often a choice rather than a necessity. I often put my hands behind my back and jump up and down to watch them bounce, or shake them back and forth, fascinated at how the flesh feels in my hands, and how much I love to squeeze them and pull the nipples when I am alone. My obsession with my own breasts is my fervent pleasure. It is not just the naïve fantasy that men imagine; self lust burns true inside so many women, but in places too painful and deep to go, so that very few can even imagine the feel of their own nipple in their mouth. The first time I did it when I was 15 years old; it caused an electric reaction in my body that still motivates me in private. Even to the tune of my red gel toothpaste played on them. It is nothing for me to suck the red toothpaste off my nipple, then commence to brushing my teeth. Though they are already as big as Annabelle's, they do not hang as beautifully, and she hides the size of her bosom in tight bras, dark dresses, and blouses that do not hug the beautiful shape of them.

Sometimes, and this desire burns me often—sometimes I would like to walk around the warm house topless with both my mother and my sister. I would like for us all to laugh at old conventions and demurities obsolete. As I stand in front of the mirror in small white undies and no bra, I remember how I have allowed the heat to ignite my mind—where I watch my mother remove her bra when she is in her underwear, and then watching her unbutton my sister's shirt, when Amanda is at her deepest worry over the fate of the world. In my imagination, I have seen my mother remove her young daughter's clothing, then clamp her mouth around my sister's young nipple. I have seen my sister's brow wrinkle in the agony of forbidden discovery, while she watches her own mother take pleasure from both of her humongous breasts, but nursing them with determined passion. In my mind, I have seen my sister unbutton my mother's dress and lift one out of her bra. I have seen her take my mother's exposed breast in her hand, and timidly suck until the flattened nipple rises the height of a small grape, sucking in and out repeatedly, until mother has to shake and call the name of the Lord to help her through the final part of it, while she backs into me shaking and trembling from where my hand had massaged her lower body, bra and single breast exposed.

Thoughts like these have plagued me (or is it comfort?) since I was a little girl—the pleasure of the most unspeakable acts, the strongest being that between beautiful, sensual mothers and their daughters. Lusts of this kind come from the heart and cannot be manufactured, but only endured in secret, where no other human being is allowed. In every person, I think, across the whole of humanity burns these lusts in the hearts and minds of women and men. It is why I know a perverted mom or otherwise middle aged woman when I see one, in whose eyes burns the same unspoken lust as mine. The hearts of men and women are evil. When I am twelve, the heart of my babysitter is evil. My heart is evil.

I stand in front of the mirror as Wicked Heart, shaking my breasts back and forth. Loving the big, double D wobble they have.

In honor of the snow, and to cover the blue fire inside, I slide into my white sweats and matching house shoes, slipped over my white ankle socks. My small, white t-shirt pulls hungrily over my bosom, and begins to take the requisite shape, to support and develop the form that is woman. My shirt is too tight as I walk past mother's room. Leaving her to this blessed morning sleep. Seventeen years of health and vitality bounce down the stairs, *sans* bra, and turn the corner to the kitchen. Pulled along by a hunger so deep.

My sister leans as I round the kitchen corner, reaching inside the refrigerator. Her jeans are especially tight this morning, as is the rose pink tank shirt she wears, her favorite color since I can remember. She raises up and closes the refrigerator, tossing a shy, furtive "hey" in my direction. She takes the eggs over to the counter beside the stove. The years of pettiness, the passive aggressive antagonism seems to have vanished with the night, and I feel no bitterness toward my little sister.

I walk boldly in white sweats and t-shirt over to my little Amanda. Shorter than me. Smaller. Smarter.

"What are you looking at?" she says, opening the egg carton.

The words 'a troll' come to the front of my mind, and to the tip of my tongue. I open my mouth, but I bite my lip and smile—snickering a little, watching her break the eggs into the pan. *in my heart my shirt is off and she breaks the cold eggs over my naked breasts.* I stare at her face closely, seeing for the first time the echo of a young beauty, who looks less like the father she never really knew, and more like the beautiful mother she adores. Someday, there will be the rare face and body of beauty. Without vanity.

"God, you're being weird," she says. "What's your problem?"

"Nothing. Just watching you do your thing. Mom."

Already, her discomfort is apparent. Disquiet. This violation of her personal space is abnormal to say the least. But every part of me aches with this need, this aching to break down these old barriers grown, the thicket that rises between siblings, nurtured by the blood of our mothers; hatred flowing beneath the surface of natural love. These are the barriers to closeness, that come only to blood kin, that are not as naturally grown between friends and acquaintances, who can oftentimes develop a bond so powerful as to defy logic and reason. But, oh! What measures are indeed required, in these desperate times we are in?

"Allright," she says. "What's wrong?"

"I..."

I suddenly hear the swirling of wind against the house, howling futures so unknown. I take the fork from her hands and push the pan of eggs to the back of the stove. Away from the heat. When I'm sure that the shock has run its course, when she knows that I have something I must do, I pull her to my body in a deep hug, and lay her head against my chest.

"Hold me tight Amanda. Please."

She closes her eyes, in full understanding that I need the comfort of her young body next to mine, that our spirits must intertwine in the snow.

"I'm sorry," I say softly. "For everything." My sniffing betrays the reservoir of tears underneath, that I take deep breaths to draw strength against.

Here we are! Two young women! Together at last in our kitchen of fear, in our house of devastation, want and need! We hold each other with conviction. Her eyes closed. Brow wrinkled. Face anguished by the hug.

"I want us to be this close, Amanda. I don't want anymore bad blood between us. I love you. I always have. I've always been jealous of you because of how good you and Mom get along. Because of how good you take care of her. Because Dad died. Because Mom wouldn't let us move. Because of everything. I've been taking it all out on you and I'm sorry. I'm sorry for all the times I was ever mean to you Babe. Okay?"

She can only answer with a loud, coughing sob, and a nod of the head. It is the full flowering of her most distant, desperate hope, I suppose. That her big sister would apologize for everything, and swear to be nice to her.

I press my breasts hard against her young body, breathing deeply, desiring the forbidden in the pit of my stomach. Wanting to turn around with my back against her, and have her hands squeeze my breasts hard enough to make me grimace from the pain. Where in my heart is such a desire born? Why must it be so?

Will her lips nurse at my breasts someday?

"When you were at Veronica's yesterday, I thought you weren't coming back. Thank God you did. Thank God."

"I couldn't leave you here by yourself. You take care of Mom, sure. But who's gonna take care of you?"

Even while the wind picks up outside, howling, screaming, I am glad that there is no more room for the biting, sarcastic silliness we wear as a cloak of honor. Along with nature, I am weary of the false speeches we make, and the sardonic bitterness we pretend is fake, but is as real as an angry lion's roar at sunset. From whence cometh sarcasms and bitter speech, but from the poison well inside? Where flows the river of pettiness and unspoken jealousies? Phantom revenge untaken, wished to be given undeserved one to another? Like the fish accustomed to swim polluted waters, we glide these waters of contempt, one to another. But where we live is too icy to dwell, and by necessity we move to warmer seas, to choke briefly on water we have never breathed before. In these new, clear waters I swim, my arms tightly around my sister in warmth and fear of the cold. I take hold of her ponytail with certainty, pulling her head back, telling her "it's you and me forever," watching her nod her head while the tears run in a steady stream down her face. I push my mouth onto hers in the pretend kiss, for now, but deeply felt as our connection by the soul and spirit.

She walks the gray high above me, somewhere on the second floor carpet. Scrambled eggs tended to, crispy bacon prepared, buttered grits, sweet strawberry preserves, light toast and soft butter. Ready for the two of them to come back down to our kitchen. I set the table nicely, china plates as white as my delusion, wanting badly one of the faux white roses from mother's boutique. But our kitchen is grand enough as it is, to host our proper inaugural breakfast. It is the beginning of a new life for the three of us, where we can live together in the peace of family harmony, the vitality of domestic bliss. I expect that we'll all grow accustomed to the Piggly Wiggly game, which I plan to invent, that the one who gains the most weight every week is the queen, because as surely as the rise and fall of the snowline down at Roanoke Island, our waists and bustlines are surely going to do the same. We are going to celebrate the new day. To eat. Drink. And be merry.

Suddenly, I hear the lonely moan of a snow ghost, in the air high above us all. It moves through the wind and the will, through the walls, until I hear it coming for me from the top of the stairs. My heart grieves cold in fear, as I wonder what in the world, with my hand over my chest, gazing at the dining room entranceway wide eyed, waiting for the ice demon to float inside and grab me by the neck, then thrust his hand inside my chest to squeeze my heart to a standstill. Down the stairs it comes—the wailing, moaning voice of the ice banshee that lives in the snow clouds, rounding the banister, flowing through the living room and the kitchen toward where I stand…

Then suddenly, the outstretched arms of my sister fly towards me—above lightning fast feet, under a pretty mouth wide open in a deep, wailing scream, and girlish young eyes frozen open in terror.

On the creeping heels of what I have learned, on what my sister has told me, I take every step in fear, each compounding on the last, until I rise the height of a mountain of dread. I stand at the top of this mountain, at the top of the stairs, with my sister's hands clamped on my left arm, echoes of the snow ghost still in her voice. How is one pulled along by the Spirit of Fear? I know how, as we float past the walls of grieving, to the first door on the left of the hall, the Queen's upper room.

I step inside mother's room as through a veil, from clarity into a fog of confusion. Mother sits quietly. Peacefully at the window of lost hope. Still. Tranquil. And though I cannot believe what my poor sister has perceived herself, I feel the same sliding along on the train, the one I rode down the aisle to my father's wake, then under the cold, cloudy sky to his burial tomb. I step closer to the beautiful woman sitting still, having epic patience for my sister who winces a high pitched, pleading whine in her voice, begging me to tell her that our mother is just resting with her eyes open, and has not become cold, grim and dead. We stand and look closely at our mother's face, as she sits cold, grim and dead.

Her blue eyes are turned right and slightly upward, gazed to the window and beyond. Her head leans back against her blue cushioned comfort chair. Maybe, she *is* at rest, her lips still red with lipstick from the night before, when she found out we were going to be buried alive in the snow. I still remember the vacant, doll like stare in her eyes, the cold, distant expression on her beautiful face at twilight, when she rose from the sofa and turned and ascended these stairs for the last time. As I watch her stare out at the window, she could very well be alive, and I know it should be a sin to not capture her in a photograph. She could very well be alive, were it not for the paleness, the remarkable whiteness of her skin, which denies even the echo of life, to betray where it is that our beloved mother could have gone. I stand and watch her in death, holding my sister, admonishing her to turn and look, pressing this until it is achieved, until she opens her eyes to stare Death in its beautiful eyes. In her tranquil expression, I see the death of fear, when the stress and terror have already torn her heart from its rhythm. Stress and terror pressed down under pressure, until it explodes into her beating heart to send a cold shock through every inch of her body frozen still. But this, followed by the warmth coursing through her blood by Grace, by what she sees outside the snowy window. The light from the Glory of God, the messenger sent to comfort and guide her from this life. This is the Angel of the Lord, who is sent to Annabellle Freeman in the evening day, to ease her mind and her spirit by the power of God, to take her hand beyond the Horizon of Fear which is this life, to raise her up from her chair of weeping, to stand with her by the Holy Spirit of God, to see her leave this life behind, to lift her up from the Earth, and to carry her soul far away from the cold, to the warmth and the power of Light, that comes from the Glory of God, that illuminates the shores of Heaven. There, Mother rests with the Lord of Hosts, where fear has no name, nor any part of it touches her memory.

We lay her flat on her back on the bed, and wrap her in the whitest sheet we own—closing her beautiful eyes before hand, crossing her hands at her waist. We had removed the burgundy dress, and placed her in a white summer dress with sunshine yellow flowers. It is the most appropriate, I suppose, that her burial clothes suggest the snow white landscape, and the summer sun we may never see again.

We thought of calling someone. But who? The dyke who masqueraded as her loving best friend, whose call and visit I dread with all my heart? The so-called parametics, and their red light wagon? By what miracle could they see themselves from the hospital parking lot to our door anyway, or even to our neighborhood? What new paths that had been carved though the parking lots and roads were already being covered again, and this time, I would gather that the plows and salt trucks have had to pick their battles well. There are no plows through our neighborhood today, and the roads are barely passable. After last night's storm, everybody who opened their doors this morning did so to a fresh, newly fallen wasteland, "waste" appropriately so, because snow was already "waist" high at the crack of dawn. We are all bound by the same necessity, for the shovels and electric plows we own, and the daily ritual of keeping the snow at bay, that threatens to seal the doors of our tombs in packed, white ice.

She lies intestate as we gather our jeans and high boots, sweaters, hats and scarves from our bedrooms. We are burdened by a task too great, beyond any we could fathom before. Activity is the mourners best remedy, even to bury a loved one in the snow.

The wind carries the snow in gusts of Summer's Winter, icy cold in these last days of July. We step out into the tranquil blizzard, shovels and pickaxe in hand, making a path through the open space of our back yard to the tall shade tree, leaves full and green against the white canvas of snow. When we look back, we see a long, pitiful, ragged path in the deep snow, from the Great Flowering Tree, to the back of our beautiful mansion home.

"It's too windy," she says, mouth nearly covered in her thick, pink scarf. Her knit hat and gloves are of the same elegant rose.

"The snow will be too deep tomorrow. We have to do it today."

"I'm scared, Belinda. Let's call 911."

"How many days would it take 'em to get here? If they came at all?"

"They'd be here eventually. They've got emergency plows. They're trained to get to people in the snow. We shouldn't do this, Belinda."

"They'll take her from us if we call. They'll stick her in a morgue somewhere. I want her here with us."

With the shovels we brought down the new path, we begin to clear the snow away from this side of the tree trunk. Together, we toss the snow aside—the cold, powdery snow, frozen dry by the arctic summer wind. This makes it hard for us to dig a space, as the snow slides in as quickly as we throw it out. It only adds to our hopelessness, our helpless floundering through this life. After an hour of digging, we make progress in the cold breezes, gradually carving a 10 by 10 foot, snow covered gravesite under the tree, surrounded by a mound of snow on every side. The snow slides like white sand into place wherever it is thrown, and some of it blows away in the strong winter's summer breeze. Above us and around us is the earthen gray of every sky in the world today; a determined, oppressive mood, sent to drive silliness deep into the soul, and foolishness even further away. In our home is the body of our beloved mother Anna, and today, in this gray world, she must be buried in the snow.

Two hours pass in our pathetic digging, until we have dug a space beside the tree trunk. But in our pitiful uninformed selves, naivité had spent itself digging through the snow to the ground we remembered, only to find it gone. What is left is only a dead lawn hidden. Frozen solid under a layer of white ice at least a foot thick.

"Are you going to try to dig through?" she asks.

"Let's go inside first."

We warm our lovely bones at the Heart of Prosperity. Feeling every muscle ache, the tingle of every finger and toe, the painful itching pulled from the edge of Frostbite's shadow. At the kitchen table, sipping warm cocoa, I can still feel what is left of the cold, rising up through my skin.

"What about her life insurance?" she says.

"We don't need it. *God,* we don't need it. We'll be able to stay here forever if we want."

"We might as well," Amanda says. "These people moving--running down south and to those tropical islands. They're just fooling themselves. Those places are starting to get colder every day. The snowfalls are longer. Your friend might as well have just stayed here."

True enough. But I know that they are running from so much more. For them, there are mountains too high, oceans too wide and deep for naught-- but a fair and hasty retreat. But for my sister and me, we must sail these waters towards irony. These icy winds of nature's fervent hatred for mankind.

My mother's body, the unnatural stiffness of it, reaches through our little resistance and taps us both on the nerve, where fear and revulsion begin. It was bad enough through the upstairs hall, but began to take root on our trip down the stairs, flourishing while we struggled through the kitchen. But even only a few steps through the snow made us realize that there will be no carrying of the body.

"We can't do it," I say, answered immediately by my sister's thinking brain.

"We'll have to drag her," she says. "No, not like that," she snaps at me. I follow her back into the house, into the gigantic kitchen. There, she tells me that we will wrap her body in her favorite gray comforter, then tie it with pieces of rope so it will not open.

Mother is bound so conspicuously, unceremoniously inside the Ralph Lauren bedding, like some poor victim of a hit man's sickness. We are out back now, the two of us, close beside one another on the snow path, pulling the grey rolled up cloth by the thin white rope tied tightly at her feet, stumbling, straining from lack of strength in our arms, breathing in the cold air, feeling the wind rising by the passing hour, while the hidden daylight slips by over the clouds. We hardly notice the thick clouds lighting up in places all over the sky, nor do we flinch at the rumbling bowls of invisible thunder.

But halfway down our destination to the tree, we feel the characteristic springs in the bottom of our feet, and hear the crashing, booming sound across the snowy land, and we know the grief is not the rumbling above, but from the ground far and beneath our feet. The earth rumbles massively, causing us to wonder how long it will be, and what small but significant damage may befall our mansion home. Even the leafy green trees shake and sway in the new breeze, and the quivering of the snowy ground below.

In the rumbling quake, we gather our wits, and we pull our mother in renewed strength and fever, the fervent power of natural fear. Through the wind and blowing snow, the glowing clouds and flowing waves of booming sound, we pull with our little might, toward the sacred ground we are destined for.

Snow

Mother is soon pulled by the two of us from the traveling path, sliding onto the white ice packed in the space under the gigantic backyard tree. The ice is too smooth, too white, too pristine to destroy by a ridiculous digging beneath it to the filthy, frozen soil lost in time. My sister takes the tiny paring knife from her coat pocket, and to my relief, quickly cuts the ropes that we had knotted too tightly to untie with ice cold fingers, then we unroll her, exposing her white wrapped body to the snow.

Mother! Thy name is irony! Woman of Beauty, who swore that all was well, you were killed by the very thing you hold so dear! While your daughters use the last of their strength for a small mound of snow over your body, they know that you died from the love you had for this life! You were killed by your perseverance inside Vanity, which caused your heart to fail with fear—when you realized the very thing your daughter warned you against was going to reach down from the clouds, clutch your heart in ice, then bury your lifeless body in the snow…and I, having not the courage, the strength, the endurance to push through the veil of false hope to grab thee, and pull thee to safety, I instead left you alone to battle a terror I never knew you had, a fear I only thought I understood, thus killing you Mother so dearly, and burying you in the snow.

In the gray afternoon, we stand at the white burial mound, feeling the earth subside. From where we stand, our trail moves from us through waist high snow, from the grave at the trunk of the big tree, all the way over the white prairie lawn, to the back door of our mansion home. From here, our house rises a gradual hill. To overlook the lawn in Prosperity.

We killed our mother dearly
And buried her in the snow

Jonathan Lovejoy

Our footsteps trailed from her grave to home
With nowhere left to go

The violent years bore us in two
Berating us with what to do
Until we killed our mother dearly
And buried her in the snow

One night while she lay sleeping
We crept up to her bed
There bade an end to days of weeping
We smothered her 'til dead

We smothered her 'til breathing stopped
We drug her out of bed
We dragged her body into the cold
Toward the winter wood

Sister and me in tow—adrift
In the wake of what we could
In the twilight snow we calmly stood
Toward the winter wood

Knowing what we had to do
Though not of what we should
We drug her body to the edge
Of the winter forest wood

Snow

Down through the winter white we dug
Into the hardened ground
We chopped into the frozen soil
Where our final strength was found—

We laid her in the dirt
Her grave raised into a mound—
We cleared away a foot of snow
And laid her in the ground

We smoothed the rounded dirt away
Where no marker would be found

The violent years bore us in two
With nowhere left to go
We killed our mother dearly
And buried her in the snow

Sister and me—we followed the trail
Of footsteps to our home
Looking each other in the eye
No remorse for what we'd done

Gazing beyond the clouds of winter
To remember the fallen one
To hear the wind carry what we'd done
Beneath the setting sun

Jonathan Lovejoy

No tears were left for us to cry
Nowhere was left to go
When we killed our mother dearly
And buried her in the snow

Now a voice cries in the wilderness
Winter winds begin to blow
We killed our mother dearly—
And buried her in the snow

Part Two

The cityscape is teaming with plows, shovels and salt men, all trying to fend off the Mighty Hand of God. In the haze of snow blowing, from the street machines to the clouds way up high, the lights of buildings can hardly be seen in the daylight. Strollers (the two-legged pedestrian kind) have abandoned the sidewalks except when passable, a rare enough reprieve from those covered in piles of snow. So many small business owners along the neighborhood streets have caved under the pressure, the years of snowfall, and the city's broken promises, over and over again, to send shovels and plows and snowblowers to keep the walkways clear. Futile at best, when even on days of passable sidewalks, there are no customers to see anyway. Only the busiest throughways still have life, as the age of the Mom and Pop Shop is fast coming to a close, being buried under drifts and mounds of snow.

In the icy cold, tourism dissolved like snowflakes on the water; parks and zoos were shut down, having no income from a curious public, no longer interested in the snowy sights and sounds of manmade nature. Opera houses and movie theaters, museums, cafés, coffee houses and restaurants had thrived as long as they could, as owners fought hard against the windy snowfalls, but finally loosing against storms that kept the snows at near disaster level, and loyal patrons were kept away. Open baseball fields and football stadiums were completely snowed in—the doors to some having not been opened in years. But strangely enough, public transportation flourished, as people grew accustomed to the proliferation of buses and minivan / SUV taxi services. The wind whipped and whirled the snow through the manmade canyons of misery. Nightlife had been shaken to its foundation, above and below in the so-called underground, as clubbers and high life partygoers grew tired of fighting the windy flurries in the night, and those that needed to gather began to do so in their homes of safety and privacy.

Amusement parks, fairgrounds and carnivals had tried valiantly, even using the snow as part of their attraction for a while, to woo people from their summer-winter hiding places to a winter carnival or winter adventure or whatever: painting some poor octopus ride white and calling it a Snow

Spider—more than one ferris wheel morphed into a Snow Wheel. Coffee and hot chocolate replaced soda and ice cream in most hands around the parks, while Icees with the polar bear logo had seen a national revival. (But is it ironic that in the snow economy, snow cone sales were a disaster?) Entire roller coasters were painted white and renamed to reflect the earth's condition: *Snow Fire* or *Avalanche* or *White Dragon.* Admission prices were cut down to half of what they were, even to accompany the presence of "Snow Queens" in the giant East Coast World and its smaller, West Coast Land mother, and their strange triplet sister Realm Across the Sea. Exotic beauties of ridiculous, conspicuous prettiness dressed in white to ride around the family theme parks in their white carts for show and park-goer assistance. Intelligent remedies, they were. Sex appeal bound and repressed in red lips smiling—blue eyes to lure fathers, mothers and children captive in fantasy. "Snow Girls" and "Snow Babes" and "Snow Bunnies" proliferated in the last days of the amusement parks, before the earthquakes began to shake the riders into free falls from the coasters and swing boats and ferris wheels, and the snows prevailed in "white storms" across the wide open spaces, and the efforts to rid the grounds of the devastation became too monumental for every Northern park in the world. Only a few southern parks still remained open last summer, those with the money and motivation, the East Coast World being the last big theme park closed, along with the West Coast Land, to signal the death of every snowy, southern amusement park who foolishly persisted until now, all pledging to close permanently at the end of this calendar summer. Even now, the big southern parks have already seen the light, and have passed through this 4th of July abandoned, buried wide and deep in ice and snow.

Snow

I climb the top of the *Snow Serpent* in kind. Walking the ice dragon coaster in kind. Gazing the sea of white where man used to be, in lasciviousness and carnality. The wind swirls around me here, at the top of the *White Dragon*, attempting to pluck me from this perch of foresight, but being unable. I am in a cloud of winter haze, to feel the high blowing snowflakes hit and melt on my face. This dragon's fire is out—the blue flame of worldliness sits idle and cold. Those who claim allegiance to hope must look elsewhere for it, somewhere above and beyond this field of white.

From the snowfall in my mind, to the present and current time, the hours are adrift—from here to the grave of Hsu Hahn. A gray headstone talking, discussing the years of her life in brief, but with no symbol of Christ anywhere nearby, at the fervent request of her mother and father.

$\mathcal{H}$igh above the eastern seaboard, the wind screams and howls away all expectation—from laymen and experts alike. The clouds are alive with sparks of energy: rivers of white heat and electric blue, spread across the entire eastern part of the country in something deeper than white noise; the crackling and rumbling of a great earth storm, but from a summer seven years in the making—a summer already buried by the cold.

Snow

A gigantic blast of what air there is left that tries to be warm, had flowed upward with unsuspected intent, as the earth gave one final warm breath to the icy north region where we live, but served only to anger the cold, arctic air poised to claim us forever. This warm blast—this last, final true tropical summer breeze as big as our collected prayers—had collided with the arctic air over the whole eastern half of the country, and the violence erupted in the atmosphere like fireworks over Satan's Barnyard. Exploding over the clouds that already live here, creating new, towering thunderheads above the gray cloud canopy. Lightning sparked up, down, through and around these clouds to nowhere, leaving evidence of themselves for no one to see, as they crackled a bird's nest of deadly wires above where we could see, with the occasional single bolt high above and away from the clouds themselves: a great arc of light whipped across the sky in crashing, bellowing thunder claps and screaming.

Below the lightning, the violent air sunk into the cloud bank like gods in combat. Great, invisible ghosts circling each other faster and faster, until they begin to fall from the thunderheads they were in, swirling beneath the cloud layer in such unearthly spinning as to be supernatural, pulling evidence of their battle downward and ever so slowly downward in white touched and tainted by gray. Pulling the sky down with them and around them in a great turning and spinning, lit up by the flashes of lightning brought with them. Their battle is concealed in the towering *snow devil*, the funnel cloud thirty stories tall and lean, brought to life by the hunger and greed of the last battle of warm air against the cold. The rainfall is doomed from its very origin, from its creation alone, to begin crystalization at its birth, falling as rain in so desperate a try, but freezing halfway to the ground; caught up in the violent whirlwind over the eastern snow plain, and blown down to earth as white ice and snow.

The last and greatest snow devil leans forward. East of the Appalachian Forest, to travel 100 miles up the coast, until over 1000 people would breathe their last breath from it. This Great Snow Twister of this century year, leaves a narrow, deep gulf in the snow, only to have its mighty efforts so quickly covered by the heavy outpouring of snow from every cloud, along with every swirling gust of wind; this so called damage path is mocked into insignificance by the greater good: the storm itself, which makes light of the deadly snow twister in the cold.

High over the eastern seaboard. Pain crystallizes inside the grey. Tears over the thousand dead in Harm's Way. Mourning for the many more that will die. Tears frozen in the new age, heavy with purpose. Too burdened in crystal to stay aloft. These are gathered by the billions, no one just the same as the other. They fall together through the gray canopy as one, but each knowing which way they will ultimately go.

A few of these move south over Edgecombe County, North Carolina. Where they drift in evening song, the melody of their warmest twilight, the harbinger of their darkest ray of night. Through the evening day, from the stars where they glimpsed the glory of God, they fall toward the lights of earthly progression, the lights of the southern city streets hidden in white. These few flakes of snow gather from the four winds, coming together by predestination over the back yard of Mai Hahn (like 'May'), who looks out her kitchen window at the lighted snow falling. I see the Asian mother at her kitchen window, ignoring the coffee boiling nearby, trying to find the memory of her two daughters, gone drifting in the cold.

Gliding the streets of Edgecombe County, where the sidewalks are almost gone again. Under the street lamps flickered on hours ago, in the twilight of afternoon, burning bright at the edge of Summer's Winter Night. Past the rows of modest homes, the line of the upper lower class, who once pushed against the glass ceiling to the middle, but finding it too hard to break.

Brick home. Small. Plain. Already covered to the bottom of the front windows with snow. Walkway and driveway partially clear. Will be well cleared tomorrow, as are these streets most of the time. People bound by the need to work for survival rather than diversion.

Mai Jun Chang. Mother of Linda Hsu, who lies in wait at Pineview.

May Hahn turns from the window at Peachtree, with no more taste for the stench of coffee brewing. She goes into the small living room to her TV and recliner. To slide into the leisure of hopelessness and regret. A life insurance widow, for now. Enough to keep her alive. Enough to exist upon. Until she must return to work to survive.

Still burdened by the curse laid on her when she was seventeen. When she left the country farmlife behind with Li Hahn Fao. Lee Hahn. With dreams of settling here. His own grocery business someday. A dream realized too little and too late, when fledgling *Hahn's Southern* was hit too hard by the snow economy. A dream over twenty years dying.

The ice barrier went up like a wall of empty promises, between Lee Hahn and business success. Through this barrier there lies no entrance. Of no penetration born, where others stand outside the Patronage of Fools, with no mercy or compassion therein. People left *Hahn's* without remorse, to gather at the Market Superstores in warmth from the cold, until it was as though he was never there. Bankruptcy, wholesale departure of goods, then a farewell to the dream of *Hahn's Southern* markets across the southeast.

This, another dead dream. The second part of Hahn's Truth, four years after the first part, which was the suicide of Linda Hsu in the classroom. That was the beginning of sorrows for them. The beginning of the fulfillment of curses, placed at their feet by Mai Chang's mother, when she spat in her sixteen year old daughter's face at their dinner table, and swore that every step she took in America would be more painful than the last.

This, I see. This, I feel. This is told to me by the spirits of the snow, when Mai Chang broke her father's heart, and condemned her mother to die alone and lonely on the farm in Hubei. Mai left with Li Hahn Fao, the silly dreamer, wanting a grocery chain in the *Land of the White Whores*, Mai's mother said. *Do you want to be a white whore like them*, she said. *To wear makeup and walk the streets in tight American dresses and high heels? To dye your hair yellow and paint your face like a Geisha whore,* she said in old Chinese tongue. *You want to die in thousand foot building with yellow hair and red lips...* then a laugh as real as it was cruel, then a slap to her daughter's face, telling her to *go and get me the punishment stick Ju Mai, so I can beat some sense into you.* Mai Chang went to get the stick thirty years ago when she was sixteen, and she stood with the back of her dress open to her mother's wrath. Mai Chang's mother took the punishment stick, and she whipped her daughter's white skin to blood.

Mai gladly left the fields of Hubei. With the twenty one year old dreamer, who had seen her outside at the country market, one warm Summer's day. They sailed the winds above the East, towards the promise in the Land of Freedom, touching down by plane, under the western Sun. In the Land of the Western Sun, in the Land of Fame and Fortune, they staked a claim down east. Lee and May Hahn, in Edgecombe County.

Lee Hahn. Ambitious. Driven. Intelligent. Virtuous. Deserving? Maybe. But Luck has no morality. And Destiny is king.

The land of opportunity. Birthplace of Linda Hsu Hahn. Child of Joy. Daughter of Hope.

Sue Hahn. Tennis player. Honor Society. Student government. One of the very few Asians who lived in residence there. Special. Unique. Destined to leave Rocky Mount someday, to carry intelligence and talent with her.

Tennis team. University of white, black and Blue Devils. English degree. A love for children. A calling to teach. Four years older than her sister whom she loved.

Four years old in the tiny apartment on Myrtle Avenue, when Deborah Lin Hahn was born. Four year old Sue cradled the child like her favorite doll.

She loved her.

$\mathscr{D}$onna Ward cruises the beachfront in luxury; hips exposed behind the white bikini cloth. The white sun burns a trail of heat through the hazy blue sky to where she and her husband play on the sands of Hapuna Beach, the white powered sands of warning. Donna splashes out of the water in the warm ocean breeze, cool on her wet skin, ignoring where ever it is that her husband could have gone. Maybe he went back to the Prince Hotel, she doesn't know. She looks down her nose at her daughter on the recliner hiding in her blackest shades, so she can gauge her mother's look without being seen. Beauty guides her mother's features into place. Big, blue eyes set well apart, eyebrows arched, nose perfectly sloped and sculpted, rounded at the tip, lips full enough to draw attention to them, to imagine them wrapped around her own finger in brief sucking. A tight, toned, athletic body with high, rounded breasts firm enough to cause wonder, and the question: *Are they real?* Donna Ward's hard bosom is as real as the fire that burns underneath, to make her brave enough to wear only a small bikini top cloth over them, to expose nearly every inch of the rounded flesh spilling out in front of her eleven year old daughter. Confident. Bold. Self assured. Morally complacent. Certain that this form of nudity is accepted and sanctioned by God himself—that to keep the nipple fully covered only, and bare feet on these white sands are the prerequisites for absolution.

Her young daughter reclines idly by. Only eleven when the sky was blue. Unaware. Unmotivated by the blue fire that burns. Eleven year old Veronica watches Donna Ward smile on this side of paradise, where her mind is not tormented by spirits of anger and dread. Where she thinks of her youngest boy Tom, somewhere down the beach, throwing the football, sailing his future through the air on a wind to the girls and to his older brother Dwayne, who's already a junior at Princeton, where Tom will start at quarterback. Donna thinks so fondly of her youngest boy. And she has to tense her shoulders once and smile from the giddiness it causes. A son who led his Vermont high school to two state titles his junior and senior year. A boy with eyes of the mother, and the handsome, square jaw of the father, and a talent for football from only God knows where, seen once in a lifetime, with grades and connections for the Ivy League. Having already thrown at a summer practice two weeks ago. Causing some to predict that he would never see his junior year in college, before he would be called to immortality.

Tom Ward. To a lesser degree—Dwayne Ward. These are the buffers in her brain, that cushion between clarity and confusion. The barriers in her mind, between happiness and sorrow. They have affixed the gulf between.

And Donna Ward turns to look at her eleven year old mistake. Her little nose wrinkled up under the stupid black sunglasses. Little body hopelessly thin. Brown hair carelessly stringy in a tragically stringy ponytail. Leaning lazily backward in the sun at Hapuna Beach. Unaware. Unmotivated by the blue fire that burns. Friends with a *tartish little tramp* named Belinda Freeman, who is *a whore in waiting* if Donna ever saw one.

Dominique Ward, a.k.a. Donna Ward, takes a deep breath in the warm, tropical air. Still not caring where her husband Jeff is at this moment. A flash of self congratulatory energy ripples through her soul like lightning, when she remembers her upcoming trip. Another smug, condescending walk through a South African village, to look hunger and poverty in the eye. To crest the wave of perceived gratitude, the thankfulness that comes from immediate gratification, when aching hunger and thirst are appeased. But who listens when a child cries? Who cares at all for their weeping in the night, when guilt is satisfied, when charity is done for the day, when their self-serving part of giving is accomplished? The phony, egotistical swooping down like some white knight or Queen Lady, to boost their own self confidence and approval for their privileged lives, to enjoy the sad gratefulness in the eyes of the hungry mothers and sick children, but having no real love for them. Using them as a social tool, a way to gain advantage for their own kind. Caring for them as it serves their purpose to be seen. To try and please God through cheerful giving, blaring their trumpets before men; all too happy to be congratulated and thanked and called a hero or a saint, for the smug and condescending walk through the African village to come.

Donna knows. And she knows them that know. So impressed by one family they know, who sold their big million door home and moved into a smaller million dollar home, and gave the million dollar difference to African charities. And now, those people feel better—finding it so easy to smile in the mirror. Having so much fun being worshipped for the grand idea, which is to throw tax deductable rocks into the Pacific Ocean to try and raise the tide, or to pour in a glass of fresh water to make the ocean fresh enough to drink. To shoot a machine gun into a flock of 1000 scavenger birds, or to pour a bucket of warm water onto a mountain of snow. To give, give and give, scattered, until there is no more left to give. To try and ease the pain of living without the true love of God in their hearts, whom some know as Christ the Lord. To weep and howl for the millions of dark-skinned poor so far away, yet feel nothing for the millions of them in their own back yard. To pretend to care enough to want to adopt children from everywhere on earth, but with no love for a single orphan child in their own country. To pledge in their hearts to end poverty in Africa, but with no concern for the Children of Africa who live here, who have need of a helping hand of guidance from New World Poverty to prosperity.

These are they who listen when the children cry, and hear nothing but noise, and feel nothing but contempt in an icy heart and soul.

And what of the children there—in the village alive with the white and black angels from here? What do they feel when they are cooed over by the strangers in strange clothing and white faces painted, hair smelling of fruited soaps and chemicals, pockets filled with curiosities: coins and keys and sugared gum, which they sometimes give reluctantly? Do they feel like a monkey in a zoo, like an ape in a cage, like a humanoid animal set to perform the dancing eyes of gratitude? What do they do when the gum is chewed and the M&M's are eaten, and they are hungry again? When the arrogant, patronizing, condescending angels are gone, who hears them when they cry again? A new cry, some of them, to have tasted the compassion of freedom, who have smelled the bouquet of privilege, and drunk the fresh waters of prosperity for a day. Who is there to wipe their tears away, when they are hungry again? Who wipes the mother's eyes, when she knows that her child is going to die from broken promises, from empty promises sent from the New World, and charity dispensed with pride? Who wipes the mother's tears, when she remembers the smell and the feel of the white woman's soft, clean hair and clothes, and the suggestion of *you are my best friend, my African Queen, and your children are my only love?*

Donna Ward thinks fondly of her upcoming trip over the African Plain. She breathes in the gust of ocean wind, shocked by the sudden coldness it entails.

$\mathcal{V}$engeance howls the wilderness Lake Champlain—across the frozen, windy sea. Over the Appalachians, down the white, windy slopes of the Green Mountains, cold pain blows the landscape of Vermont. The North Wind breathes through a town named for the flower fields of Spring, leaping over the railroads of Whitehall, stretched long from where we are buried in Prosperity. The North Wind grows. It blows hard past the borders of our region, looking for those who have sought to escape. This wind knows. Among those who have gone the road south and west, down through Arkansas, where the snows fly thinner through the air, across the hopeful cities and towns toward the lower Midwest. Chasing these riders in their chariot. Grieving to see them frozen alive on their journey.

The road west crosses the line into Oklahoma, where the flurries play under clouds less menacing. Clouds that have seen the darkest days of the white storms, unlike any other place on earth. The big skies of Oklahoma are covered gently for now, in the aftermath of violence from days and years past. They breathe a small sigh of relief, the three of them, miles and worlds away from the graves of their brothers and sons.

These are the flurries of resurrection. The fleeting brushes of hope gathered and blown, snow not thrown by the angry gods from the clouds in the Northeast, but rather the flurries of gentle gusts over the prairie, brushed from the powdery miles of ground. These are snows unmelted. Permanently frozen this year, assured by the summer high of 31 degrees, and the wind chill of ten degrees colder still.

These three are a family. Nervously leaning on one another. Gliding through the warmest possible summer on this part of the earth. They travel the partially cleared highways of Oklahoma, in awe of the Barren Plain, the snow covered fields to the horizon. This sight is too magnificent for words, like the beauty of art and music. It is enough to carry their spirits to a calming state, where the pain of regret can move more easily through. They glide the Summer Winter, these three, to eastern Tulsa County, to the town of Broken Arrow.

One of the three—the father, seems to remember what was said of this place five summers ago, after the twisters killed over half the 80,000 population, that God didn't name this place Broken Arrow for nothing. It is where the treaty between God and man was broken again in the modern day. A reflection of Eden and Gethsemane. This was the first Armageddon, some said, when destruction was delivered not by the will of man, but the Almighty Will of God.

They drive through Tulsa County, these three, through the snowy remains of Broken Arrow, where even five years after the fact, the ruins of houses and buildings still lay. This is a ghost town. A town once filled with life and promise, now filled with death and despair, awashed in emptiness. Abandoned by Hope itself. Left to freeze under the crest of newly fallen snow. Left to die.

They cruise beyond the frozen, dead streets of Ghost Town, these three. Moving south past the Broken Arrow city limits, to the country where land was bought and sold in cheap quantity and fear. Donna Ward's father Jack Stone, the real estate millionaire, smart enough to by land where they were giving it away—this time in Tulsa County, Oklahoma. Fifty acres of smooth grassland and a large brick rancher home, a place he loved to visit once in a while before he died. Calling it a Sea of Tranquility. Leaving it to his daughter in the will, along with 10 million dollars to boot.

They cruise the land, these three. Healthy. Wealthy. Wise. In the place where the scarred earth is covered, as is the memory of 44,000 people dead. In Tulsa County, Oklahoma—where the worst outbreak of twisters in history took place five years ago, only one year after these unnatural phenomena began. These fields were covered in light snow then, still a grassy plain in a light, white blanket—with tornadoes of all sizes and strength formed across the prairie for miles. For two weeks, the storms criss-crossed Eastern Oklahoma. Having a special curse laid for Tulsa County, when the twisters hit in broad daylight one afternoon in Broken

Arrow, until guilt and everything else of value was gone. People stood at the doors of their homes with video cameras, watching some of the funnels come to life even in their front yards, snaking through like some giant gray serpent from the sky.

They travel this cursed land below the city, these three. To the bottom of Tulsa County, until their destination arrives. A long, light colored brick rancher home. Black shutters, white columns. White door. A house accompanied by only a tree or two, surrounded by an endless expanse of ice and snow. They arrive at Destination Hope, these three—the mother disembarking the rolling chariot first, to gaze far and wide the frozen tundra of Oklahoma. Soon, the three of them are away from the white Sequoia that brought them here, all looking over the snowy field of white. They gaze the open field, these three, to marvel their Season of Tranquility.

*I*n the theatre of her mind, she plays a drama of the Truth—that truth unfolded to a fluttering in the wind, shaken as puffy ice crystals of Revelation, each containing the secrets of her universe untold, and unknown to the hearts of women and men. Each flake of this new winter fallen, aloft on the cold breezes downward, some illuminated by the deadly blue light from the clouds for a moment, then to drift in the lonely cold of gray again. In her heart and spirit, the snow dims in her mind's eye, to allow the first part of the truth to burn in clarity from her soul—for Mai Hahn, the latter day snow burns away, by the light of her vivid memory, when Lee watched his oldest daughter collect her degree, already committed to travel, to teach fifth graders in a distant northeast. When Lee, May, and Lynn watched her walk across the stage and collect her ticket to ride.

Under a burning blue Carolina sky, in the stadium filled with Blue Devils—mothers and fathers, sisters and brothers, every Blue Devil relation and aquaintance known—to watch the graduates get their tickets to ride Vanity's train to Hell, the Hahn family hugs their successful daughter so tight. A mother in pleasant, nervous indifference. A father in fearful, obsessive pride. And a younger sister in tearful, obsessive love.

"Why do you have to go so far away," Mai says to her lovely daughter that very night—after the Blue Devil Graduation. Her accent is Far East.

"It's the best opportunity there is for me. A Vermont private school— wealthy kids—I couldn't be luckier."

But luck has no morality—and fortune is fleeting. And what power does a curse have, what momentum does it gather along the bloodline, as it is passed from a mother to her daughter? A sudden possessiveness—a hot, cold jealously somewhere deep in a green and white fire, causing her to rather see her daughter fail than leave and run to the arms of freedom.

"You'll break your father's heart if you go so far," she says, New World English burdened by the Old World. An accent just thick enough to betray native origin. "I forbid you to go. You can get a job here."

"I'm a grown woman," she says—pretty Asian features enhanced by a stylish gray sweatshirt, with the Blue Devil university letters displayed. "Every time I try something new you always try to stop me or discourage me. You didn't want me to play tennis, and it helped pay for my tuition. You didn't want me to be in student government, you didn't want me to be a cheerleader, and I shouldn't have listened to you on that one. Do you know they asked me every year to be a cheerleader? You're the only reason I didn't do it."

"I didn't want you making a fool out of yourself—dancing half naked for teenage boys and their horny old fathers and grandfathers. Besides that—you always had the time for your studies didn't you? How would you have the grades for this University if I had not been so strict? If it were up to me you would have only done your studies and nothing else. You could have graduated 1st in your class. If you had listened to me, you could have graduated from the Ivy League instead of here."

"Who are you kidding, Ma? You wouldn't have let me go so far away. And what's wrong with this school?" she says, pointing at her sweatshirt. A proud, wry smile hidden. Staring at her mother for an answer.

Mai Hahn answers with a forceful *hmm*—by a judging, suspicious glare, and a return to her dinner on the stove.

"If there's one thing I regret, it's not being a cheerleader. I could feel it every time I went to a basketball game. I should have cheered four years in high school and four years in college."

"That's for Deborah Lin. Not you. Lin's not a funny face like yours. She has my face. You have your father's face."

"What's my face go to do with it?" she says laughing. Jaded to the pain.

"That is why I did not let you cheer."

"Because you didn't think I was pretty enough?"

Mai sips from her short glass on the counter. The wine flows pleasure to her blood.

"Let *them* be a cheerleader, I said. Don't take up a spot from a girl who deserves it more than you."

There have been times over the years, when Linda Sue has felt the pushing—towards something her spirit knows to be a dividing line. An edge. But it has never been a point of aggression to another person. But rather a violence turned inward, like wind and waves on a rocky shore, to the slow and gradual loss of self esteem, happiness, and even hope for the future. For Linda Sue, there are times when even the sound of her mother's voice grips her, to push her towards this edge. This limit.

"You think you can make it in Vermont on your own?"

"I'm a grown woman, Ma."

"Hah! Who told you were a grown woman? Everyday you were in school you call—*hi ma I miss you ma I like to come home ma*—I tell you, Li Hsu, you should have gone to school on the other side of town and lived here with us. Now you think you'll go to Vermont and start a new life without your mother."

"I'll still call you every day, Ma."

"It's not the same. And you never too old to be punished for disrespect."

Tingles, phantom itches, crisscross the landscape of Sue's skin from her shoulders to her ankles. She lowers her eyes.

"You might as well be in another country up there. What is in Vermont anyway except snow?"

"I've been there already and I've seen what a beautiful place it is. The town is called Prosperity."

"Hmm. Naturally."

"There's a...I don't know... a richness there. You can feel their appreciation for the finer things. They know there's more to life than paying bills. I look forward to becoming a part of that."

"Richness? I'll bet. You going up there to look for a man, aren't you? Gonna shake that big booty. Go ahead and deny it. Where you and your sister get such a big butt anyway? Especially you. Make you easy to catch a man."

"There's got to be more cash in the gum bush than that."

"What?"

"There's more to life than men and marriage."

"You a dyke?"

"Ma that's awful. But if I were a *lesbian* there wouldn't be anything wrong with it. Would there?"

"I don't know. I worry about your sister sometimes. Her room look like a sorority sometimes. But Lynn not like you. She got a good head on her shoulder."

"I just need to get away from here," Hsu says. "Rocky Mount is dead. I really hate this city. There's a weird spirit that hangs over this place. It's a spirit of poverty. Violence and failure. A city on the rise my *ass*."

"You watch your language, Li Hsu."

"Dad's store is never going to make it in this city."

"Your father knows what he's doing. The store will be fine. If you had any respect for your Mother and Father you would stay here and help us make a successful business."

"I have to teach."

"You have to run away. You have to run away from wisdom. From counsel and discipline. Read what it say in that book you love so much about honor thy father and thy mother, that your days may be long."

"Oh, Lord..." Pretty Asian eyes roll. A deep sigh.

"But I tell you the truth...and I want you to hear me good... if you leave this family to go to Vermont, you will bring shame and dishonor to us. And your days will be *short.*"

"I don't understand you. Most mothers would be proud. And you act like I'm doing something wrong."

"You listen to your mother and you live longer. You don't, and I see your body in a coffin."

Li Hsu allows her spirit to be tickled by her mother's prophecy. Old world ignorance. Passed down the family tree to here and now. To die in the light of knowledge. The light of modern, new world wisdom.

"Look at the tears. Always the tears. You are a weak, free hearted, push over. You a sweet little funny face who belong here with her mother. If you go to Vermont, the curse of death will follow you like a dog."

Li Hsu gazes downward, her mother standing close by. As hard as she tries, she cannot keep the water from overflowing her vision.

*A*gust of wind nearly blows us off our feet as we walk. Our trip through this storm is ill advised at best. Maybe it is our soul's relief—the facilitation of its undertaking.

We walk from the grand white house on Tulip Garden Road, blazing a trail through the snow to Mom's boutique, chopping into the new snow with every step—along the road that is barely passable. There are no cars foolish enough for out or in, no remaining tracks from those of us who are gone away. Every soul that left before this new storm is long gone, the trail of their departure covered up in the newly fallen snow. Amanda and I are warriors this time—we battle in bravery the elements of this fevered winter, as we make our new path from here to eternity.

We are out here every day. Plowing the field, so to speak. The plow being the electric snow blower, and the field being one of ice and white. Many have learned a hard lesson about neglecting the shovel and the plow after the Earthquake's Revelation, which is every light and deadly snowfall. We learned as far back as five years ago that these snowfalls are not passing curiosities to be neglected until the next melt—we saw clearly that more and more often there was no melting at all. Unless one wishes to be buried in an ice tomb, one gathers the tools of the trade, to move the snow away from wherever it is that you want to walk from the front door. And these storms are such that their duration is as otherworldly as their intensity—making the shovel and the plow a daily and necessary ritual during a storm. To let 48 hours pass without clearing a path from the door is, in some places, suicide.

This is one of the out of the way places. Where we walk, live and breathe. Like everywhere, even on the hills of Prosperity Garden Terrace, money and privilege mean less and less every single day—and after the biggest storms, this is just another neighborhood. Another gated community buried in 10, 15 and 20 feet of snow. Very few neighborhoods, especially where snow was already common, are bolstered by any municipal effort beyond the busiest streets and thoroughfares, and those as anonymous as we are content to live and die alone. It is as impressive a sight to stand on the streets and lawns of the nation's capital, and marvel at the carefully landscaped efforts to keep paths to knowledge and wisdom open, as it is to cruise the rows of poverty houses and anonymous suburban blights to see the opposite: to see the snow drifted high enough to bury the forgotten alive in their homes. But there is an arrogance, a heightened spirit of entitlement and war for control in the capital city that flares up year round—so that casual walks down Pennsylvania Avenue and through the White House Lawn remain possible, as every inch of it is kept shoveled and plowed down to no more than a few inches; sometimes piles of White House snow are hauled away by the truckload to keep it clear. Or the steps of the Lincoln Memorial after a night of high plains drifting, where the wind blows in memory of one century's '63, and its historic absolvement of the afore century's '63, snows of the battlefields where walked the Man of Lean, to snows of the modern day precipice at his feet. These steps are laboured upon. Driven by the burden in the hearts of men, to keep every step clear that rises to a mountain of light—the burden intertwined with that of survival; the preservation of life, and the postponement of a tragedy in the afterlife. This is the instinct for survival, but not just their bodies, but that which is civilization itself. They are nicknamed the Snow Guard, as even their gray and white camouflage fatigues suggest, and to allow the snow to win is their Death and Dishonor. They keep the steps, the courtyards, the frozen waters of the National Mall, the balconies, walkways, throughways, gardens and lawns of our national conscious clear, believing every penny of the snow treasury that buys clarity for the headstone crosses at Arlington is well and worthily spent.

It is an echo of this same consciousness that pushes us. That drives us through the wind and snow—past the frozen land where the duck pond used to be—past the hopelessly open security gate. Down the road not more than two miles further, to the row of restaurants and clothing outlets that used to be, and where some stubbornly persist until now and the near future—where one fancy boutique has been struck a death blow. From the memorial of a century, to the snow covered lawn of our king, to the crosses on the stones that whisper names no one can hear, over the empty miles north to where we are, we trudge our way through the lot at the empty strip mall—to Freeman's Jewelry and Boutique, to retrieve a memoriam that I remember.

Not really certain of what we're looking for, we unlock the door to Freeman's Jewelry. Our initial steps are covered in snow, but are hardly given to the idea of melting. The powdery snow falls off our knee high boots to the carpet. What wonders and valuables lay in the glass cases—tens of thousands of dollars in gold and diamond rings, necklaces, bracelets, earrings and the like—are protected by a silent alarm from here to downtown Prosperity. But such is not a necessity for this and so many insignificant, out of the way businesses around here; all protected and guided by the same spirit that bestows our town its name—that no one can penetrate the Angel Guard, as complete as the one who guarded Eden with the flaming sword. No one who would do that is even aware of us anyway—and those who live here have no need to rob and steal.

We walk aimlessly in the gray dark. Past the jewelry, towards the crystal figurines and ceramic statuettes, moving through the small space toward the back of the store. The porcelain dolls heighten my interest some, causing Amanda to find the light switch. The fluorescent lights flicker life into the little space, reminding us that there was once a thriving little fancy business here. We notice the few art prints on the shelves and walls, carefully chosen and placed as important—to forego the look of an arts and craft store, though many empty frames of all sizes are leaned against a wall nearby. The store bears the look of a fancy nothing—a small, shimmering flash of beauty, with no pain and substance underneath.

Such a store is fit to be run by a rich man's wife, while he spends his days buried under a mountain of stock market talk and trade. My father's first million had come from his own blood and sweat—while the rest had come from the labour and pain of other wars fought, lives lost and gained in concrete jungle madness, fortunes made and lost by buttons pushed and clicked. A Wall Street broker he had been for 10 years—saving every extra penny ingeniously—investing those savings with knowledge and enough wisdom to build a 10 million dollar fortune in just as many years. What modest, lower middle class living my parents did before they came here was from my mother's own jobs. Always managing this store or that one, comfortable in every high level beauty and department store known. With her looks and education, and a personality fit for a king, she rebuffed offers of all kinds, executive and otherwise. Faithful. Vigilant. Chosen.

I finally turn my attention to the Wall of Reason in the back—visible upon entrance to the store and during the walk to every inch of this flat gray carpet. The wall is my father's Southern Christian upbringing, my mother's good sense, I think. Allowing them enough spiritual awareness to know and feel the truth even in worldliness.

I wander in front of the wall like a shopper. Gazing at every fine wooden, marble, gold and silver cross in awe. The pure white marble with the golden Christ figurine surely catches my eye. But these are not all crucifixes, as some would be inclined, for this is not his Holy Temple, nor is the snowbound earth required to keep silent before Him. It is an old idea left over from my father's childhood in my grandfather's furniture store warehouse, where he always kept a selection of oak and pinewood wall crosses for sale. My father remembered that even when the furniture was hardly selling, somebody always came in to by one of those plain wooden crosses. My father had flirted with this idea right before he was killed—of a side business that sold every kind and color of cross imaginable. *"There's a cross for every heart,"* I once heard him say, though it was only in a dream that he said it. How astute such a casual dream sensibility, I suppose, being that every heart is born with a light or heavy cross to bear.

But none of these on the display wall I see are quite fit to tell the tale, or mark the place for all eternity where Annabelle Freeman could have gone.

There is one American Indian bride among the white ladies. Her ivory leather dress is trimmed in royal blue stitch, longsleeved, white tassels under the sleeves and at the bottom over her white boots. Her expression is calm, touched by Melancholy unseen. Her beauty is such that I wonder how she lasted a day here unclaimed. I turn to look at my sister, glad she is so enamored by the Indian Bride and the other dolls. Enamoured by something other than what the world has known for seven long years, and will know in measures too great to imagine. I know, I feel that there is a battle waged to be won, a battle between God and Man in our snowy future. Of who shall be the victor? At what cost shall the loser suffer?

As if on automatic, I move toward the smooth, gray door to the back storage room. The room is darker and colder than even the front—filled with boxes and metal shelves of unused, unsold nonsense like Canada Geese and metal gazing balls pretty enough to be out front. I don't see anything here like what I remember. Nothing fit to be the memoriam for Annabelle. I suppose I'll gather two long pieces of wood from my father's work shed at home like I should have. I'll nail the wood, and fashion the marker as I should—

But my suspicions are suddenly leapt from behind the shelf in front of me, leaned on the floor on its side against the wall—projecting itself into my heart with fear.

On the trail to Golgotha. We are a sight to see, though we could hardly be seen at all in the white noise—the rising wind and snow. There are two young fools. A girl and her younger sister, both carrying a white wooden cross together—one at where the beam crosses the staff of 9 feet—the cross beam being taller than she. She rests the heavy, white cross on her aching shoulder, while the bottom rests on the shoulder of her doomed companion. The woman in white guides the cross and heaviest load therin, while the girl in pink bears the lightest part—both hefting the wood from the snow at their feet. The wind swirls at them hard, over and around them, gusting until the pink girl stumbles and falls flat to the ground, causing the weight of the cross to double in the white woman's hand and fall painfully and heavily to the ground. In the gust of icy wind, the figure in white runs over to her rose pink companion, distressed—helping her to her feet in the blizzard wind. She helps the long wood back to the shoulder of the Rose, then the White Raven flies back to her place at the head of the cross. She lifts the beam back to her shoulder, and they continue their march through the open gate to Tulip Garden Road.

Such is the cross I wear upon my breast

These eighteen years, through all the changing scenes—

And seasons, changeless since the day she died.

Helped along by the unseen, my hands burn as I swing the lowly pickaxe, having already cracked through the ice layer to the dry, black soil underneath. But the black ground is frozen still, needing to be chopped before we can shovel the small, two foot hole. Somewhere between the tree and the head of my mother's cornice above the ground, I dig into the earth. The wind whips and howls from the west, from the direction where we came from, carrying our cross down the snowy pass. How many of those that remain here peered from behind their curtains of fear, to look certain death in its white eye of crystal, to see us trudging our lonely, burdened little selves through the swirling, squalling snow?

My rose companion stands faithfully by me now, Indian bride still tucked deep inside her jacket. Here, in the last week of July, the wind howls the coming of Armageddon, and a frozen fortnight—renewed by a winter storm unlike any the world where we bury our dead has ever lived to see. I hand my sister the pick axe, taking the garden shovel from her. On my knees, I begin to clear away the dirt and broken chunks of ice, determined to dig a hole 24 inches deep. Every strike in the dirt is a blow against the death wind, and its desire to see us on our backs and frozen. I notice that along with the rising wind is a rising cold, driving the heat further and further from where we breathe. Every breath is harder than the last, until our lungs begin to burn, and crystals have began to form on the scarves over our noses and mouths. But I will not stop, I will not give up this fight, until the 24 inch hole is dug at the head of my mother's burial ground.

Blow, West wind! Weep and howl the misery from your journey around the earth! Scream the burden of death you carry, cry the agony of your defeat at our tired little hands as we dig, dig, dig our way through the frozen arctic ground! Pain carries me through the digging, even while I stand and rest from such a tiny task, pushing my sister's hand away in a flash of old temper, but quickly grabbing her hand and saying, *you can help me raise the cross,* then tapping her affectionately on the head. I finish the little job at hand, until the yardstick goes down 27 inches below the surface. We make our way back to the wood we bore, this time with *me* at the foot of the cross. We both lift while I guide the beam over the hole in the ice—*raise it up!* I yell over the wind, and my rose companion pushes with all her might until the beam begins to slide below the ground. I go to where she is at the cross beam, and we both push with our hearts and souls, straining upward. Raising the cross upright. It slides amazingly far down, enough to ease our heavy burden to light. The white cross leans over the space in the ice where we marked. I raise it upright, adjusting it slightly, gazing through the cold—burning eyes unaffected, making sure the arms are spread properly over the grave. *Put the dirt back in,* I say, holding it tight, glad that I listened to my rose when she told me to use the tiny garden shovel.

The hole I dug is narrow enough to be strong support for the cross, so that there is hardly any lean to correct. I hold the cross steady in the wind, watching Amanda on her knees quickly filling the hole in around it. *All of it,* I say, helping her pack the dirt into a mound around the base of the white wood. With our gloved hands, we gather snow from around our gravesite and cover up the dirt completely, until all traces of it are gone. Then I step back, far from the mound of snow over my mother's body. The wind whips and whirls my disbelief, as I lower the scarf from my face and breathe the arctic air bravely. My open mouthed expression, my stillness in the raging cold, calls my rose companion from her station, and she hurries from the cleared area at the grave out into the high snow where I stand. We hold each other tight, unable to speak. Staring at the seven foot white cross rising majestically above the snow.

Part Three

*W*ars flow the river of time. Rumours of wars navigate the icy waters. Tanks roll like Armageddon through the desert fields of snow. And though the heavens have opened, where the Wrath of God hath poured softly on every wind, these men cannot cease from their wrongdoing—from their hiding in diplomacy like Oddyseus and Achilles' ghost in their Trojan Horse, later to pour out upon the sleepy opponents in wired fever for blood. Men whose intentions are borne in the pirate ship that rises from the east, burning blue and black fire, who gather their pleasure along the shores of Death and Destruction, to increase the suffering of the women and children, with no regard for the lives of the husbands, fathers, brothers and sons that they took. Men who ache and writhe in Hell on the frozen earth, the burning that plagues a life without the King of Heaven, and the Prince of Peace in their hearts forever. They endeavor to bring evils that must be, to hear no cry from above or below except their own cry for battle, the lustful craving in their bodies and souls for blood. These men are called upon, but by their father who is the Prince of the Power of the Air—to war against the Holy Spirit of God in the world. These spirits move upon human compassion. Hiding in natural good will—moving from place to place in their war against humanity. Getting inside the safe places. The fortresses, where they pour themselves out in legion just beyond the sight. They affect human behavior towards divinely appointed negativity—those evils that Christ himself said must come. But woe unto them, he said, by whom the offence cometh!

Cheryl Ezman haunts these snowy roadways. Local real estate millionairess, divorced mother of one. Five years older than her spiritual betrothed, who was thirty five when we laid her to rest. Cheryl Ezman. Former co-owner of Ezman Properties—her interest bought and sold in her divorce—Ezman Properties now bearing a new name. She treks through the knee high snow. Through Prosperity Garden Terrace. Driven. Pushed forward by what drives so many forward in life. Desires. Wants. Needs too wide and deep to fathom. Too inexplicably powerful to ignore.

She steps down from her tiny palace on Honeysuckle Garden Road, to the streets of Tulip Garden. A place where the snow drives higher than most. Where the wind screams louder from the Walls of Gray, down to the tombs in the Valley of Shadows. These tombs are the whited sepulchres. Unseen in passing. Hidden by the judgment of the Almighty.

Cheryl Ezman walks the streets of Tulip Garden. Burning. Devastated. Destroyed by a frustrated, unrequited something or another; the longing so deep in her blue and blackened spirit. These are the spirits inside. Hiding in the horse of human compassion. Born of loneliness. Nurtured by fear. A seed blossomed to the fullness of itself—here at the end of the present age before Armageddon, when the sun was darkened, and the Moon no longer gave her light.

Cheryl walks the streets of Prosperity. Pulled along by desperation. Driven by instinct.

The clock chimes the Window of Time—opened to the third hour of the afternoon. My sister and I rest from turmoil—where grief and mourning have settled in, and the realization that our beloved mother is gone. We sit on the plush sofa quietly, my feet and legs reclined up in luxury, while Amanda sleeps with her head in my lap. I feel ownership, a possession over her that permeates all. My spirit aches the need for us to ride this storm out together. To be at one another's emotional whim—to exercise privileges of one another's beckon call.

Engrossed by the summer commercials on TV, their stubborn and direct assault on reality—in my heart I know that somehow we will not be allowed to rest at the moment, as indicated by the chiming of the clock and the *doorbell,* and then a desperate and determined knocking. Oh, there is so much to fear, from a fateful knocking at the door! Bewildered, I reluctantly retract my reclining seat, which wakes my sister from the edge of sleep. She hears the second knock, and sits bolt upright and looks at me confusedly. In fearful confusion. In a confused fearfulness, I get up from the shadow gray sofa and follow the memory of the knock across our living room to the front door.

I pay close attention to the movement of this moment. Watching my hand reach out to the press-down door latch, feeling it go without effort—a flash of memory! To the night only a week ago when I tried to leave my poor mother and sister! Flash again to my present, as I watch the front door of our little mansion open upon my immediate future in the cold. Standing there, beaten by the freezing, biting wind is the proverbial figure dressed in black, trimmed and accessorized in the loveliest royal blue hat, scarf and glove cloth imaginable. White skin contrasts the blue scarf, and eyes the color of the summer winter sky. My mother's best friend and companion. Aunt Cheryl we once knew.

Instinctual happiness comes to the surface, *fungalooga* and terror, to power my lips into the phoniest smile I have ever given, and to reach my hand in pretend gladness out to hers. I see the delight and relief in her eyes as I take her hand—pulling her from the jaws of ice and white death to a place of warmth and light. But even while this is so, as she steps over the threshold—I am transported to the heart of memory, and I am pulled backward through time to the days of my father's passing.

In the Heart of Memory, my mother flies to Florida in the heavy snow flurries, watching them grow lighter with each rapid passing of the miles, until the sun shines over the beaches of southern waters outside her plane. She rests easy, knowing that she will find peace, harmony, innocence and tranquility in the arms of her own mother, while her 12 and 10 year old daughters must wait safely in the cold, taken good care of by her best friend. This friend, Cheryl Ezman—who is Aunt Cheryl to me at the time. I can still smell mother's sweet perfume mixed with shampoo. I can still taste the mint on her beautiful mouth, the sweet hugs and kisses at the airport. The memory of Cheryl's compassionate, pseudo-supportive hug to her; secret gladness disguised in charity while she patted and rubbed my mother's back and kissed her hard twice on the cheek and once more on the lips in front of everyone. Cheryl Ezman. *Ms. Lezzi Ezzie* at the airport. Stealing her best friend's children.

The seconds slow down to the hours, as Cheryl steps into the present, this cubicle of luxury—minutes transformed to days in the heart of memory. These days have turned to night in the new snow where I am twelve and my sister is ten. Even now, I wonder when I was first chosen by her and why, rather than my sister, whose face and body were so thin and innocent rather than mine. Maybe that is why. Because she was not a little Carmen such as I, whose look made me ready and ripe for the picking. My black hair was long and full bodied; here in the Halls of Memory, I am twelve with long and full bodied black hair. My skin is as fair as day, and my eyes are the blue of a tropical sea. With no makeup, my young lips are as pink as the rose, so full and soft to the touch. Driving home from the airport, my face burns an imprint in Cheryl Ezman's mind while she drives, the lovely face of innocence, before the fulfillment of promises, when my young body has yet to grow, and my breasts are not fully sized and grown. Their premature largeness is only the echo of future growth; the nipples only the innocent part of what they will be, with puffy areolas still lighter than air, and not as dark and large as they will someday become. My hands are small and white—that of a weakling young girl, with hardly the strength to squeeze the juice from a ripe orange. My hips are still narrow, not their future hourglass, with buttocks the decided and bubbly little shape of a girl on the edge of discovery. I am this young Carmen, uncorrupted, who sits in the passenger side of Cheryl Ezman's car while she drives home through the slippery snow, holding my hand and rubbing her thumb back and forth across it. Why, Cheryl, do I sense a tremble in your hands? This, I do not know. My sister rides quiet in the back seat unawares—of the trembling I have come to know.

The snow was at times slushy back then. Which made it so dangerous in the morning after it had frozen over during the night. The dirty, mushy snow was frozen solid that morning, as we rounded the corner into the neighborhood that was so new to us. We had just moved in that same summer of my father's funeral, when the summer roads and streets first bore the permanent look of pure winter. Cheryl eases us down the streets of Prosperity Garden Terrace, not to her own little palace but to the doll house on Tulip Garden. An empty house. No longer filled with the laughing voice of a husband and father. The empty house, where a widow's ghost flows through the walls of grieving.

We walk the snowy lawn, us three. Two daughters and their guardian. In the aftermath of trauma. On the edge of a new place of grieving, unlike any we have known before. We walk the snowy lawn. The grown woman beside the little woman, and a little girl close behind. They walk the unseen path, laid out to all descended from the Garden of Antiquity. Touched by the curse meted out to mankind. We walk the snowy lawn. Acquainted now with the Spirit of Death, having taken the father deep into the earth. Then to sweep down and take our mother into the sky when we need her the most, to leave us alone, us three. To move through this space, abandoned. We walk the snowy lawn.

The sun glides behind the clouds of memory, until the day is spent. Cheryl, Amanda and me are done with the evening's discomfort—the settling into the new dynamic, which includes getting used to our mother being gone. She is our mother for now. Our guardian. Our protector. She is responsible for what happiness or sorrow there is to bring. On the very first night, she tells us both that eleven chimes are the outer limits, when we have to go to bed. We tuck Amanda in together, then she escorts me to my room.

On my back in my bed, my black hair contrasts the white nightgown, the pillow, and the white of my young face. I look up at Auntie Cheryl, comforted. Cozy in the strangeness of her presence here, taking care of us while our mother has gone. *I've noticed how your mother acts toward you sometimes,* she says, sitting on the edge of my bed. Looking down into my face. *She lets little Mandy get away with everything. Well, I love Mandy too, but I wanted you to know that you've always been my favorite. You're smart. You're beautiful. If you ever need to talk to me about anything, I'll always be around.* She touches my nose and makes me smile, then she tickles me hard enough to make me laugh. *See? All better.* Then she leans down and touches her lips to mine, moaning innocently, shaking her head a little. This kiss is noisy when she stops. She does it again, this time holding it there longer. Still moaning, though with knowledge. The feel of her voice vibrates my spine to my bottom. *You've got big soft lips*, Auntie Cheryl says. *Does your mommy kiss you a lot?* Yes but not for a long time like us, I say. *Then this is our special kiss that only we know about, okay? One more time? Only this time, you kiss me.* She lowers her head and I raise up and kiss her on the mouth, too afraid to keep going, too afraid to stop, but just holding it there for what is a nervous, blessed eternity to her body. She smiles the false innocence of corruption when I lay my head back to the pillow, then a kiss goodnight to the forehead and a pat on my upper thigh. She sings the cherished *sweet dreams honey* from at the door, waving at me, then turns to depart my room, leaving me to ponder the feel of a grown woman's lips on mine, and the vibration of her voice in my soul.

As I walk the warm Halls of Memory, I see us in Cheryl's intrepid car again. Taking young Amanda to a friend's house. From there, they will ride a wave of joy and pizza party happiness, as they are perpetuated by the forces of innocence and youth. We listen to music on the way home and we talk, but she smartly mentions nothing of our secret kiss, so as not to spoil her place as Auntie Cheryl in my life. The woman I trust. My caregiver. My moral guide. The replacement, in the absence of my mother. Already, I know not to ever mention to mother or Amanda that Cheryl and I kissed on my bed last night three times before I went to sleep. I am 12, when her spirit comes to me. I am aware of her in my mother's bed last night, laying nude on top of the covers, door locked, hands clasped at her stomach like the dead, her swollen breasts drooped to the sides of her body, bulbous, naturally elongated and enlarged, big and stretchy enough for her to swing and bounce to oblivion, which she has done for herself on numerous, regular occasion, often flopping them noisily up and down while she excercises in the nude. This chord flairs the key of G minor, kept remarkably flattened and hidden beneath her clothing. Even now, on my mother's bed after our kiss is shared, she anchors them up with her arms as much as they will go while she is flat on her back, and she begins to wobble them back and forth expertly without touching them, resisting a stance in front of the mirror and a feverish flopping of them back and forth.

Amanda and my mother have been kindly, so unkindly disposed of, and our dinner is eaten and enjoyed. The TV whispers of future tragedy, while I am enraptured by the beauty and bubbly smile of my new best friend. *Mastermind* is our game of choice on the living room floor, below the shadow gray luxury of our plush chair and sofa. After we laugh, I feel these spirits of melancholy perversion descend, carried along the timeline from her youth, when they were given to her by an adult female babysitter. It burns the grassland in blue and black flame, across the prairie landscape of her mind. These spirits descend from the clouds, to where we live and breathe.

It's good to hear you laugh, she says. *We can't always be happy but it's still good to laugh isn't it? The world is changing so fast. Its building up to something really big and scary. I think this snow is a sign. It's not going to stop. But we still have each other don't we? And we can always protect each other and make each other feel better. My mother died when I was your age, so I know the pain and scary feeling you have. I'm just really glad that I've got you here with me.* I'm glad you're here too, I say. *I enjoyed our little secret last night,* she says. *There's more secrets I'd like to show you. They're a lot of fun. Things that we can share between us forever.* I lower my eyes in something not unlike shame, but not as complete. I think is only shyness; a naïve confusion as to the depth, the breadth of this frontier. *Come on, let me show you.* She takes me by the hand, but not in frivolity. I am twelve, being led by this thirty five year old woman up the stairs. She purposefully does not smile, to better enjoy my uneasiness. To prey upon the energy that flows from my discomfort.

Up the stairs I climb. Hand in hand with my Auntie Cheryl. She lets my hand go and drops pretense, and she beckons me to our huge bathroom. We stand in front of the mirror facing one another. Part of me is in sheer, girlish delight, having no idea what is going to happen. She unbuttons my pink shirt—staring me in the eyes, watching the fear of revelation overtake me. In the fog of this, at the precipice of new life, at the crowning point of what is meant to be, I think I hear the words *you're big enough to be out of this training bra already.* She reaches inside my bra, and I feel the hands of Autumn brush my nipple, to raise to life nerves I did not know I had in my body. She then folds her navy cashmere tee up to the top of her chest to reveal a white bra so filled with flesh as to be unbelievable, over an hourglass shaped waist in tight, slightly faded blue jeans. This Nova Curve she shares in common with my mother, her best friend, the Anna bird flown, whose hips are even more remarkable than her own. The fire that ignites inside me, I cannot know. It is an azure flame. She skillfully reaches in her bra and pulls them out one at a time, smiling slightly, but hiding the glee inside. I have never seen such a sight as this—big, long and bulbous tits with large, dark areolas. Her nipples are nearly flattened into them, inverted as is the psychology that carries them. This is the mind of one whose focus flies opposite, and so must remain hidden from public view. Her breasts exposed, she opens my pink button shirt wide and slightly off my shoulders, and in the mirror I think I see that girl's bra being raised up. Two very firm, very young breasts grown too large for their age are exposed to the air in the house. The girl in the mirror has an awestruck expression, suddenly tempered by a closed mouth and tucked in lips. My antagonist tells me to turn to the mirror, and we stand there as an overdeveloped woman and girl, staring at breasts brought into the light, while we remain fully clothed elsewhere. She turns me back to her, and she tells me to take one of her breasts into my hands. I don't move. She gently says *go ahead honey, it's alright. It's just you and me.* And I instinctively lift her left breast up with both hands, squeezing it at her direction, kneading the soft tissue like a handfull of bread dough. *Now I want you to kiss it*, she says. And I do this, avoiding the nipple, kissing the white flesh everywhere but on the areola, until her impatience takes hold. She says *you can the kiss the middle now,* standing with her hands far back on her hips. Hold the bottom, she says, and *kiss the middle until you want to suck it.* I do this, my own breasts still showing, kissing around and on top of the flattened nipple, feeling her impatience growing. Then I notice the darkened areola draw in tighter, wrinkling the flesh, while her breathing deepens underneath a pained expression. I look up nervously, with little or no understanding, glad for her patience, but feeling my mouth open on its own, and pull her very large nipple into my mouth. It seems to me the size of a grape as I pull it in repeatedly. Sucking on it hard enough to make a popping, kissing noise in the air around us. Her eyes are closed. Her brow deeply wrinkled. Cheryl Ezman takes a deep and trembly breath, in disbelief of her own actions and the corruption of her best friend's twelve year old daughter. I am suddenly at one with this, enjoying the feel of her erect nipple in my mouth. She tells me to *suck a little harder, like you're trying to get milk,* she says. This, I do. It makes her open her mouth and take a deep breath and grab her other breast with her own hand and look down at me. She pinches her other nipple fully. Grabbing hold again of restraint, she puts her hands back to her hips. Then she leans down, her own breast hanging, and I see the woman in the mirror take the girl's young, firm breasts into her hand, and as I see it happen to the girl in the mirror, I feel a warm, moist suction clamp hold of my nipple—and as it pulls, a lightning bolts the Triangle of Needs, my sensuality from my groin to my bowels, then back again to where the warm, moist sucking pulls away. Expertly. So much more expertly than I, her head bobs the Fellatio of the Maidens, up and down until I hear my own breathing get away from me, then I am unable to stop my body from trembling a small seizure. She grabs me hard—hugging me to her naked breasts, repeating over and over *just breathe honey, I understand, Momma understands,* then she removes all of my clothing—my shirt, my bra, my jeans, socks and underwear. She turns me to the mirror and tells me to look at how beautiful I am. She stands behind me, shirt still up, holding me. Gripping me tight enough to pin my arms to my sides. I am nearly dizzy. I see that my face and neck are flushed. From behind me, she leans down and turns my head to hers, and she coaxes my lips open with hers, and firmly sucks my tongue deep into her mouth. Of the pleasure it gives, of the relief it bestows to where I live, I am unable to say. It feels as though the lightning might come back at any time. Then at last, unable to do otherwise, she undoes her jeans just enough to reach inside and pull the small, thin member attached by a strap around her hips! Hidden underneath her jeans all along! She tells me to spit on her hand. This, I do. Then she takes her middle finger and pushes it into my bottom, where one point of lightning was borne. I know to stand still and quiet. She tells me to relax. This, I do, while she pushes her finger slowly in and out of my bottom. Of the pleasure this contains—of what agonizing this is to my body—I do not know. She whispers in my ear *lets relax now, now we'll relax together*—and I feel my spirit opened, and the icy cold of the unknown begins to burn from my bottom to my groin—this feeling grows, as she rubs the middle of my swollen vagina and pulls on my nipples, as she slowly pushes the thin member deeper into my backside. As she does this—I begin to feel a fervent bouncing against my buttocks, and I hear her beg me to *let Momma teach you baby, let Momma teach you to feel good.* As she thrusts and rubs, I feel the lightning coming again, and this time I fight with my voice to control my own breath while the seizure happens, and I feel the thrusts go harder against me, and I am unable to hold my eyes open long enough to see the torture on the face of the woman that shakes against my back, and screams the sound of pure, helpless depravity into the air around me.

hrough this hazy fog—this foggy haze of memory, I find a hand reaching out. I grip this hand for dear life and I pull... seeing her winter gray eyes emerge in knowledge, gazing at me in unknown wisdom amidst the flash of energy, which has me naked on our dining room table on my back, while she is naked standing. Leaned over me with her mouth clamped over my nipple and pulling it up in sucking motion, while I at the same time oblige her heavy hangers in hungry sucking as well. In reality, she hugs me without a word, in this phantom energy, kissing me hard on the cheek, implanting the cold from outside into my body.

From her fear catatonia, my sister breaks free, running across the room with no smile, her prematurely massive bosom bouncing in fever and revenge for every one of the fifteen years she has lived and died. I know that the bounce of them has lit a fire of warmth inside Cheryl Ezman that she has fought like a warrior to conceal, and she smiles with open arms, while my sister nearly runs into her welcome embrace. *Aunt Cheryl*, she says, brow wrinkled, squeezing her cold, snowy body intensely, without pretense of intention. I watch in poker faced joy and relief, while my sister grips this woman under her shoulders, hugging her back so tight it becomes something close to clawing.

Can you feel it, Cheryl? The massage of my young sister's fingers through your coat? Can you feel it, Cheryl, the pillowy pressure of my young sister's breasts against yours through your coat? Which of us, Cheryl, will be first? The first to take Amanda on her walk down the path, where the white leaves will gather and fall at her feet? Or will we conspire the unthinkable, to give in to the eschatological winds that beckon, to act as only the end of the age can require? Which one of us will hold her arms from behind, while the other kisses, licks, sucks, bites and twists her breasts without mercy? Is this our future reality, Cheryl Ezman? Or merely the curse that courses through my bones? Which one of us will shake first, Cheryl Ezman, under the power of my sister's screams? What fevered perversions are these, Cheryl, that you have burned into my body? What deadly thoughts are these?

Yes. Remove your coat. And give it to me. Join us in our Dance of the Milk Maidens! Become our snowy queen!

"I almost didn't make it," she says. "I knew it was crazy to come but I had to. It's a blizzard this time, you know. I thought I was going to have to stop and build a fire."

Her Londonian reference is without effort, nor allusions to amusement. I take her black coat, seeing the crystals melting. Feeling the drift and cold.

"That snow's gettin' a little high by that door—isn't it Honey?"

"We'll get it tomorrow."

"Tomorrow might be too late. Where's my Anna?"

What questions freeze the blood? What answers squeeze it pumping again?

My busty little sister opens her mouth to speak hellos to her bustier Auntie Cheryl. In her dark gray cotton turtleneck, their foundation is gargantuan. I am amazed at how she can be so relaxed and self confident. Above her small, curved waist, all of her forty two years are on heavy display. "Oh, never mind," she says. "She's like a hermit when she gets in this house." I watch her walk in a shapeliness that defies logic. Like pure lust on display. In charcoal gray shirt and pants of black. I wonder what fire burns hot enough to make her walk such a distance in this storm, without even a sweater to cover them underneath her jacket.

"Hey Anna, get down here!"

"Aunt Cheryl—"

"It's alright. I'll go get her."

She walks up the stairs. Taking them slowly by maturity, which is restraint and decorum. Civility walks up our stairs. In relaxed, unapologetic philosophy. A product of her time. Living the energy of her calling.

"Anna Freeman stop hiding from me. I've got you now girl. You can't get away." She disappears from the top of the stairs down the upstairs hall. My sister and I stand in the middle of the big living room. Frozen. Motionless. Unable to twitch a muscle. Like two snow rabbits caught by a spirit. We feel her fruitless journey down the hall to my mother's empty bedroom. Bed neatly made. Floor vacuumed without footprints. Blue rocker recliner unsat in by the window.

A spark of fear flashes through. It dashes through the air from the door of my mother's empty room, to grip us where we stand.

What kind of a game is she playing? she says—coming down the stairs. Smiling. Trying not to seem afraid or bewildered. What is the source of fluttering she feels, as she descends the stairs to us? Seeing our eyes stare. Deliberately misinterpreting the warning in them.

"Where in the world is your Momma? I can't get her on the phone, now she won't come out. I know she can hear me. Is she mad with me about something?"

The genuine concern on her face, and her hand pressed unconcerned over her big breasted heart nearly gets to me.

Cheryl! Why do you look for my mother! Why do you look for the dead among the living!

She starts to walk toward the kitchen, which sparks my tongue to speak.

"Aunt Cheryl—"

She turns. Her expression finally burdened with the bewilderment she had fought so hard to deny. "She's not here," I say.

"Not here? What do you mean she's not here? Where did she go? More importantly *how* did she go?"

"She made it to the airport before the snows came," I say, wondering why it is I have to lie.

"The airport?"

"She couldn't deal with the storm this time," Amanda says. "She was talking to Grandma Eva a couple of nights before. Grandma kept asking her to come but Mom kept saying no. But after the last big earthquake—something changed. She became completely afraid."

Without compassion, I watch the denial in her face turn quickly to anger. "Why the devil would she leave without telling somebody? And what are you two still doing here?"

A sempiternal pause…

"She'll be gone at least a month," I say. "Somebody had to stay and look out for things. You know how much she loves this house."

She tucks her pretty lips and turns to the side, towards the kitchen. Toward the back patio door.

"I just don't understand. She always tells me everything that's going on. Maybe I was too clingy or something. If I'd given her some space maybe she wouldn't have run from me."

"When people are scared they run," I say. "It didn't have anything to do with you, believe me. I told her we weren't going with her no matter what. She was so scared that she left without us. Which worked out great anyway because she was afraid to leave the house empty."

"Well, I assume you talk to her all the time, right? When is she gonna call again?"

"Um…it could be any time now."

Relaxed and as comfortable as a heavy breasted woman can be, she crosses her arms underneath the supersized, sagging shelf that is her bosom. Still looking toward the kitchen dangerously from our view, confusedly from her own. She takes a deep breath. Amanda and me both watch the shelf rise and fall.

"Damn this diet," she says in defeat. "Please tell me you've got some yellow cake in that kitchen. Not Devil's Food, either. Yellow."

"We've got cupcakes," Amanda says. "Come on"

"Uh…you two stay here," I say. "I'll get 'em."

I move quickly from the living room to the kitchen, cursing Fate for dragging her through the snow to our hiding place. What is Lezzie Ezzie doing here? Part of me is glad that she'll never realize her dream, her life's ambition to have my mother pinned naked underneath her screaming. Knowing full well that Annabelle Freeman was not salty in the least, that her pendulum did not swing out that far. Keeping the touches and pinches and moaning kisses in lightness and comic, feminine delight. Resisting the urge, so many times in this very kitchen, to walk over to the stove or counter where my mother stood and whack her on the bottom, then press her groin to her wide buttocks, and grab both my mother's perfect breasts from behind.

As I open the ridiculously, tightly sealed supermarket deli industrial strength plastic holder for the cupcakes, the whirl of white icing twirls my mind back to our tragic reality.

The three of us have eaten the cupcakes gladly, as the spirits so generously divined, allowing that a sugared confection is melody for a hungry, weary soul. Washed down by sweet waters once gathered from a Mountain's morning Dew. My sister and I have shared many curious glances over this snowy afternoon lunch, until we both knew it was time to stop or make Cheryl more suspicious than she already was. But her quiet acceptance of what we told her had only been quiet contemplation, and she is ready to begin her game anew.

"When is Anna coming back? Did she say?"

"No, she didn't."

"I'll bet she's planning to stay and never come back," I say. "But I'll be 18 in November and I'm not going to Florida no matter what."

"You really think she might stay?"

"Yep. I wouldn't be surprised." After I lie, I hide behind the biggest gulp of Mountain Dew I can take.

"Well, since we haven't heard from her yet, why don't I give her a call and say hi?"

On roller coasters, there is always that one place. That one drop that is so severe, it will determine the course of every life who experiences it. A fearful, terrible plunge to the depths of happiness or sorrow. I ride forward in this brief time, coasting the energy of Cheryl Ezman. Falling to my death.

"I wouldn't do that," Amanda says.

"Why not?"

"You'd be wasting your time. Mom forgot to take her phone. And they're never home this time of the day. The snow's normal in Florida this time of the year. People are still out and about."

My sister opens up another cupcake. To divert Cheryl's attention, I suppose. But Cheryl stands up in full, busty form and walks to the front closet by the door. Reaching inside the unzipped pocket. She walks back towards us with the phone in one hand and control in the other. The shape her gray turtleneck colors when she draws the deep breath is incredible. Her hand is now resting far back on her waist. A pose I became so familiar with when I was 12.

We both sit still. Staring not into space or at the widescreen LCD, but watching her hold the phone to her ear as if we were watching it happen on a movie screen.

"Hi Babe this is Cheryl. Call me as soon as you get this okay? Bye."

"We told you she forgot her phone."

"Oh yeah. You did say that, didn't you?"

I watch the veil of civility grow thinner, until I can hardly see it anymore. Behind the fading veil, I see a beautiful forty something face, framed by shoulder length brunette hair. And I see a pair of winter gray eyes, sparkling with knowledge of intention, suppressing a piercing scowl, where before only the delighted fungalooga smile had been. Her pretty mouth is relaxed into something not quite yet a frown.

The crackling outside is the gentle splitting of the sky in two, followed by the rumbling, booming crash of it fusing back together again.

"Do you know your grandmother's phone number?"

Quiet.

"Girls, I want your grandmother's phone number."

She sees Amanda lose her façade and gaze at me.

"What's going on here? Why won't you let me call your mother?"

There are forces here that I can feel, that press down on whatever I want to say or do to relieve her suffering. Her pain is lack of knowledge of the truth, which is the agony of unenlightened perseverance. When those that are empowered hide knowledge from the powerless, to jerk them around like suckers, and watch them cross a thousand bridges to nowhere, then jump through a thousand hoops to no avail.

She walks towards us. Arms down, big breasts drooping, face and mouth now doing the same.

"Did she tell you not to let me call her? *Answer* me."

She glares at Amanda on the order, taking a step towards her. The change in her face is remarkable. All the pain, regret and unhappiness she has ever known taints her lovely features.

"I said, I want your mother's phone number and I want it *now!*"

Amanda's expression takes characteristic form. Wide eyed. Lips tucked in. Though I can already see my future self at her side, at the moment I am frozen. But as I feared, this woman dashes forward toward my sister like the lightning in the skies over Prosperity, and grabs her hard by the shoulders. The look on Amanda's face terrifies me. She shakes my sister harder than I thought possible.

"You give me that phone and you give it to me *now!*"

She is as angry as a snow leopard. But I have no choice but to jump in her attack, wrenching her hands from Amanda's shoulders and stepping between the two of them.

"Don't," I say. Shaking my head no.

"I don't get what's wrong with you two. Why are you doing this?"

We can only stand still. Mouths half open in fear. Under the gigantic bosom, she starts to rub her arms together. Like an addict.

"Girls... I...I thought we were closer than this. Belinda I thought *we* had an understanding. You're mother's like a sister to me and I need to talk to her."

Quiet. Our betrayal is epic. Cheryl begins to talk aloud—contemplating an alternate course.

"Let's see… Annabelle Crews… her mother's name is Eva. I can call information to get the…"

She pauses. Looking up at the ceiling. The clouds press down upon her efforts, where she sees loneliness and despair to infinity.

"Belinda Freeman… you give me Eva Crews' phone number… or I swear to God and Jesus I'll beat it out of you."

Upon a warrior's sigh, I push my sister back with such authority. Such gentle roughness, I move her back and away. I undo the buttons on my white collar blouse, and take it off to the tight, white T shirt underneath. I drop the white blouse to the sofa. The middle aged woman glares in disgust at the big seventeen year old girl. A young woman who stands ready to defend her sister's honor, and that of her departed mother.

"Aunt Cheryl please…" Amanda says.

"Belinda don't make me have to do this. Give me the number."

"I can't."

My voice calms her to battle mode. Her expression locks in the uneasy tranquilty of battle, and she rushes toward me—

"Aunt Cheryl she's *dead!*" Amanda says.

With one hand on my shoulder and the other clawed at my face, she stops cold and pulls back, not even feeling my fingers at her throat and tangled in her hair. I had planned to live the fire of my heart, and give to her every bloody bite, black and blue blow and bruise I had stored over the years, until she was broken and weeping from the pain alone. Is that why I allowed the situation to turn to chaos? How badly did I wish, did I need to fight another woman? This woman?

"Anna's Momma died?" she says, sliding her hands away from me, alarmed by Amanda's grief torn expression. "Why didn't you just tell me? I would have understood. If her Momma died then—"

"Mom is *dead,* Aunt Cheryl."

It is written that the types of fear are many, and uniquely distinguished. Cheryl feels the cold in her body again, but this from the departure of another. She looks at me. This time in pleading. My lips are tucked, and what compassion there is left, she sees. I nod my head, piercing her heart again. She winces, then begins the requisite denial. Shaking her head slowly. She backs away, looking at us as we drift toward her in spectral form.

"Come to the kitchen," I say, suddenly supportive where only a moment ago I was surreptitious and serpentine. We take her hand, this time as a companion through a snowy wilderness. We take her by the hand and arms, both on either side of her. Escorting her to the late afternoon light. With a free hand I pull the ivory curtain string, sliding it open. Then we watch the beautiful woman open her mouth and draw in a cold breath, the last on this side of her lifeline.

I stand behind the woman, gripping her tight around the waist and bosom. Pinning one arm immobile. Amanda shackles the other. We feel her spirit darken, and we watch her face twist in the same grief and fear we have known. We feel her body tremble and shake her loss, as she breathes the words *No God, please no*. I hold the woman from behind. Gripping her tight while she leans forward then back against me in pleas and wailing. We feel the strength. The power of grief tearing her body.

And we bear the woman steadfast and upright. In her darkest hour.

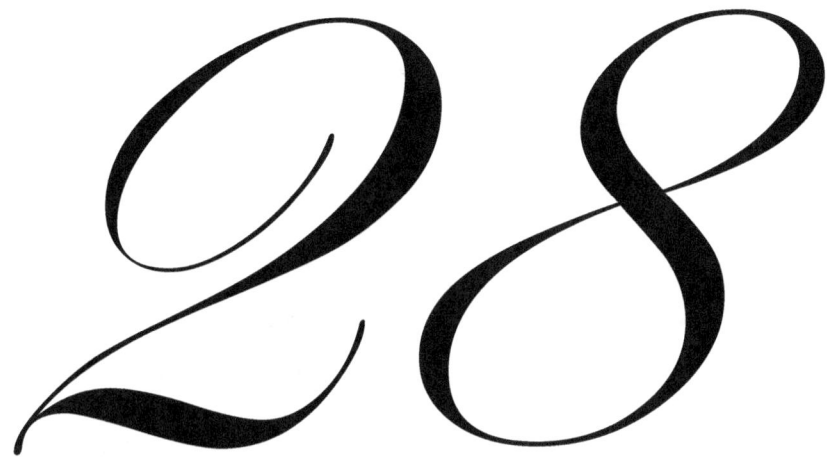

There is a universal tear now, that exists between motherhood and womanhood—it is decreed in the last days, that women can only be one or the other, with nothing left in between. Those that try to mix the two are unpleasantly surprised, when they are unable to balance the mother they are, with the woman they so heartily wish to be. If you choose immorality over purity, watch and see the corruption enter your life and poison your relationship with your daughter—she who is the offspring—the unmolded clay, the unwritten page of the future. But more and more, with each passing year, women are choosing to follow their nature deep inside, that says *you are dying, Dearest—the woman you were is dying.* And their survival instinct is kicking in all over the world in the form of liberation and independence, the age of *hot mom dot com*—where daughters have no moral light to guide them. Mother does not submit to her husband—so why should I? Mother does not dress modestly, so why should I? Mother does not have the mind of Christ—so why should I? She strives in the corporate madness, bound by necessity of modern times—by men who cannot satisfy their lust for life, by men who cannot treat them with the respect and civility they deserve. By necessity, He tore a chasm between womanhood and motherhood, so that a girl must decide early in life which goal by which she will aspire. But most navigate these woods unaware, comfortable in the delusion of Mother Woman, believing that they are somehow one and the same. But there are others who have felt the tearing in the universe—the modern split between the two, and they go on sinning, allowing the woman to creep in and grab the mother by the throat, until she is well choked and dead.

"I remember the cross," Cheryl says. "Freeman and Swan Crosses. Your father's crazy idea. For some reason, your father loved crosses. I think maybe it was just…"

"What?"

"The fear of death. Maybe he knew he was going to die. He used to say, *'I don't know much about religion but I have a feeling that Jesus got it right. This Cross means that he died for me so I can go to Heaven when I die.'* I never really thought about what he said until just now. He was a born again Christian."

"Was Mom?"

"I never heard her talk about it like that. But she was so sweet. So giving. So friendly and full of love. She had to be."

"She was," I say.

"How do you know?" Amanda asks.

"We were arguing once about selling this house and moving down south. I remember her saying *'as sure as Jesus died on the Cross for my sins and walked out of that grave three days later, this house will <u>never</u> be sold. And Hell will freeze into a block of ice before I let you leave.'*"

"Sounds like she was really angry."

"Towards the end she was always angry. Irritable. But it was partly my fault. I never realized how scared she was—"

"She died of pure fright," Amanda says, a hint of terror on her face. "She was so scared that she had a heart attack and died."

"We don't know that. She might have died anyway. Even if there was no snow."

"The snow killed her, Belinda. I know it did. And now it's gonna get us. It's gonna reach in here and it's gonna grab us all when we—"

"Come here, Amanda," Cheryl says. I watch with suspicion while my sister stands up and walks over, huge 15 year old breasts covered in her baggy sweatshirt. She nearly falls into Aunt Cheryl's arms, unashamed. Unafraid.

What can I do? Scream, *get your lezzie hands off of my sister? I know what you're planning to do?* I only have the strength to slide over and join them, leaning my head onto Cheryl's shoulder—more in understanding than grief. Almost envious of where it is that my beloved mother could have gone.

Somewhere above the clouds, there is a traveler or two, speeding along in a jet plane, in awe of what glory is the evening day, when the sun is below the cloud horizon, and the trail of orange light divides Heaven from Earth. In their eye, they see the star that shines above the equator, the tropics where the snowfall was once the lightest, but grows heavy under the weight of time passing, and days when ice will cover every brown and green corner of the world. These planes go on, in stubborn hope and persistence, believing that the reprieve is around the corner, and that the sun will shine warm again. We all breathe in this same cold longing, exhaling a frosty breath of denial and despair.

I breathe this air in my mother's room upstairs, in the gray room with Cheryl Ezman, while Amanda lies on the couch downstairs, lost in a blessed sleep. Cheryl stands at the window transfixed, her spirit held by her vision of the angel at the window and the ghost of her angel in the chair.

"Your mother was the best part of who I was. She was everything I had left. And now, I'm not going to make it."

"Don't talk like that Aunt Cheryl."

"I loved her," she says, gliding to her place in the chair. "But of course you knew that, didn't you?"

"Of course you love her."

My intentional oversight, my uncompromising understatement makes her smile to a near laugh. Her look, when she gazes at me, is the intolerant glare of a grieving woman.

"My adopted mother," she says "…except for my adopted mother, you and your mother are the only truly beautiful women I've ever known. And I mean not just pretty or sexy, but cosmetically, asthetically pure. Like a queen and a princess."

"Have you looked in the mirror?"

A pause…

"My adopted mother was a beautiful woman. Very quiet. Sort of sweet. But I… when…"

She pauses, as if what she had wanted to say required so much more—as if compromising, soft recollection simply would not do.

"They slept with the door open. They never showed any affection when they were together. I was an only child, but I had friends. She let me go anywhere I wanted. I was a cheerleader in the 9th grade. I played volleyball in the 10th grade. I did charity work for the church and the school."

"Why'd you quit cheerleading?"

"You won't believe me."

"I will, I swear."

"I quit," she says, nearly laughing at herself. I quit… because my tits were too big. Everytime I jumped I nearly hit myself in the face and I was only 15 years old. God, I looked like a stuffed pig in that cheerleading costume. Amanda's in a lot of trouble because hers are just as big as mine were. You're lucky though. You've got your Mommas perfect breasts. Big enough to always be noticed, but not big enough to be laughed at and stared at and made out to be a circus freak. Yes, I was popular with boys…these things started growing when I was in the 6th grade. By the end of the 7th grade they were already hanging to my waist. By time I was 16 I was always the biggest in the room. Bigger than every teacher even. Bigger than everybody except Lillian. Hers were so big that she looked frumpy and misshaped in her clothes, because she tried to keep 'em hidden in loose shirts and dresses. Oh, the things people don't know. The lengths we go to, to hide who we are…"

"…I think Lillian had low self esteem. I wonder who gave it to her? Lillian Helderman. Lilly Helder. Church lady. Foster mom. Adopted mother. One night when I was outside in the evening, I couldn't have been more then 12 or 13, I noticed her through the kitchen window wearing just her skirt and bra. Let's just say that except in pictures, I've never seen anything like it. That giant white bra, too tight, flesh spilling over. Flat stomach. I see a brown polyester skirt for some reason, I don't know what color it was. I think that if she had known I saw her, the embarrassment would've killed her, I bet. Maybe her breast magic rubbed off on me. Just by me being near her. I've got magic breasts. The kind women pay thousands of dollars to butcher themselves for. Amanda's got 'em too. I corrupted her already."

She laughs, and looks at my confused expression.

"Who knows, maybe I'm doing the same thing to Amanda. You've got your Momma's boobs. High and tight. A good D cup. But Amanda…"

She looks down at the carpet. As though admiring a picture of my sister held fast in her imagination. Her memory. She looks down at her own breasts, and rubs her shirt gently, unashamedly over them. They rest low and gigantic against her body, underneath the gray fabric.

"*A large bosom is a calling, and a curse,* Lillian said. *Behind closed doors they are a gift from God—the greatest pleasure a woman can have.*"

"Your <u>Mom</u> said those things to you?"

"… My adopted father worked for a small real estate company. He had to drive to work two hours every day and sit in an office. He left at eight, got home at eight. 8 to 8. Monday through Friday, every day…

"…I was only 13 when it happened the first time. My real mother had only been dead for a year. She died of lung cancer. Maybe smoke from my granddad's pipes and cigars that killed him when I was little, I don't know. It didn't take long before *I* was adopted, you can *believe* it. It was first come, first serve on this one. That little Carmen. That little 12 year old tamale with that hot little face and hot little body. Look at those eyes. That long black hair. Is she Greek? Italian? Is she half Mexican? What an exotic little thing she is. Her father was half Cherokee, ooohhhh, that explains it. All my life, Belinda, people had a special, second look tucked away that they took out just for me. One day, I just got tired of hiding it. I cut my hair and started wearing the tightest shirts I could squeeze into…

"Back when I was 13, it was about 4'oclock in the afternoon, sun was hot and still high in the sky. It was July, just like now. Of course, there was no sign of snow that day. Lillian calls me in the house. I go inside—I don't see her. I guess she's in the laundry room. She comes out of the bathroom holding a big white towel and an enema nozzle. Her lips are kind of tucked in. She's in her big white bra and underwear. Shaped like a pure hourglass, she is. I can still see her thighs jiggling on every step in the hall. But she didn't have a nasty walk that girls and women have now. Her hips didn't move back and forth and side to side. I just remember her putting that towel on the end of the table. The table was practically in the living room, the house was so small. What little bit of a kitchen there was wasn't worth anything but cooking in. I watched her pull the shades down. She closed the front door and locked it. I got pretty scared. I can remember saying, *what's the matter?* I thought I was going to get a whipping for something, even though she'd never whipped me before. She says, *we're gonna play a little secret game I've always wanted to play*. Even now when I think about it, it's so hard to accept. Sometimes I think I dreamed it Belinda...

"I was wearing a denim dress with a white t-shirt underneath. It's funny, I was 13 for a whole year and that was the only day I still remember what I was wearing. She says, *"we've got to get naked to play this game... I promise it's the most fun you'll ever have...* I took off all my clothes in front of her. I said *are we gonna take a bath?* She said *not this time...* and she put the white towel over the edge of the table. She sat down in one of the chairs, then she grabbed both my breasts, and licked the whole nipples like ice cream, over and over. Not sucking, just deep, heavy licking. Moving her head back and forth slow and fast and slow. I remember it was so wet, her mouth must have been watering. I still remember. It felt like a shadow. Like a shadow moved inside my body and took over. I wanted to wet myself. I wanted to relax and piss all over myself. I think I closed my eyes and took deep breaths because I *had* to. She didn't even suck the nipple yet. She just licked it. But she licked it hard and soft and quick and slow, Belinda. She flicked her tongue on my nipple like a damned snake and it felt like I could have turned into a ghost and floated up to the ceiling when she did that. I swear to *God and Jesus* I think I did that anyway. She licked me *hard* Belinda. With the top of her whole tongue like my nipples were pure ice cream. She licked me like she meant it. Like there was nothing in the world she could have done to stop it. To say it was the best thing I ever felt... it's like a starving homeless woman saying a gourmet steakhouse filet is the best thing she's ever ate, what is the fucking *point* but yes, I remember it being the best thing I had ever felt in my life...

"When she stopped licking she reached up and pulled my head down for a long, deep kiss. I just remember feeling like my body was going to pop away like a soap bubble. I almost couldn't stand it. Then she got up and made me put my hands on the table, then she let spit fall in my backside, then she took the thing... the enema thing, and she slid it all the way up in me..."

I am a partner in Cheryl's disbelief, as I watch her cover her mouth and look out the snowy window, her face burdened by confusion, a bewildered shock in her eyes.

"It sent something to my whole body Belinda. Like the shadow inside became one with me. I couldn't believe anything could feel that good. Then she leaned down, from behind me, and sucked my nipple like she tasted strawberry. She actually grunted when she did it. Like *nnmmmhhh*. That deep grunt you get when something is so good to your body you can hardly stand it. She grunted once so deep when her mouth was on my nipple. I felt the grunt vibrate the nerves in my whole body Belinda... I know it was something she needed, something she had needed for so long. How long? Ten? Twenty years? I still remember her grunting, the way her brow was wrinkled like she was frustrated, almost angry at how good it felt in her body. Every time she sucked my nipple in, and she sucked it in so deep, I had to breathe harder to keep from making a noise."

Cheryl! Cheryl Ezman! I cannot help thee, woman of straw! Woman burned in the blue and black fire, then frozen by the ice and snow!

"... then she touched my...my *clitoris*. It made me push back against—
it made me hump against the little white *enema nozzle*...then she sucked
on my other nipple and Belinda something happened in my body and I had
to cry out to keep from dying...I still remember it like it was yesterday, I
swear in God's name I remember every bit of it... then she hugged me
tight but she kept pushing that thing inside me. I've been doing that to
myself ever since. I almost always have to do that to go to the bathroom.
Have you ever heard of such a thing?"

Cheryl looks at me, straight faced, as if I might somehow have an
answer.

"...a few minutes later we started kissing again, and that feeling was
coming back to my body. She told me to take off her bra. It took me
forever to get her bra off but I know she loved every second of it. Feeling
my weak little fingers pulling and fumbling with that latch. I finally got it
off and when she turned around... it was... it was unbelievable. Her
breasts were bigger than mine, probably a J cup, if you can imagine, and
they hung low just above her waist. Her areolas were sort of pale but they
were very big..."

I watch Cheryl make a continuous circle motion over the front of her
breasts, while gazing into her memory. Her pale eyes are glassy. Vacant.

"I didn't know that something like that even existed. I was just like
everybody else. I thought she just had a big body under her blouses and
dresses but I had no idea. I remember the way they hung and swung back
and forth when she bent over and slid her underwear off. She made me
grab 'em and clap 'em together and bury my face between them. They
smelled like deodorant inside. They were so big and heavy. Then she told
me to suck the nipple like I was trying to get milk. I remember that when I

looked up, she had her head back and her eyes were closed. Her hands were on her hips. Just like mine were that day. Remember?"

"Yes."

"This was obviously something she had been thinking about for a long time. Or something she saw somebody else do. She said *pull it deeper in your mouth, Honey*. And I did. I held on for dear life. For the life I had. And for the one I lost when my mother died. I closed my eyes and I just clamped on to one and kept sucking. I did it until my cheeks were sore. And just when I was going to stop, she put her hand behind my head and held it there. So I just relaxed and kept going. She breathed really loud and deep for a long time, like she almost had an orgasm. Then she took the breast out of my mouth and sucked on it herself, then I sucked the other one. There we stood, both nursing her big breasts at the same time. I was 13, Belinda. The feeling I got when I sucked her nipple… when I watched her suck her own…"

Cheryl stops and closes her eyes, shaking her head like a conniseur who remembers the most heavenly taste of wine. Is it Lillian Helderman's kindness, or her perversion which carries such electric appeal to her?

"She sat up on the dining room table, on the white towel with no clothes on. She laid down on her back and opened her legs. She told me to stand on two phone books. She gave me the enema nozzle and told me to hold it between my legs, *like a little white penis sticking out*, she said. On the phone books, I was just tall enough for it to be in the right place. I remember she was shaven. It was red and very swollen. I remember so vividly… it was swollen. She told me to spit onto her… onto her anus. I did, but moisture had already dampened it. She said *put it in… put your little cock in my ass*, she said… she took hold of it and guided it in. Then she made a sound like a dying animal. Kind of like a wailing, hopeless sound. *Hold it tight between your legs,* she said... *now push it in with your body in and out... watch it go in and out of Momma's ass... push it in hard push it in harder Baby finger Momma's clit just once just one time—put your thumb right there on Momma's clit... okay that's good... hold my legs up baby... keep pumping... keep pumping my ass baby...* then she started making that noise again, the sound of her spirit dying, I could hear it. I didn't know what I was doing. I was so awkward, the thing kept slipping out from my legs until I had to hold it with one hand. There I am like a dumb little shit, fucking the shit out of my foster Mom... my adopted Mom... and she says *fuck the shit out of me baby... bang it harder up in my ass... hold on to it and go as hard and fast as you can... that's it that's it that's it make me cum make me cum make me cum* and I'm banging it in her butt hole as hard as I can—she's laying on the white towel, legs in the air and... and when I stopped to readjust, when I banged it in one more time real deep, not really thinking about it, she yelps like a kicked dog and her whole body jerks once like she'd been stabbed with a needle and she squirts something out of her thing right up into my face... I swear I don't know if she pissed in my face or what. I don't remember smelling urine—I just remember having to wipe my eyes. I didn't know what to do so I just kept banging again, and she said *oh God keep going baby make me cum again make me cum again make me cum again,* and while I banged her in her ass with that little white dick like a dumb, clumsy little bitch, she yelped again and her body jerked again, and the piss or whatever shot right up onto my stomach. I swear it looked like she was hurt or something so I took it out, and she laid there on her back trembling like she was hooked up to a live wire. Her legs were still in the air a little but they were shaking until she lowered them and closed them. I just stood there. I stood there and watched this beautiful, demure woman that everybody thought they knew and understood, laying butt naked on her dining room table, shaking from an orgasm her adopted daughter gave her from anal intercourse. I watched Lillian Helderman lay there and tremble for at least another whole minute. Trembling like she was laying outside in the snow…

"…I asked her was she okay and she just took my hand and squeezed it so tight she cut my circulation. Her face was flushed. After a while, she lowered her legs and stopped trembling. Her legs were hanging over the edge of the table. She asked me what time it was. I told her *fifteen minutes after four.* She told me to come around beside her. She pulled my head down and kissed me. She told me to nurse her breasts again.

"And I did."

Numbness pulls me to my feet, to drift me over to her chair. I take her hand, standing nearby, listening to the wind weep and howl outside our window.

Snows drift from the grave of Annabelle Freeman up into the sky. These drift aimlessly across Prosperity, Vermont, until they are dropped by the winds that carry them. The winds continue their hopeless journey west, beyond the whirling flurries of its birth, past the doomed corner of the world. In hopeless longing, these winter breezes blow, in sorrow for what they know, and for what pain and tragedies they have known. On this calling they fly, bound for lands far west of here. Traveling the last hours of this July, focused on a future unseen to man, but of inherent fore-knowledge to them. The wind knows Donna Ward from days and years past, and the blood of her future calling.

These summer breezes are icy cold, and they tell me of mothers and daughters. The Unseen Dynamic, of life and death, and everything enjoyed and endured in between. The sufferings of unknown passions, burning the flesh and blood of so many who are hidden. They live on the streets of Everytown, in every neighborhood, every suburb and urban blight, like bright stars scattered over hazy distances, across a sea of dim and dullwitted bitterness and loss, the other stars whose burning is not as hot or as close to be seen, these mothers whose bodies burn the forbidden fires of lust and hatred, directed not at their sons, nor their husbands, nor any sister or brother or in-law thereof, but whose lust, love and hatred patterns burn, to screech a screaming inferno, to corrupt their daughters in forbidden pleasure or pain.

Yes. These cold winds I have felt, like so many who walk the earth unknown, their true selves seen by none but God the Father, these women whose bodies have twitched at a misplaced touch of affability or anger. These women who have straddled their daughters when they were too young to ask questions, when they were eight or nine, laying on their stomachs on the floor or on the bed, or who have looked and craved their daughter's fervent misbehavior, and fulfillment of promises of a spanking, paddling or a whipping as payment. These are the women who nursed their daughters far beyond the age of reasonable accountability, in any enlightened culture, or who punished them with corporal fever when they were grown. I hear tell of these secret women, these Amazons, the

Valkyries, the Lady Barbarians, through whose blood runs the heartbeat and desire of a man. This masculine diversion burns them with hunger, to salivation when they see their daughter in her bikini, her bra, even to her cleaving wedding dress and beyond. A lustful agony burning so many, but who are hidden so far from one another as to be alone, who satisfy the lust they crave with beatings, scourges, where the leaves of the Autumn Woods fall ivory to the ground at their feet.

Donna Ward stands alone. Breathing the lonely, dusty smell of approaching doom and devastation in the snow.

Donna Ward is a victim. Carried along on these Winds of Eschatology. Unvictorious. Unable to remove herself from the river that flows—that goes from her family's origin across the sea, down to the mother who abandoned her when she was twelve, after a young lifetime of abuses that left scars outside and in. Is this the demon inside her natural desire, that focuses it to intensity, until it burns a wire inside her brain? This wire radiates heat to certain places, until all she can see is her daughter's face, and all she can feel is the hatred it gives. This hatred is agony inside, fueled by the grieving she never lost when her sons were killed. Where are the barriers, the levees in the storm that flows from one pole to another in her mind? This side is not protected from the raging hurricane off shore, that forms and threatens and dies in cycle, having not passed in full over her core of civility. What levees are these that have crumbled forever? The gravestones that remain are not enough; they will fall in the power, in the wind and rain of what is to come, as the rain freezes when it swirls into the air, howled on breezes that crackle in winter lightning and thunder.

Donna Ward looks across the prairie. At peace with the gray she feels above her, and the endless ocean of white she sees.

I've never seen anything like this, Jeff Ward says, on the near side of snowy footsteps come and gone. Footsteps she had heard, even felt in her electric brain. *It's like Antarctica.*

"It's not that cold."

"I'm talking about the landscape. It's incredible. Just pure snow as far as the eye can see."

"Maybe this wasn't such a bad idea."

"It...it feels different here. It doesn't feel quite as much like...like death," he says.

Donna looks at her husband through suspicion. Wondering what churns beneath civility.

"I don't know if this is Heaven or Hell," he says. "Whether we're alive or dead."

"What difference does *that* make? A world covered in ice and snow? Sometimes I still have pinch myself just the make sure I'm still awake."

"It is like a dream."

"The world is a nightmare, Jeff. Truth is, sometimes I wish I *were* dead."

"I thought we agreed not to talk like that on this trip."

"*You* agreed," she says, hands on her hips, sweater pulled smooth and tight over her bosom. "Are the boys asleep?"

Jeff Ward decides not to divert her from her accidental peace, where calm and reason resides the Halls of Denial. "Oh, God. I did it again didn't I?"

"It's alright," he says. "I still do it to. But this could be the start of something new for us. You and me. Especially you and Veronica. This is our chance to be a family again."

He is Naivité. Moved to the rare hug about his wife's shoulders.

"I want you to promise me Donna—the next time you feel that hatred rising, the next time you feel like it's going to happen I want you to talk to me. Let's not take it out on each other anymore. I want you to love Veronica. She needs you more than ever, Honey. I need you. With the way the world is—with what's happening. Every year they say it's getting better and its actually getting worse. I don't remember the last time I saw a blade of grass. And we all know that this is going to be the worse winter we've ever seen. What else have people got except family?"

Together, they stare across the white, barren landscape, at a loss for what words there might be to describe such heavenly beauty.

These dreams go on when I close my eyes—
Every second of the night—I live another life.

Heart

Dolls dream the perpetual sleep of the dead. Eyes wide open—they are a part of what drifts and flows around us, watching us as we live. We can never remember whether the arms were up or down, whether the hair was loose or plaited, or what spot on the chair or carpet these dolls lay, whether they leaned against the right arm of a chair or the left when we went to bed.

The eyes of her Indian haunt Amanda as she sleeps, to pull her into the other world, the one only accessed by sleep.

In this vision, so wide and deep, Amanda is unfortunate enough to see and feel the height, depth and breadth of reality, which is the snowy back yard of our white mansion home. In her vision, she senses her Indian bride, her Indian guide *Elizabeth*, an angel sent to compel and guide her in a form she knows and loves. This angel, a bride in unearthly beauty, with long, silken hair as black as pitch under a new moon, dressed in leather cloth as white as the driven snow—this angel is there to protect her heart and soul from the fear, the terror which might seek out her life in this body. The angel watches over Amanda Freeman, when a blue hand bursts through the packed and frozen snow, clawing fiercely until the arm breaks through. Then the beautiful woman moves through the snow. Climbing, crawling, walking, falling, swimming, pulling, desperately dead and blue skinned in the snow. Amanda's fear rises, held at acceptable abnormality, lest her heart cease to beat.

She watches the figure open a locked back door by the magic of a mere touch. She walks gracefully through the dark now—smooth, ethereal command, no longer awkward, nor clumsy in desperation. A calm, quiet, forceful manifestation of demonic power, unencumbered by the cold, unhindered by the blowing flakes of snow through the open door behind her, undeterred by the sound of the rumbling, trembling earth beneath her frozen feet. She glides effortlessly in the dark, through the dark kitchen she glides. She slides through the winter air, unaware of whether this was her home and pleasure. A measure of malice resides, to coincide with the lack of compassion, and desire to steal, kill and destroy her daughter's sanity. Without vanity, she takes every step in determined tempo, the soft padded thump of each resounding through the house, as though insulated and directed into her daughter's heart and hearing. In the cold agony of her calling, the blue woman steps each step upward, landing at last on the second floor hall, aware that her daughter has awakened in this dream and lies motionless on her back, frozen in a scream that will not come. Then the footsteps lift and move themselves, until they are transformed into a cold, dreadful knocking at the bedroom door. There is always so much to fear, from a fateful knocking at the door. Then Amanda perceives the blue woman open her mouth and eyes wide, to utter a sound from her blackened tongue, a sound of ice and winter—only the deep, gruff moaning crescendo that grows, until it is the voice of certain death to the living.

And when the Lord has mercy on the daughter's poor voice, a scream bursts forth into the house like a fountain.

Amanda's scream had gathered us up from our weary sleeping bed. From separate, grieving night rooms, the living woman and I had hurried to my sister's bed, where she lay screaming in the dark.

We sit in the middle of Amanda's bed. The three of us, locked in fear and grief again. On either side of my sister we rest in a passion, with her hugging me tight, while Cheryl sits pressed against her as well. We know that likely it is no longer a question of whether my sister will sleep alone, but which of us she'll sleep with and for how long. *I saw her come out of the grave,* she had said—*her hands were blue,* she said, until I told her not to speak of the blue woman in the snow. I hug my sister tight now. To absorb her grief and fear, glad for Cheryl's determined, focused support, no matter its purpose and intent. To make us feel better is all that matters.

I am able to close my eyes because Cheryl is here. Adrift to remember the dream I was just awakened from by the scream. The dream of a blue summer sky, with a scattering of white clouds over the horizon. I walk the long road in this vision. A long, dusty, country road south, somewhere far and away from the pain of snow. A black pickup truck with an unknown driver passes by, raising the welcomed dust to my nostrils, which I breathe in gladly. The road stretches on to a path of plush, green summer trees, just beyond the tall, silver silos of grain with a large red and white barn nearby. The truck goes on until it passes out of sight. On either side of this long road, the grass is greener than what I can bear, to border the road from another sea of green, the ocean of summer corn that grows as far as I can see. Down the road where I walk, some distance apart from it, there is a row of forest trees, so small from their great distance away. The sky is so blue, the sea of grass and leaves so green, that I can hardly distinguish of what place this is, whether it be earth or heaven.

And then a strong, warm breeze blows over the rolling fields of green, blowing warm, so blessedly warm upon my face, carrying the dust away, until there is freedom in the air I breathe.

Then from the distance beyond the trees, I see the sudden gathering of dark gray clouds, and I hear the siren wailing of a girl (or is it a woman's scream?), the noise pushing the clouds so rapidly into the peaceful ocean blue, moving a shadow over the green below. The wailing voice reaches into my heart again, and I awake from this dream a second time, realizing that the warm breeze is only the heat from the vent over our heads, and Amanda is on her back between Cheryl and me, trapped in another pitiful, hopeless scream.

*H*ere, in the seventh summer-winter before Chaos, financial markets around the world have begun to explode, the chain reaction that starts in only one place, to rock the stability of what structure or form lays beside it in false security—causing a sudden and immediate blast and loss of itself to oblivion. What economy there remains around the world is left to ponder what once was, as so many jobs have suddenly become obsolete, as so many people are inclined to disbelief, that car sales have fallen down to nothing, as money is no longer wasted on such multi-thousand dollar foolishness as a shiny new house toy on wheels, when what one owns already is beyond sufficient enough. It is the greatest time for automobile mechanics in modern history; a one-time five hundred dollars to a mechanic, or that same five hundred done 50 times to a car loan company? To shudder the thought. The largest and first industry to go in the snow economy saw the big auto manufacturers quaking in their snowboots, as the collected lots of new and used cars filled to ghostly connections in their minds, from their high rise offices to the factories which bore the burden of the corporate lash, where the robots and flesh machines stood cold and dark and lonely with inactivity, to send images to the corporate mind of the ghostly seas of color, these real acres that lift and come together in their frightened minds as an ocean of miles of empty car lots, this emptiness being the people who would normally pretend they could afford the house toys on wheels. These snowy acres are ghost towns. Filled to bursting with painted boxes, metallic and the finest plastic toy machines on wheels, that once rolled black tar streets in pride and necessity, in lascivious laughter and gain. These SUV's of old, those luxury automobiles from the highest to the low, those fine road monsters that trucked whole families to whatever place and private cakes they baked and ate; one to another those Moms and Dads, sons and daughters in new rolling power machines over and over, from one year to the next, money thrown away in changing toys to roll and play in.

These acres of lots and dealerships. From the snow capped mountains of Colorado, over the snowy plains to the sandy beaches of South Florida, where even now the waters lap the shores in ice and bitter cold. Save for the lonely rich, who still wander out into the snow for Diversion's sake alone, to plop full mountains of money for fun, to enjoy the privilege of riding a new toy away in the snow. These acres of car, truck and SUV lots stand empty of souls, as the mouth of these storms has opened and swallowed them whole. These that manufactured the rolling vehicles. They were the first to weep and howl their lost gold, as some found solace in the cold air downward from their high rise rooftops, and others drew comfort from the end of the barrel of a gun. Their wives let this new comfort come to pass for them in vogue, and the fashionable proliferation of pills and a glass of wine. These are the comforts of a concrete stone for a pillow, and the mound of dirt as a blanket for their bed.

And in some of the rarest cases, the snowfall is a welcomed covering. Over the permanent landscape reminders, as the earth itself had tried so hard not to be apocalyptic in its warnings, confining the damage from the frequent earthquakes to an open field, or even a long country road or two. Few sights in the history of the world had been more fearful, than what the farmer in the open field would see, when he saw the exploding dust line approaching him from the distance, as the earth crackled and spit dust high into the air for at least a mile along a violently opening fault line, as though someone had exploded charges every few feet through the open, dusty terrain. And when the dust clears, there is left in the earth a long and ugly raised scar, as if it had been cut by the pressure erupting from underneath, and now the broken skin is left to heal jagged on its own. Along more than one Midwest country road, there is this raised fault line occurrence, making the little traveler's road on either side of the dirt mound impassable except on foot. Long lines of raised dirt once scarred the unpaved roads, remarkably and often confined to the borders of the road itself.

The early days of the snowfall saw the appearance of these raised fault lines everywhere on earth; even the long, paved roadways were not spared, as more than one highway had to be closed and rerouted because of the raised broken line of asphalt that made them obsolete. Sometimes, unlucky travelers in the east would have to evoke the name of God and Christ, most notably along old highway 64, when the raised line of earth appeared one morning on their rainy trip unaware, from inside the dense pine forest and roadside ditch, then across the big stretch of highway diagonal to the other side, to the detriment of a giant metal powerline tower dead on the ground, all the way back to the forest on the other side. These daylight travelers luckier than so many, those having run into the hilly terror at night. All over the world, the raised earth scars betrayed the pain and agony, the suffering endured by the trembling earth itself. Seven years beyond this, lies covered the evidence of these bygone scars, so thankfully buried and hidden in the snow.

And what alternatives to the raised faultlines were they, or appearing as the arrival of a small canyon, or a terrifying new border in a neighbor's yard, dividing one property from another. The inexplicable appearance of the cracks were unnerving indeed, not always preceded by an earthquake, sometimes removing a whole line of houses from the urban blight, or slicing a course through a giant parking lot from the crying woods to the dying shopping center entranceway. Helicopter cameras and reports were so busy in those days—showing the world what it could no longer turn a blind eye to, that they were *not* the masters of creation, and the unseen forces of time and history had their own will and purpose, having an important announcement to make. This—in the form of hills and mountains gently cracked, and the lady fisherman's awe in disbelief, as she stands in the middle of the dry pond or lake bed, gazing at the fissure in the ground, fascinated that it hardly seems wide enough to have let every single fish and drop of water through.

In the morning hallway, outside my sister's sleeping room, we surrender to the daytime shadows, and the ghosts that drift in from the snow.

"Your mother was a dream queen."

"Hmm?"

"Pills. I noticed that she has all kinds of sleeping pills. Maybe her death wasn't an accident."

"Are you saying she took an overdose?"

"One of the bottles is almost empty."

In the darkened hall, revelation appears in shadow form, to taunt and torment us of the possibility.

"She wouldn't have left us like that. Especially Amanda. I think fear and grief got the best of her. You should have seen her face the first night this storm came. Remember the night the snow started, but it didn't really do anything until the next day? That beautiful evening snow? I was threatening to leave with Veronica Ward. Something we all should have done. She tried to force me to stay but I'd already made up my mind. She met me at the door that night. I got so angry and scared that I hit her. I was beating her on her head while she held on to me. She wouldn't let go. I heard the fear in her voice that night. It broke her down to nothing, I saw it on her face. It was in her eyes. Like she was crazy. She even tried to make us believe that it was just snow, and that it was beautiful. And the thing is, she was right. It was beautiful. I couldn't make her believe that... that we're all in trouble this time."

"I know. But she accepted that, remember? I went shopping with her before she died. She bought 2 months worth of food for you guys. She was ready to make it through this. She even mentioned that old house your Dad wouldn't sell down south."

"She did?"

"She said it was in North Carolina," Cheryl says. "Martin County, I think. Talked about how hard it was getting to hold on here."

"Did she ever say anything about moving there?"

"She said she felt like she… like everybody was being driven out, and it was her job to stay and fight for what was rightfully hers. She said, *I'm not gonna let this damned snow take my house.* I said, *what about that North Carolina house?* And she said, *you and Belinda talk so much about moving, you almost got me thinking about it.*"

"You wanted out of here, too?"

"I wanted to leave a year ago. And this January I almost did. I tried to call your mother's bluff. I was gonna pack up and move to Hawaii if I had to live in a grass shack when I got there. I even showed her my plane tickets. She got that look on her face that only she could do. Where she kind of tilts her head, looks off to the side and raises her eyebrow. Like she was thinking, *whatever rides your train, baby.* When she made that face, she had a heart of steel."

"I know. She made it the night I first told her I was leaving with Veronica. I thought she was so tough. I thought she could take anything. But she was faking. She was *gangster* fake."

"That's just it. She had to have killed herself, Belinda. No way was she scared enough to have just died of fright. She was tough enough to hold a smile and be pleasant and friendly, even though the whole world is in Ice Hell right now."

"If she wasn't scared then why would she kill herself?"

"Pain," she says. "The pain of living."

"Trust me, Aunt Cheryl. She had changed. She *was* afraid. The last couple of days, she was a zombie. She was in front of the TV all the time. Listening to everything they said about this storm—"

From somewhere far and near, we listen to the deep, quiet looming of noise, as the aftermath of a great explosion.

"Was that thunder or a quake?"

"I don't know… I think it was thunder."

I open the door in Amanda's room, surprised that she is still asleep.

"She's in a deep sleep. I can hear her breathing."

Cheryl walks to the door and opens it again. Softly. She stares many seconds longer than I. Looking for something.

"What's the matter?"

She shakes her head, awakening from whatever fog she was in, closing the icy morning door. Daylight is the shapely, sleeping girl's companion. Amanda's full figured slumber is a warm fire in Cheryl's bosom.

"When I first saw your mother's grave… I felt my heart skip a beat. The spirit of death is cold. It touches us when we aren't ready, just so we'll know it's there. So we'll know that God is watching. But the pain in our hearts warms us. It protects us from the fear of death. It makes us ready. Like the soldier on the snowy battlefield. Grieving for the sound of his wife's voice. The feel of her warm body next to his. The pain of her absence, the agony of it is his bravery. His fury. His boldness in the face of Death. The loss of freedom is a fire that drives him forward in the snow, to point the gun, the sword, and shoot or stab death in its black heart, so he can live to fight it again. For just one more day."

"I'm not a soldier," I say. "This snow scares the Hell out of me. And I don't know how poor Amanda's gonna make it. All she talks about is the end of the world."

"I've thought about it myself, you know."

"The end of the world?"

"Pills. And a glass of wine."

"Oh. What keeps you from doing it?"

"Everyday it's something different. But a few days ago, I realized I had run out of things to look forward to."

"What stopped you?"

"I remembered your mother…"

I watch Cheryl lower her head and wince hard, as against a stabbing pain.

"I remembered Anna. And I thought about how even if there was a chance that—"

"That she loved you?"

Cheryl closes her eyes, unable to hide the depressive anguish of a wrinkled brow.

"When I saw your mother's… your Momma's grave… I died."

"For some reason, Mom's death gave me strength. I miss her but, with the way things are, the way she was before she died, I feel relief more than anything else. God help me, but sometimes I think… sometimes I think I'm glad she's dead. Please don't hate me for saying it."

Cheryl walks over to where I lean against the wall, looking at me in the eye. On the nose. On the lips.

"Hate? My Anna's daughter?"

She shakes her head. Her pale eyes are a sky in winter. Her soul is deep, simple turmoil.

"I live. I live for what closeness there might be left between us. Whatever games there are left to play."

In her voice, I perceive the masculine side of womanhood, the whirlwind that is a hurricane in November, of those that once raged our stormy seas, before their life was touched by the cold—confining themselves to our memory, of days when the sky was blue.

What dreams are these, of the heart, soul or mind—that bear the full weight of prophecy? The dream is a full vision, in uncompromising force and clarity, which shows me my sister naked as a jaybird on my mother's bed on all fours, with my naked Aunt Cheryl behind her in the style of a dog. Amanda's buttocks are still, but pushed hard back against

Cheryl's groin. Cheryl holds Amanda tight around the waist. Her face is wet with tears, flushed, burdened by sorrow, her groin pressing tight against Amanda's buttocks—her breasts laying heavy on Amanda's back. The look on Amanda's face is the pain of lost virginity. The agony of a need unsuppressed.

Then suddenly, in keeping with the power of a dream, Cheryl's hips twitch and lurch forward one perfect time on their own, but hard enough to jerk Amanda's whole body, and I see Cheryl's face strain as her mouth opens to let out a violently loud, depraved scream of pleasure so intense as to cause her pain. I see the muscles in her neck straining, even her arm muscles as well, her breasts hanging big and heavy from a tight frame, her buttocks dimpled from the squeezing forward, until it seems that Cheryl's entire body is held in the pain of the most intense climax possible, one that leaves her face twisted in despair and disbelief, even while Amanda pushes back in unwilling gladness to receive it.

I wake up quietly from this. Undisturbed. But in full knowledge of what I have seen, whether I have been shown by Destiny or Desire, and of why it was shown to me. There is a spirit that possesses Cheryl Ezman's body, to create an unearthly lust and ability, and now I know without a doubt why she felt she had to come here, whether my mother would have been here or not. It is the call of the wild, as to a snow beast within, that draws one from their fortress of loneliness and solitude, to where the meat of their bloodlust waits to be hunted.

And how many years since I was 12, how many of these five years has she boiled in the lust of society's fervent, fearful undoing, in the sin of these last days in the snow?

I arise. Awake from a late morning sleep. Already, I can feel, I can hear, I can smell that they have been awake for sometime—in the aroma of breakfast and forbidden company. Though they gather such welcome laughter from the morning comedy they found on TV, underneath it flows the stream of desire, along the current of devastation and despair. Cheryl sits in loose, long white t-shirt borrowed from Amanda, her legs exposed high up—the smooth, ivory skin of her thighs noticeable. Amanda is dressed the same, in her characteristic rose pink cotton.

"Amanda," I say. She sits dumbfounded in a smile, on the edge of another laugh at *Three's Company*. "Amanda," I say again. "Can you finish watching this upstairs Honey. I know it's a pain but—"

"How come?"

"I need to talk to Aunt Cheryl for a minute. Go on, now. Please?"

She is not going to budge. Wanting to hear what we might say about life, death and mothers buried in the snow. She doesn't move. Until Cheryl touches her on the arm with a quiet *it's alright Babe, go ahead. I'll be up in a minute*. Amanda takes a deep breath, two days from 16, but already more of a woman in her body than me. Cheryl keeps gazing dimly at the television, the images of the two women and their roommate so timelessly compelling.

"I know what you're trying to do, Aunt Cheryl."

"Right now I'm trying to finish watching this show. I can't hear it…"

Cheryl rudely turns the volume up too high for me to do anything about it. So I just sit here, looking away, to the bay window my mother loved so well.

"I understand," I say, gazing at the snowline two feet high across the window. "She's my sister. And she makes me feel the same way."

My ghostly, depressive tone is enough to unnerve her away from foolishness. I hear the volume go down. What I had believed was impending conflict was surely nothing of the kind. Death needs no noise, no violent utterance to make do.

"I don't know whether or not it's just me. But sometimes when I look at her, I just want to push her up against the wall and... and rip her shirt down. I want to stare at her big... white tits until she too embarrassed to move. Then I'd... I want to slap the Hell out of her for no reason."

I slide closer to Aunt Cheryl. The ear she hears me with is pity.

"Sometimes," I say, "I just want to lay on top of her and bite her breasts until she is crying and begging me to stop. I don't know where it comes from, Aunt Cheryl. I'm not a dyke. I'm not a lesbian or a pervert. Am I?"

Cheryl looks back to the top of the stairs, to where the seeds of our immolation grow.

"She'll be 16 in two days," she says. "That's too close to being a woman. I... it should be while she's still a girl."

"No."

"You said you understood... Belinda—"

"I know, but... I have to protect her—"

A sudden laughter, the full voluptuous innocence of 15 year old maturity *ha haws* at us from the upper room.

"I'm not wearing one, but I brought two with me."

Her voice is low. Almost whispery.

"I swear I don't know why. I swear to God and Jesus I don't. Maybe I thought… your mother and me… I've got two harnesses. One for me. And one for you."

"No…" I shake my head this time, trying so hard to be strong against the dark spirits that plague us.

"We won't hurt her… I swear. We'll make her understand gently, so gently we will."

I pull away from the vortex of Cheryl Ezman's spirit, the spinning, the turning that is the sucking motion, that seeks to spiral me downward, to a place I only thought I was prepared to believe in. I go to the snowy bay window to escape, followed by my kindred Nemesis, the projection of my maturest dream. She turns me around in front of the window and presses her lips hard to mine. I can only breathe, my eyes still open to see, hoping not to receive her unholy commission dispensed with whispers, touches and quick, passionate kisses at the window.

*I*s this how filthy hearts and minds have become? In this, mankind's final hour? To even allow such a thing to enter our minds can only be symptomatic of the earth's snowy condition, and the general feeling we share with the rest of the world, which is—*what of it?* What force is there in Earth under Heaven—that seeks to destroy the veils and facades we carry? What force is there in the gray and white earth under heaven, that seeks to lift mankind from the slumber of hypocrisy and moral complacency, to reveal what evils he is capable of? How many homes around the country and around the world are frozen under pressure, where the snow is a dreadful weight pressing down, to cause to reveal the white or black hearts that live and die inside? It seems such an automatic, page of life dramatic, end of the age traumatic so symptomatic of the times—that the prophecies must now be fulfilled; that as it was in the Days of Noah, so shall it be in the coming of the Son of Man. The earth is again filled with violence—physical violence of the body, and all manner of perversion therein. Even I, still remember in disbelief some of the things I have seen and heard by report, sometimes on the news magazine shows and the private things they make public. Burning the theater of my mind now is the image of the two women: they were prim and proper local news anchors at the desk in the morning, who understood what churns beneath cultured civility, but who were powerless when the surface of theirs was broken, and the blonde anchor reached over and pulled the brunette's hair down in pure rage, and they both stood up like two white tigers on hind legs, ferocious before a regional audience, and then before a national audience ad nauseam. When it first began, the brunette had tried so hard to maintain a calm expression, until the pain of her hair being pulled was too great to bear.

Yes, somewhere along our snowy path, the two of us have turned the corner, and now we walk the path of foolishness, heavy laden with sin and carnality.

These are the days of Noah, as prophesied by the Son of Man, for as it was in the days before the flood, so shall it be in the time of his coming. There has descended on the world a spirit of wanton recklessness—a spirit of violence itself—that manifests in the gentile and the civil, until their ordinary behavior becomes extraordinary, rising and expanding without effort to the unspeakable. This spirit falls in purity in the snow, undiluted, unclouded by delusion, but true in purpose of intent. From every corner of every cloud above falls the poison snow, drifting down atop and around every house where innocence once resided, to see it attacked and burned or contaminated—until it must corrode and rust and rot away.

It is the beginning of the sorrows of mankind, when the centuries of divine neglect must return to call, and collect the recompense that is due. Retribution falls in the poison snow, where the clouds were seeded by the Prince of the Power of the Air. By the will of the Almighty, the clouds grow full with ice and death, which now falls gently in the wind, accompanied by the cloud ceiling flashes of blue and white lightning in the sky, and the roar and booming rumble of thunder from them. Snowfalls such as this were never imagined by mankind on the earth, given as a sign of the approaching rapture, and the second coming of our Lord and Savior. This poisonous snow falls undeterred, to fill the beaches with ice and cold, to spread itself from shores to many miles into every ocean in cleansing. Unseen, those spirits that caused the snow move among the humans in pure, crystalline malevolence—touching every human in the vulnerable parts of the mind and soul, to affect their behavior with negativity and shades of the forbidden. These beings lurk in the shadows, in the dark corners of the human heart, to affect the unsuspecting with ease.

Breezes blow warnings to us in the icy cold, as the entire earth tastes diversion likewise as we, its attentions and affections drawn and misdirected to the unspeakable. The woman and I hear these icy morning breezes, rumbling the outside of our mansion home, to try and shake it to its well-to-do foundation in the cold. Confirmation of the end time speaks to our minds and bodies, when the woman goes to the closet and pulls the bag she had brought with her; when she endeavored to masquerade as innocence, and the extension of our mother's desire in form. Our mother's love for us, she drifted in upon; as the soldiers in that great horse of myth and legend. These demons, these heart and soul memories bestowed, are now here to claim two further causes; two others in dumbness, sorrow and damnation.

From the bag, she lifts one fervent harness, where attached to it is a realistic member the color of skin, fashioned to the look and feel of its calling. It excites me to an end I did not know before, and she can see the surrender in my eyes and my spirit. She takes the back of my head and pulls me forward, until I know to open my mouth and place it around the head of it. I do not close my eyes while I look at her, the both of us in our mourning cotton house shirts, and I wonder what will I say, what will I do if Amanda sees the fellatio of our Winter's Demise. I stand at the front closet in foolishness, my black hair in loose ponytail, nearly choking on the realistic member in my mouth. Cheryl tells me to take off my t-shirt, which I do by the classic crossing and uncrossing of my arms. She tells me to remove my underwear, which I do. *Step into the straps*, she says, which I do, and she supervises the Chiming of the Whirlwind, the origin of unknown violence and perversion in my body. I stand amazed, exposed, trembling from the cold inside, and the uncertainty of what we must do. I watch her remove her long shirt in the like manner, her arms crossed and uncrossed the same as mine, unable to accept that a shapely, fit woman can have breasts so gargantuan. I watch them pull and swing so heavy, so white as she leans over to slide her underwear off, then reach back into the bag in the closet, removing the second member, done in the same ivory skinned likeness as the long and hanging one before. She slides into the extension of who she is inside, this madness brought forth as she closes the closet door.

I watch her walk over to the bay window. As plain as what eyes outside would dare to see, but knowing she is protected by the gray light of day, the heavy snowfall, and the daytime darkness inside our window. I watch her stand naked, Amazonian, drawing power from her heavy curves, her extreme and irrefutably feminine curve of breasts and hips, her bottom made so wide by time and maturity, wide set to an infinity exceeded by no other woman of such lightness in form since Annabelle Freeman. Hers is a body rarely seen by man, so rarely imagined by polite society, except by those who have given place to art and sin. Breasts and hips from a woman so far away in her timeline, the origin of her exotic blood and form, the Native American nuance of her appeal. I watch her turn away from the snowy bay window, gazing at me straight and deep, mouth relaxed enough that her lovely white teeth are visible. *We'll go to her room*, she says, and I stare at her eyes to see the resolve and determination in them. she walks past me in drift, as I turn to drift behind her in human form. We walk the carpet in fever pitch of leisure; the long, slow steps of our strongest life's calling, to become a part of why the world as we know it must come to an end. I watch her hips as we climb the stairs, fascinated that such beauty truly exists in the unaided nude, the naked woman's body seen in person rather than captured on still and moving film. Her hips switch and sway smoothly in front of me as we take the mourning stairs, both of us strong in the knowledge of what it is we have to do.

Rising high above reason, with every step closer to the last days insanity, we reach the second floor carpet, to begin our ghostly trip through the daytime light down the hall to Amanda's room. I hear the foolishness of TV from in her room, the laughter of spiritual blindness and degradation from the speakers. I watch Cheryl take a last, bold step to the door of my sister's room, knocking on the door, knowing that Amanda cannot remember the warning given by her mother from the grave, when death came knocking at the door. I am in a hazy fog, such a foggy haze of anticipation and thrill, my own nipples so hardened from the what pulses through my virgin body. These are the last days, I know, from the sound of the door that clicks softly when the knob turns. These are the last days, I know, when the door swings open, pulling with it the air from around us for a fraction of time, then I can suddenly breathe when the vacuum goes away again, and the current of air draws us floating from the hall into her room behind her as she walks away, miraculously having not seen the two phantoms at the door.

There is *something in the way she moves,* the prophet sang, which speaks to me in the voice of the somber and wisened cello, as I see the witch grab the pink rose from behind, shocking her by holding her arms immobile. I feel her mouth the words *Aunt Cheryl what's wrong* with her last free breath, as she takes her first breath as a dead soul when she sees me naked with the realistic member hanging down, walking so casually over to the noisy and foolish box of violent color. She stands there, being held so tight by the Woman of Snow, her mouth open wide in shock as I walk back over to her. She tucks her lips in, and I see the echo of laughter in her eyes among the astonishment, which incenses the spirit in my body possessed, and I slap her hard enough to make her cry out. Her tears fall instantly. Her little voice is so choked up as she asks *why, what did I do, I didn't know the TV was too loud Belinda, I'm sorry, please...* and I am shocked to something close to a visible twitch in my groin when Cheryl grabs my sister hard by her throat and chokes her to quiet, saying *shut the fuck up* in my sister's ear. Amanda's tears flow freely. *Take her shirt off* Cheryl says, and I am powerless to resist grabbing it in near anger; her youth, her naiveté, her innocence suddenly nauseating. I pull the shirt, the rose fabric violently off over her head, then Cheryl grabs her by the neck and hair, saying *take her panties off. Take 'em off!* she yells, staring the busty young girl directly in her eye—*don't look at me like you don't understand,* she says, *you busty little twit, I know you've got it in your body too, I can feel it.* Amanda can only gaze through a waterfall, seeing Cheryl's beautiful face through a wall of tears, saying *Belinda please,* then Cheryl grabs her nipple and twists it. The sound Amanda makes, the violent struggle that ensues inspires us to emotions we have never felt, where there can be no mercy given. She begins to slap, to hit Amanda in the face so amazingly hard as to make me lose my breath in this, with the three of us nude in Amanda's room, while we wear the hanging members, and begin to beat her on the head, shoulders, face and back. *Hold her up,* Cheryl orders, which I gladly do, and I am not surprised when she slams her knee hard into my sister's abdomen, causing such a sickening blurb of a yelp to escape from deep inside her spirit. We hold her bent over, still and quiet as she whimpers and breathes hard, spit falling once on the floor. We move her over to the bed. *Get on top of her Belinda*, she says, which I feel I must do. *Belinda I'm sorry, Belinda please*—she says, breathlessly, until Cheryl grabs her hard by the throat again. Cheryl lays down on her back, pulling Amanda down on top of her face up. Amanda lays face up on top of Cheryl, flailing confused, frightened. *You do it Belinda*, she orders. *Do it*. And I know it is something I must do.

I lay down on top of Amanda, prying her legs open while she cries, Cheryl's hand still around her throat. I take the large member in my hand while she shakes her head in Cheryl's grip, and I slide the head of it through the open gate, then I push firmly and steady until every inch pushes through my sister's scream.

I lay there. Trying to remember how to breathe. Smelling the crossed aromas, the scent of her hair and new sex, the smell of Cheryl's heavy, musky sweat. *Turn 'er over, but leave it in,* Cheryl says. We work together athletically, smoothly until I am on my back under Amanda, the member still so deeply, so painfully inside—shocked by the sudden, hard slapping noise of Cheryl's hand on Amanda's white bottom; a hard, repeated spank in one spot—*hold still—I said hold still* Cheryl says, *just scream the pain you dumb bitch*—whacking her so cruelly on the bitch syllable. I feel the lowering of her life, lost expectation as she lowers her head and cries the only spanking she as ever received, tears dropping onto my shoulder, yelling loud through pain and confusion. I hold her close on top of me, now to comfort her, telling her it will be alright and to just relax and breathe. Pitifully, she shakes her head and breathes too hard. Then Cheryl gets behind her in the style of a bitch dog turned butch, her gigantic tits resting on Amanda's back, letting spit fall down to Amanda's bottom, sticking her finger once inside, making her wince the pain. Then Amanda feels the head of Cheryl's penis go into her backside, which causes her to yell so loudly and pitifully far beneath a scream, such a gruff and weakened plea for mercy that I pull her head down in support and offensively belated compassion. I hold Amanda while she wails the pain, as the beautiful woman pushes the full length of herself into Amanda's backside.

Then I must move. From an energy too deep to know I begin to squirm, feeling my own member so deep in the front of her, as Cheryl pushes hers so deeply into the back, and within two minutes along the timeline, the gifted woman of snow ceases the hard pumping on her own, to where her movements become involuntary, and the muscles in her body tense up as she strains to endure the wave of energy exploding from inside her groin, and begins the high pitched, animalistic cry of a woman condemned.

*V*ain algorithms plague the theatre of my mind. I watch them roll the snowy highways North and South, as some foolishly strive to escape damnation. Mothers and daughters, brothers and sisters, husbands and wives in their pretty cars and trucks, speeding slowly—slowly speeding along the interstate roads that are clear—hoping to get safely to and from where they are going. I hear the same rumbling beneath the earth as they, and perceive it rolling across the snowy countryside. From where they drive, so many rolling along in ice and complacent rhythm, they see what fires the electric lights of fear, sparking inside the clouds that stretch to the horizon; and every now and then, so many or so few are awestruck by the appearance of the lightning itself, and not just the flashy echo in the clouds. *Snow lightning,* as these cold sparks are now familiar to us, but still causing a spark of genuine fright in the soul.

I see the sky blue minivan that rolls along, carrying the judge and his wife leisurely south, from Berkshire Green, their upper middle class mansion neighborhood in The Garden State, rolling down to their daughter's middle class poverty, nestled somewhere near the bottom of Virginia. The judge rides along in fat portfolio luxury, hardly a day's worry in his past, so that the snow's arrival is a mere inconvenience for them. The fine fifty something wife sleeps unsoundly, a passenger luxuriously driven, rolling the snowy highway south, to where her daughter waits to be judged and ridiculed by passive aggressive bitterness and underhanded delight. Every compliment will be a backhanded slap of contempt; every insult a forward thrust of the knife, but not to kill as just to draw blood, but to cause pain, inner weeping and gnashing of teeth.

The two judges roll steadily along in the snow. Unimpressed by the wrath and power that lights the clouds so brightly, and fills them with such a rumbling voice of doom. The upper class mother awakes, riding million dollar comfort—in middle class disguise—looking back at their younger daughter who is always there, though 30 years has not seen fit for her independence, nor to take her away from her parent's home. The judge, his wife and daughter, striving the interstate south to see the other daughter this July, for the fortnight into their coldest August night. I see them rolling along; the Lion, the Witch and their Wardrobe of sin, wherein their feeble hearted Princess Pureheart resides. They roll along, these three, hoping soon to make it across these last miles into Virginia, their younger daughter fearful of what snows drift from the flashing clouds.

—*Boy, God is* <u>*mad*</u> the daughter says, prompting the mother a sleepy glance to the beautiful afternoon scene—and a self assured, superior dismissal by way of *What's God got to do with it* from the Judge, joined by the mother's skeptical *if there is a God*—

—*Granma says that God blessed us with everything,* the daughter says, and the mother says *God helps those who help themselves*—and *God didn't get us where we are, we worked for every penny of it*—*that mess you're talkin' is for poor, lazy ignorant people: God doesn't give you anything, you have to work for it,* the mother says—

—*God, what God, there is no God,* the father says behind glasses and a thick moustache, but with such good natured arrogance, such high minded self assurance and conceit as to be scornful, and mocking of the presence in the clouds. *God,* the mother says under her breath, remembering the married daughter's foolish Faith, and she laughs so heartily, such a high pitched, gleeful cackle that she startles the daughter in the back of the minivan, when suddenly a streak of thick light snakes from the clouds as the quick laugh subsides, striking like a hammer into the engine block from high above, blowing every wheel off the minivan and raising it up in the flow of afternoon traffic in a shower of white sparks. The car flies a sky blue streak forward and diagonal across the median—according to the people in the cars around it that see. To the Lion the Witch and their Wardrobe traveler, there is the sense of being pulled slowly up from the ground and a loss of which way is up, in a muffled blast of noise and the sensation of having their ears blown out of commission. The beautiful sky blue minivan flips down onto the highway and rolls into oncoming traffic, and is slammed into—head on by the passing silver sedan, and the cars behind the sedan react accordingly—skidding and smashing into each other like rolling bricks of glass and metal. For a mile, I see the cars crash and pile into each other, while the other side of the highway rests in uneasy calm and patience—as the traffic that was behind the burned and blasted minivan rolls to a calm and peaceful stop—their easy rest made so inevitable by the memory of the thick, white lightning bolt from the high clouds, and the blue minivan hurled across the snowy divide.

In the theatre of my mind, the gray and frosty haze, I see a minivan as blue as the sky above the clouds, crumpled and twisted upright and unrecognizable as before, with every tire blown off and away, with a blackened, melted space where the front and center part of the hood and engine block used to be. And as the wind grows, as the windy haze blows before my eyes, at the very last I see blood and ice, and the whereabouts of a dead lion, a dead witch, and a dead princess—inside their crushed, crumpled wardrobe of life and sin.

*V*ain algorithms plague the theater of my mind. I drift awake from the news of what I heard just last night, of sky blue minivans on the highway, and funerals for lions, witches and the like. In the bathroom, I stand at the mirror, weighted down by disbelief, unburdened by the sickness that was in my stomach less than a minute before.

I had begun to struggle when it was over, and begun to push my way out from under Amanda and Cheryl (no longer Aunt Cheryl), and I hurried in here to unburden myself of the sickness that churned nausea in my stomach. Now, I stand at the mirror. Still naked. Still wearing that which pertaineth to a man. Unable to touch it. Unable to bring myself to remove it and throw it away. I gaze into the eyes of mine—into the face in the mirror—eyes that own every part of who I am. I look into these eyes, these tired eyes, that once may have had the spark of young life, but which suddenly look foreign to me, touched and cursed by sin. In the mirror I see a beautiful, young woman nude—wearing the instrument by which this evil had come. Am I too sickened to move? Or too fascinated by what I see? I feel as though I have crossed a line—as though I have leapt from a precipice a mile into the air, and there is too much fear and sorrow to bear.

I reach down again and run cold water into my hands, taking the biggest drink that I can. All I can hear now is the sound Amanda made—the pitiful, hopeless, fearful sound when I penetrated her virginity. The main melody, counter pointed by the howling noise when Cheryl sodomized her while she was still penetrated by me. She was a lamb we had led to the slaughter, that lamb worthy of sacrifice—without spot or blemish, and we had unmercifully cut the throat of innocence, and bled the purity from her soul. This melody I continue to hear, to the pitiful wailing of disappointment she made, when I raped the virginity from her body. This was not a scream of pain, but of disillusionment and despair.

I loosen the straps at my hips, and slide quickly the big penis thing to the floor. From my groin I remove the blue and black fire, burning away and down to the floor. I stand still and look down at it, still hardly able to accept that this is done, that a human life can take such a turn as this. Then

I look back to the mirror, at these Eyes of Mine. Reddened, bewildered. Condemned.

What spirits torment the heart and mind? What demons torment the soul? Those that have sought to destroy me are at play inside, having achieved their desired effect in my life. They dance and whirl around me like the water in my face, and that which cascades in my hair and down past my shoulders and back. I hurry and open my eyes in this shower, knowing full well that demons have less power when eyes are open. In the daytime darkness, in the aftermath of what I've done, I open my eyes to face reality, that I am a victim of the end time violence and perversion sweeping the globe, and I am no better than so many who have lost their lives to the justice system, and sentenced to earth's manifestation of outer darkness, where there is daily weeping and nightly gnashing of teeth. But the prison I am in holds no bars of steel or walls of concrete, but extends the length and breadth of Creation. I understand now, even before I will close my eyes tonight in that first sleep after the raping, that there is indeed a place called Hell on Earth.

I turn the shower off. Listening to the water drip from my evil, naked skin. All that I see when I close my eyes again, all that I feel is the tormented soul of Amanda, whose very scent is still so strong in my nostrils, and the look on her face burned so hot into my brain. To ask myself, *what have I done*, would be only to anger God himself, and the angels that sit encamped around my freedom. What grief there is in the world to bear, that which escaped me so easily when Mother died, now comes in like a cold, ghostly hand, touching, caressing the back of my neck and my spine, through my lungs and a small arrhythmia attached to my beating heart.

Invisible leads are attached to my feet as I pull them up and step out of the bathtub onto the finely tiled floor. I was once so enamored by this gigantic cave of a bathroom with the vanity lights and raised Jacuzzi by the small bay window overlooking the side yard and line of giant cedar trees. My heart grieves somewhere past the window, into the snowy breeze that circles to where she is buried, and to the tall white cross that watches over her. From here, I can see the whirling snow flurries just beyond the window, dancing and swirling about, so lost and bound by the whim of the wind. The will of the wind blows hard and cold this summer, in the last hours before innocence turns 16.

I cover my damp nakedness in one of the huge, plush towels. In the mirror, I see the beautiful, exotic face of guilt, so humble now, so much less assured than before, lowering her eyes in embarrassment, at the pornographic beauty of what she sees, the wet raven hair and ivory skin, the bewitching eyes and full lips, the smooth neck and exposed arms, shoulders and chest just above the bosom. Though the towel is quite large, it only succeeds in covering my thighs near the top, leaving me exposed as the bathroom whore that I am—always on fire between my legs, since as long as I can remember, often immersed in phallic and Sapphic fantasy, sometimes to completion of the panting, trembling cycle of violent thought. What of the silken brunette hair, shoulder length? Eyes from when the sky was blue, eyebrows arched to heaven? What of the nose, sized and angled so Aishwarya Rai, diverting attention from itself to the smooth cheeks and full lips below? Now, the reflection watches me roll the weapon and its harness neatly, ever so neatly and deeply inside a towel. I roll it up into a clean little package, that bears no resemblance of its true self, of the death and utter destruction it carries inside. But even as I do this, I know the girl in the mirror likes what she sees, and envies to wear the blue and black fire again. But I am sickened down to the core of my spirit, knowing full well that I am going to throw this thing away at the first window of my soul's opportunity.

Clean and neat, I put it in the towel and leave the bathroom behind—hardly able to lose touch with the reality of what I've done. I walk down the hall toward my room, stopping at Amanda's room to hear the sobs from inside. The fierce protectiveness ensues, but why? It's like putting out a cigarette after the fire has burned your house down—go ahead, smoke! Go ahead, be disinterested in your sister's cause! Care nothing for her emotional well being now, just like you did before your Shower of Folly! Your ridiculous attempt to wash off the sin and corruption from your white skin! Why go through the rubble of what you have destroyed! But in belated, benign benevolence of intent, I open the door as if I am going to rush to my sister's rescue, but suddenly taken aback and stopped deadly in my tracks, when I see the two of them together naked, sitting on the edge of the bed facing away from the door, Cheryl's naked arms around Amanda's naked shoulders—both their backs exposed down to the bed where they sit. I am struck by the Stockholm-ness, the sado-masochistic strangeness of what I see, as Cheryl lends such deep and abiding comfort to the snow girl, whose soul she just burned with fire. I know they heard me in the room, but their dynamic is so solid, so completely preordained, so heavy with sorrow that they do not want me there to disturb what ties they seek to bind. Even now, I am horrified, as their naked backs distract me, the contrast being remarkable between them; from the short brunette hair, tiny curved waist and big wide hips spread to hourglass infinity, to the sandy brown ponytail and narrow shoulders and boyish cylinder waist and athletic hips of the other. I wonder if Cheryl's other hand, the one I can't see, massages my sister's big, round breasts, which I know someday will be even larger than Cheryl's own, to rival those of Cheryl's adopted mother Lillian Helderman. Lilly Helder. Lilly Helter Skelter. Lilly Held Her. Silly Lilly Held No Shelter. What is the irony, that the girl Cheryl passed this perversion to so skillfully, so violently, has breasts that will be as heavy as the woman who passed it to her? Cheryl's squirting mother— Cheryl's new hurting daughter? Both with bosoms more gargantuan than she? What Ironic coincidence, what coincidental irony should plague thee, O Cheryl, as you comfort the daughter of your dreams?

I close the door gently—foolishly, walking away to my own room. A room blessed or unblessed—I don't know—to be in the back corner of our grand house, directly adjacent to my mother's room. I step inside my refuge and close the door, quickly sliding the thing in the towel under the bed, even in quiet disbelief besides. Like the murderer who hides the weapon so dangerously nearby, I hold onto the instrument of my sister's murder, a weapon so decidedly unmentionable.

I open the towel from around my body and drop it to the floor—too ashamed to look at myself in the mirror. White, tight French cut underwear pulled hastily on, then a white sports bra, then I slide into the white sweats, fit so snugly to the shape Annabelle gave me. In the mirror, I catch another glimpse of these eyes, looking so remarkably like the woman we knew.

Men. They have so little protection from the pain of emotion—so easily lost in the brutality of the moment—unable to endure the agony of rage—fighting, cursing, walking out of the room fuming. While women are able to suffer the biting pain of hurt feelings, the green burning fire of a jealous rage, or the cold, stabbing blade of guilt while the look on our faces, the tone of our voice—our pleasant mannerisms can deliver the calmest, most easygoing pleasantry ever witnessed. But we too, are mortal, and these pains can be tucked away but for so long—burning and stabbing our insides until there must manifest a sign somewhere, of our infinite suffering inside. This I feel in my trembling hands as I pull my wet hair back to pin it.

Then suddenly, I hear a rushing mighty wind outside, as the July winter brushes hard against the back of the house.

"*H*appy Birthday to you… Happy Birthday to you… Happy Birthday dear Amanda… Happy Birthday to you…"

Two days removed from tragedy. We sing a song of birthdays. A two woman chorus, a Chorus of Ghouls. Trying to sing happiness into the ghost of the life we took.

Cheryl and I clap in the luxurious living room dark, both of us pretty in our dresses and pinned up hair, smiling so great a fungalooga smile against the pain. Amanda so demurely smiles and brushes a strand of hair behind her ear. Gazing for a second at the sixteen candles of the pink vanilla cake. Made with Cheryl's unchanging hands. Hands of Straw. Of dirt. Of blood.

Amanda pulls as much air into her lungs as she can, as if in fear to disappoint. She leans over in front of me, as a slow motion breeze blows forth from beautiful sixteen year old lips, and she moves her head back and forth—up and down and around near the Flame of Youth, blowing without as much as one second wind, until every single candle lies smoking in defeat. The two of us, Death and Hell, clap and scream a joyful delight unheard of for such a *L*onely, *I*solated, *F*ocused *E*vent as this.

We both hug her individually, holding nothing back by way of human affection, the woman saying *"Happy Birthday Baby,"* closing her eyes in joyful pretense, then offering what is left to me. I hug her so tight, saying "Happy Birthday," in a voice just over a whisper, laced with so much of the anguish I feel. And the earth too, reaches up as it knows how, as it too sees fit, as we feel the requisite invisible springy waves in our feet, and we hear the sound like an explosion booming and rumbling around us. I see the joy melt from Cheryl's face like thin ice on a hot window, and I feel the Spirit of Fear come to plague my sister's heart once again.

"God says Happy Birthday," I say. We both chuckle a bit. Cheryl tucks her lips—suddenly demure, walking to the white bay window curtain, sliding it open in lieu of unnatural light. "This is from Mom and me." I watch the bewilderment come over Amanda's face as she takes the little white jewelry box from me. She opens it and sees the tiny cross of gold, attached to a solid gold chain. Cheryl stands at the window in my mother's navy dress. Arms folded. Unable to smile. Amanda takes up the necklace from the box in requisite fascination, but genuine, I think. She knows this is not some trinket I found at the mall with Veronica last week, or some little what not from our mother's dead store, but the engraved letters on the back confirms what she suspects, that this simple gold cross was formed a half century ago.

"Annabelle," Amanda says.

I take the cross necklace from her and clasp it around her neck. "It belonged to Grandma. She gave this to Mom when she was 16." The simple gold cross hangs beautifully from the gold chain, in lovely contrast to her white button down blouse. Her black satin skirt is the true author and finisher of her maturity. Her tiny hoop earrings are golden.

"Mom would've wanted you to have this, Belinda."

"It's yours, Baby. For the rest of your life."

She touches the cross against her chest. Somewhere in her vision, formed by a quiet breath drawn so deep, forms the ghost of a woman she loved, risen from where it is that her beloved mother could have gone.

"Hey," Cheryl says. "Come here."

Her voice awakens us from our standing slumber, with me behind Amanda hugging her tight, dreading the Autumn of the White Woods, and craving our return to innocence. We walk over to Cheryl at the window, two dead girls, lost in humility. Cheryl points outside in the gently falling snow, to where the two shiny, brand new snowmobiles sit idle. One, black trimmed pink as the rose—the other, forged in blue and black fire. Amanda and I both mouth the word wow, while Cheryl gazes through eyes of winter.

"Happy Birthday."

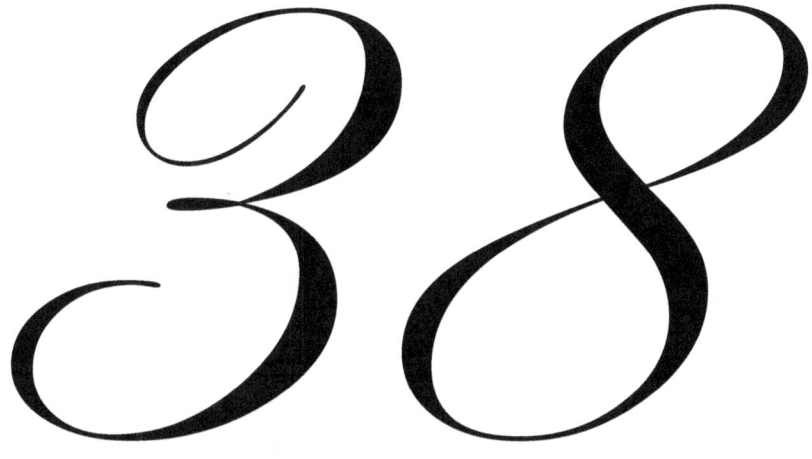

$\mathscr{S}$ixteen is the age of accountability, I suppose. That universal place along the timeline of every life, where there is no longer a question of moral responsibility. Where sometimes, the tragedy of human existence extends far beyond this hopeless life we live, to fulfill the prophecy of some that say there are demon possessed children in Hell. Of what manner of child can this be, I wonder, that would cause the Spirit of the Almighty to turn the loving side of himself away, and judge this child in the lake of fire and brimstone?

I am plagued by the reality of lost innocence. I see it and hear it in my sister's voice, in her new, worldly mannerisms and emotional aggressiveness, perhaps born from suppressed rage underneath the fungalooga, the super aggressive smiles and happiness displayed. I see this, as she so happily, so symbolically throws her leg over the back of Aunt Cheryl's snowmobile, the two of them choosing the one glossed entirely in black, with the beautiful lines of deep rose pink so skillfully trimmed throughout. I watch this sixteen year old girl announce to the snowy landscape by body language alone, that *yes, I am a slut for Aunt Cheryl,* grabbing her so unashamedly around her waist as we begin our trip around Prosperity Garden Terrace in this summer's winter foolishness. The look on Amanda's face is the thrill of determination and joyful discovery, as Aunt Cheryl cranks up the snowmobile like a professional racer of the thing, with the total skill and reckless abandon of the masculine channeled through the feminine. And I fumble and click around with mine until I get it started, gliding slowly through the snow behind them into the streets of this town. I ride far behind the two of them, afraid for some reason to go any faster, as if it would somehow cause me to fall and break my corrupted neck.

We follow the cleared car paths around the neighborhood, so noisily, so conspicuously visible from the mansions and pristine houses going by, the woman and her newly devoted girl slave in pink, while I ride my *slow*mobile behind them, my depravity hidden behind cloth as white as a snowbunny, my machine so much more appropriately the color of blue and black fire.

They are moving along so much faster than I am capable, having only practiced on this thing for a few minutes before our journey. Up ahead, I see the girl in the rose pink coat raise both hands up briefly, imagining that I heard a delighted scream in the air over the roar of this engine, whether I actually did or not. My mind is ablaze with the sounds from them this morning, Amanda's birthday night having been spent in Aunt Cheryl's bed.

Is it as though I had been locked out of their depraved little world last night and this morning, Aunt Cheryl making sure to take her whole slice of the new sixteen year old sweet cake, and share it with absolutely no one, not even the nosy spirits that ebb and flow through our suburban castle. What they did last night, they did with the lights off, which can hardly hide their white skinned secret from the spirit eyes that stare.

There was no hiding the lengthy kisses, the two of them trading positions on top, until eventually, Aunt Cheryl had to slide the member up around her young lover's hips in the dark. Kissing Amanda's neck and her breasts while it was done. Having just enough ambient light from the suburban glow outside to see the member tightly secured in the dark, laying down flat of her back, to continue the deep and powerful, licking tongue kisses and wet lip sucking, the two of them breathing so loudly as to like sound like they were having a baby instead of the orgasmic neck and face licking session they were having.

There was no hiding from the spirits that stare. The feeling in Amanda's body made more severe by her member strapped on, that causes her to take hold of it by pure, raw instinct in her sixteen year old dark, sliding it into the grown woman laid upon her back with her legs wide open, their horny breathing suddenly stopped cold, followed by a soft, plaintive wailing from the older woman, as though the sorrow of the ages has been made to pour from her spirit.

There is no hiding the sound of the bed knocking, the fervent mattress motion, the tell tale sound of sacredness or sin, the sound of what lust hath conceived in the dark. There is no hiding from the spirits, the sight of this heavy breasted woman pressed down on her back, her arms pinned to her sides by her busty young tormentor, driven forward by the unbridled, honeymoon lust and power of youth, slamming herself down into the woman without mercy and without ceasing. There is no hiding the sounds born from this trauma, where heavy breathing is replaced with heavy whimpering, and the leading edge of begging from the grown woman's mouth.

Oh, there is no hiding from me what you have done, Cheryl Ezman. When the regret you feel because of the monster you have created begins to strike fear in your soul. When you realize that no, you have never actually been *fucked* like this before, with a member so Amazonian, a pair of breasts so Olympian, a girlish face so innocent and beautiful. What is the sound I hear, my dearest Aunt Cheryl? Is it the sound of revelation in your voice, when you realize that the feeling beyond this plateau may be a place you cannot go willingly, a place you cannot endure without madness? The spirits are privy with me, Aunt Cheryl, as we listen to your breathless begging begin, which are the words *"Amanda please...please have mercy..."* which comes out Amanda *blease, blease* have mercy. But you are pleading with the moving train dear woman. Begging it to stop in futility, which is sixteen year old lust unleashed, which is the spirit of Pandora in fervent aggression. You notice that you are unable to wrench your arms free, unable to writhe from her grip and pounding. Realizing in terror that you are going to have to go through this, as punishment for your deviance, and your corruption of innocence in the latter day. You cannot hide, dear woman, the sudden change in your voice—that goes from what is spoken to what is unspoken, your voice's response to the lightning strike in your body, which confirms your worse fears that yes, this is the top of the roller coaster honey, and yes, your journey toward the bottom has begun.

These are the ghosts of depravity. The spirits that see and caress your flesh, that send the grieving wave through your body, causing you to begin the long, wailing siren of regret, that morphs your spirit into one of epic weeping, as a lifetime of misery is expanded into your body. And these selfsame spirits have no mercy, until your weeping is accompanied by a loud, high pitched soprano shriek of pain and terror from above you, to ring your ears with Pandora's Trumpet, and the blaring of its hellish noise into your brain in the dark.

No, Cheryl Ezman. There is no hiding from these ghosts of depravity, the sight of both your legs up beside the young girl while she lays still on top of you, your legs shaking uncontrollably in the aftermath of trauma, while you weep and sob the pain of a lifetime of misery unleashed into your body.

From the screams I heard last night, to their heart's revisitation the morning after, I am heavy laden with the memory of Cheryl and my sister, as Cheryl endeavored to take every ounce of what innocence the busty girl had left, finishing it off with a craving in the shower, which I stood by the bathroom door and listened to without guilt this morning. So glad that the door was unlocked when I turned the knob, to listen more easily to the sounds drifting over the crystal waterfall and steam.

It is fascinating to watch this sophisticated, successful and beautiful woman disembark her gliding black and pink chariot in front of her house on Honeysuckle Garden Road, trudging through the waist deep powder to get inside to her old school answering machine, to take another trip down futility lane, to see if young Lacey Ezman had left a unique and special message for her. This is the false hope and desperation that has driven her forward these last eight years since her divorce and loss of custody, believing somehow that the fifteen year old girl will recant the story she told her father back when she was seven, and choose to leave her father's house in upstate New York, and run back to her and pledge her eternal loyalty and forgiveness. Hanging feeble hope so heavily on a maybe spoken over a year ago, that she might want to come and stay with her mother for a while.

"Leave that message on my home phone," she said. *"I'll be waiting for it..."*

For over a year, as the world has been plunged deeper below the surface of an icy tomb, Cheryl has held her breath and held out hope that soon, she would be able to continue what she started on her daughter during a fateful visit a year ago. A secret that has fed fuel to the fires which began to burn the Lezzy Ezzy mind, born from a visit to the snowy streets of White Mountain when her daughter was fourteen. A secret seven years in the making, leapt seven years across the timeline to just last year, a secret that the daughter has sworn to hold tight to her bosom, while the world is buried deeper in ice and snow.

While Amanda wanders happily from the living room to the strangely cold, uninviting kitchen space, I allow myself a steady gaze at the lovely woman at her answering machine, listening hopefully to the first of two messages that are stored there until the day of Redemption, watching her demeanor go south in winter repose, when the second voice is that of some ridiculous man who has not been able to get her bosom out of his mind, having succumbed to the weight of them in his aching spirit. As she clicks off the message and goes to the kitchen with nary a fungalooga smile in place, I wonder which part of the double tragedy that is her life was on her mind this morning, when I heard her take the last part of my sister's innocence in the shower.

Was it the prevailing shadow of Lillian Helderman, the giant breasted foster mother, the J cupped breast goddess, who first introduced her to the shower game one Sunday morning, when her husband took his rare trip out of town for a weekend business trip 'til Tuesday? Was it the standing repose of her fourteenth year, when the forty something year old Lilly Helder stood in front of her, Olympian breasts mashed full against the fourteen year old's prodigious little D cups, the two of them pressed in a deep kiss, both rubbing the other feverishly down below? Or is it the looming shadow from the snow world in this condemned northeast, when Cheryl passed this shower game to her daughter Lacey, with the two of them engaged in this self same, breast pressed kiss?

When Cheryl did this with the hungry, enthusiastic young slave of hers this morning, which part of the double tragedy burdened the theater of her mind? Was it the Vesuvian breasts not meant to be seen, the mature beauty of her Christian foster mother? Or was it the big, puffy areolas of her daughter's B cup baby bosoms, and the feel of her hands between her daughter's legs, while her daughter's tongue was pulled so deeply into her mouth?

Which of the two tragedies from her timeline laid the heaviest burden at Cheryl's feet, as she rubbed her little slave, my little sister's body so feverishly down below? As her lips were locked to my sister's, as their breasts were mashed together as tight and bulbous as they would go? Which of the two tragedies burdens the tension in her muscles the most, as she begins to whimper from the fear of what is about to happen to her body?

And when the tension breaks at last, when the energy explodes into her flesh, when she begins to grunt and groan for dear life, shaking, lurching forward, doubling over, at last breaking the kiss so she can breathe—which of the two tragedies, which of the two shower games was placed again in her mind, as my sister rubbed her mind and the center of her body into oblivion?

I watch this beautiful woman drift past her new student and protégé, her new living practice dummy and orgasm machine—drifting out onto the snowy patio to make a call on her phone—so disappointed that she has to leave a message, and tell her daughter how much she misses her, and how she checked the house answering machine again for their special call, and for her to please call her on this phone tonight if she can. I watch Cheryl Ezman's desperate plea end in voice only, continued in the same quiet as the snowy landscape around her as she clicks the hopeless call away, gliding back into the kitchen with the naïve, pathetic sixteen year old busty, who sips a glass of Tahitian Treat with the glee of a cheerleader in the snow in the days before hope was faded, and the world began to be sealed up tight in its icy tomb.

$\mathcal{T}$he modern mother daughter dynamic plagues the theater of my

mind. As I leave the two of them to their giggly delight in the kitchen,

morning snack hunting to kill their hedonistic hunger, I am drawn up the

stairs of this far suburban place—a place where my mother spent more

than one secret day and night, allowing whatever buried taboos there were between them to take place, whether it was my mother's lips at Cheryl's nips, or the palm of Cheryl's hands across my mother's world class hips—these are the walls of privilege, that hold the shadowy secrets that churn beneath cultured civility.

I am haunted by the modern mother daughter dynamic, as the ghost of Linda Sue Hahn touches my spirit, to take me down the eastern seaboard, then due west from the shores of Hatteras, to the small brick house of May Hahn, when her oldest daughter turns seventeen.

"I tell you every year the same thing. I won't have a daughter of mine hop around like gook clown for horny white men."

"Ma, that's <u>stupid</u>. Cheerleading is a <u>sport</u>," she says, wiping the tear squeezed out in the pain of pure anger.

"Cheerleader is sport for <u>whores</u>," she says. *"Excuse to make big butt naked in short skirt. How you get ready for college with baby in your belly?"*

"What?"

"You heard me. You get half black baby in you if you become cheerleader."

The look of shock, awe and bewilderment on her daughter's face is a perfect storm of disbelief and confusion.

"Don't look at me like you don't understand," her mother says, lowering her voice to a sinister, breathy tone. *"You want big, black muscle*

boy to rape you in back of his car. He get you pregnant and then I have to pay for you to get <u>abortion</u>."

"*Oh my God,*" she says. Mouth open in apocalyptic shock. "*Oh my God you're crazy.*"

May Hahn's face softens. From judgmental rage, to the calm of uneasy acceptance.

"*Go to your room.*"

"*Ma I didn't know you could be this stubborn. This <u>ignorant</u>.*"

"*I said...go to your room.*"

The seventeen year old, eleventh grade scholar turns on a current of deep, inner turmoil. Gliding angrily down the hall, past her thirteen year old sister, who watches the scene in something close to fear.

The small house suddenly resounds with the loudest door slam in its unknown history, and the sound of a young woman's voice screaming the word "*bitch*" inside the locked room.

"*Debra Lin,*" she says to her younger daughter, without even looking at her. "*Go to my closet and bring me the punishment stick.*" And this, she does, in the days before the driving snowfall. A beige caning rod, flexible and strong. Lifted from the shadows of secret, from somewhere inside May Hahn's bedroom closet.

"*Come with me,*" she says to Debra Lin, who follows her mother in tucked lipped reticence and nervous humility. Down the hall they drift, to the door of the angry teenager's room. Tapping lightly on the door with the stick, saying "*Li san. Open this door. We have to talk.*"

"*No!*" the girl screams, turning her stereo onto her classical music station, blessed by Rachmaninoff's single flash of brilliance, to inspire history toward the rest of his lovely delusions of grandeur.

"You open this door," the mother says calmly... *"or I will get big hammer from shed and break it down."*

In the bedroom, the girl breathes an angry sigh, rolling her eyes, standing up from her desk chair and moving reluctantly over to the door.

Li Hsu Hahn opens the door to her Asian mother, who stands there with hardly a motion, until the two of them have exchanged enough energy of understanding through the look. Understanding at what barriers have been crossed, and the revelation of those still yet to come.

"Turn that music off," she says.

And upon the current of bitter resentment, of direct, determined defiance, she breathes a deep sigh of disobedience, which sends a spark to the older woman's hand, powering it to whip-flash a blow across her daughter's face, making Li Hsu grab her face with both hands in a shriek of pain and fear, accompanied by the theme of white mountain glory, the famous variation in Rachmaninoff's rhapsody, as her mother continues to whip the cane across her head, about the shoulders and every part of her arms and her back. This, to the expressive melody for the ages, booming in grief from her daughter's stereo, with an endtime message delivered from the throne of God, as to what tragedies are coming upon the earth, to presage the fires of the Second Coming, as it is foretold by human behavior.

"Debra Lin," the mother snaps. *"Turn the music off. Now take off your sister's clothes."*

In the pain of childhood naiveté. In the burning of bewilderment. Thirteen year old Debra Lin Hahn begins to help her seventeen year old sister pull her tight, royal blue t-shirt off over her head, exposing the plain, white C cup bra and white skin underneath.

"Take off her bra."

And when the older sister reaches back, to try and take it off herself, the mother whips the cane onto her hands, striping them with a fire that makes her snatch her hands away.

"Debra Lin," the mother says. This, sending the young girl forth on her mission, to undo the straps on her seventeen year old sister's bra. She exposes her sister's firm, mature breasts pitched up to high C, then helps her take off her jeans, noticing her sister's breasts hung down to perfect cone shaped triangles as she bends over, the natural hang of bosoms firm with youth and support. In frustrated defeat, she slides her own underwear away, still bent over, slipping out of them slowly, handing them to her younger sister, who places them neatly on the bed, along with the t-shirt, jeans socks and bra.

"Disobedient brat," she says. *"Think she a grown woman because her butt get so big and fat. Because your tits so big and round."*

And upon this, the mother places her cane so softly, so deftly upon the bed, telling her daughter, *"Put your hands behind your back."* And this, she does. Her face red with emotion, expression burdened by suppressed anger and humiliation Face stained by the trickle of a single tear, and a loud sniff of pure defiance. This tear of mother daughter violence shed, while the thirteen year old looks on in shock and disbelief, as her mother removes her own tshirt, to reveal two of the longest breasts on this side of creation, hung so low and flat against her body, breasts touched by macromastia passed down to her from the old country, that swing like bells tolled in the name of discipline, as she leans over to place her black t-shirt on the bed, and retrieve her punishment stick, her long, thrift store flower skirt still in place. Breasts in the key of G major, but made more extraordinary by the sheer length of them, and the mashed flatness they display.

She walks over to her naked daughter. Cane held so tightly in her hand.

"What happen to number one daughter, when she call her mother...ignorant bitch?"

The next instant is filled with the sound of a fervent shriek, as the mother brings a series of blows down upon her daughter's breasts, raising the cane up far back on each hard, rapid blow in succession. She does this on each of her daughter's firm, round breasts in irregular pattern back and forth, until her daughter can only shake her head back and forth in defeat, hopping up and down and screaming with angry determination. But in the midst of this storm of pain, she holds her hands clamped behind her back in stubborn resolve, determined not to let her mother have her total defeat. Swearing that at least in this, in her hands held behind her back, she will not let her mother win.

"Shut your screaming," she says. Whipping another strong flurry of blows across the front of her daughter's breasts this time, which very nearly makes Li Hsu have to give up and hold her hands to her breasts in defeat.

"Debra Lin. Cover your sister's mouth."

This, the little girl does, flinching when the mother yells *"Harder!"* Covering her sister's mouth with authority, with one hand behind her sister's head as an anchor.

And the mother continues the whirlwind of painful breast blows, with the burning of flames from somewhere along the timeline, filling their space with her daughter's new and angry screaming, muffled by the palm of her younger sister's hand.

And when the barrier of these one hundred and fifty blows has been breached, the mother stands calmly. Studying the determined bravery in her daughter's teary eyes. Listening to her gruff, muffled sobs held in behind her younger daughter's hand.

"Let go her mouth," she says. *"Let me hear her call her mother… ignorant bitch."*

But the only sounds heard are those of sobs and weeping, punctuated by the occasional sniff in angry defeat.

"Now, turn around. Put your hands between your legs. Hold your legs together."

And the first blow stripes the truth across her backside and into her spirit, causing her to let out a loud, growling yell under strain and duress, as though she had tried with all her might to hold it in, but was unable.

Upon this chord, the mother repeats. Touching the cane skillfully in warning before each hard, determined blow. Marking her daughter's skin in the burning of violence, and the agony of blue and black fire. Groaning, growling and heavy breathing accompany nearly every blow, until the grunts are held in check by force of will, replaced by a heavier, louder breathing, and a greater twitching of her fleshy bottom in reaction.

But as though called forth by predestiny, the seventeenth blow causes a change in the rhythm of sound, bringing out a long, wailing siren of pure pain and sorrow unleashed, marked by a spot of blood upon the red welt raised and grown. And the sadistic fires in the mother ignite in their fullest measure, as she touches the cane to the bloody welt in warning, bringing the eighteenth blow down upon it again, to bring another wail of sorrow and defeat from her daughter. But this, being only the signal to the mother to continue, striping bloody welts up and down the daughter's backside until the fortieth blow is achieved.

And upon this is her daughter's surrender, as displayed so completely in her voice, a voice of total lamentation, repentance and regret.

May Hahn gazes her thirteen year old daughter's tears. Walking over to her devastated condition, raising her little Asian face up to hers, giving her a kiss on the lips, and a soft rubbing across her hair. Then she steps over to the front of the punished one. In front of the one brought down from the towering heights of rebellion.

"You cheerleader?"

"No," she says. Shaking her head 'no' with enthusiasm.

"What about…ignorant bitch?"

And upon this, is brought forth a stream of heavy sobbing, shaking her body from head to toe. Along with deep, genuine apologies spoken.

"That's my good daughter. My number one daughter."

Topless May Hahn steps close to her daughter. Hugging her tightly, cane still firm in hand. Feeling her daughter's surrender flow out of her body in trembling, and out of her voice in sobs and weeping.

Part Four

This is one of the lonely places. A place heavy burdened with regret. A wilderness of epic grief and sorrow.

This is the Oklahoma prairie. A snow covered, post apocalyptic landscape. Where the scarred, traumatized countryside is now a field of pristine, snowy white. A sea of tranquility. An ocean of uneasy calm from north to south. From east to west. The ease, the quiet of post trauma, as far as the eye can see.

This is a house in the field of snow. Where a father, a mother, and a daughter live in false hope. Drowned in a fog of perpetual tension. Lost in endtime chaos and discord. Where the love of family has waxed cold.

The father has taken a rare, and risky trip to the far city. A shopping trip braved alone, in the guise of buying more toys and gadgets for house and home. Money sent to medicate the misery of his life.

In the space on the Oklahoma prairie, the mother and the daughter are left alone to ponder. To wonder how it can possibly be done. How they can cohabitate in the same space without violence. This, the violence of feeling. Of emotion.

The days of their cultured civility are numbered. Growing shorter with the passage of time. To where every conversation is a match at the edge of a fuse. Inevitably lighting the sparks of volatility. An invitation to the dance.

In the lateness of the afternoon hour, the mother returns to her daughter's bedroom upstairs. To the door of her upper room. Feeling the rise of late afternoon, early evening appetites calling. Secretly loving her daughter's touch upon the spaghetti pot when it happens. Telling her through the door, "I thought I told you to get downstairs and cook dinner for us. Your father will be home soon and dinner should be prepared."

In the silence of betrayal. The quiet of epic disobedience. The mother pounds on the door in a rage. Screaming at her daughter to open the door. Feeling her daughter's profound satisfaction. Her victory.

In the calm of predestiny. At the shores of what is meant to be. The mother stops the futile pounding on her daughter's bedroom door. Lowering her head in the calm. The tragic calm of uneasy acceptance. Embracing what is meant to be. Having already anticipated the course of action. Pulling the tiny key from the pocket of her tight blue jeans. Sliding it into the knob. Resting it there. Taking hold of the knob with one hand. Turning the key with the other. Drawing this smooth motion into reality. Feeling the bedroom doorknob turn with pristine ease, as if moving on its own.

The mother walks into this enclosed space. The forbidden space of her daughter's room. Placing the key in her pocket again. Closing the door behind her. Locking it.

The daughter sits up from her reclining position. Watching in shock as the mother locks the pictures and sounds of the television away. Silencing their space to a vacuum

"What are you doing in here," the daughter says. "Dad told you to leave me alone. You can cook the spaghetti yourself."

In this same, tragic calm, the lovely woman undoes the first button on her lavender shirt. Undoing each button. Until there are no more barriers to cross. Until every button is unlatched and undone.

She lowers her eyes from the pathetic seventeen year old girl. From the bewildered eyes of naiveté. Taking her shirt off, letting it fall unceremoniously to the floor. Taking the lavender t-shirt off underneath. Exposing her bra. Leaving the round, firm breasts bound for battle. Their tragic key of C minor unplayed.

The mother unbuttons her jeans. Bending over, sliding them off. Kicking them away with her white sock foot. Sliding the socks off last. Tossing them away.

In lavender shaded underwear too small. Pulled over hips too wide for her toned, tight frame. The woman walks toward her daughter with quiet determination. Committed to act. To do away with the pretense at last. To cross the last boundary into tomorrow.

Calmly. Forcefully. She grabs her daughter's white, button down shirt. Pulling with determined intensity. Ignoring her daughter's angry resistance. Managing to successfully rip the shirt halfway open. Pulling it angrily over her daughter's head.

"Take 'em off," she says. Quietly. Pulling at the front of her daughter's jeans. Managing to get them unbuttoned. Braving a slap and a push to her face. Taking her daughter calmly, forcefully by the hair. Displaying her love of the gym with aggression. Hauling back, slapping her daughter's face with enough force to knock her off her feet back to the bed.

To the music of her daughter's hoarse, rough scream of shock and fear. Grabbing the girl's pants again. Sliding the zipper down. Yanking, pulling, slipping the girl's tight jeans from around her hips. Accidently pulling her underwear halfway down. Yanking. Pulling. Sliding the pants down and away. Ignoring her daughter's pathetic attempt to kick. To push her mother away.

This is one of the lonely places. A place filled with violence. With hatred.

The mother flops herself heavily upon her daughter. Overpowering the smaller female. Pressing down her weight and strength upon her. Sliding her hand quickly between her daughter's legs. Squeezing her hard in her proper place. In her improper place. Listening to the daughter squeak a squeal. Listening to her squeal a pathetic squeak and sob. Mouth open. Eyes blared open in shock and disbelief.

The mother lays fully on the daughter. Pushing her legs open with her own. Braving the daughter's breathless struggle. Her mousy pulling and scratching at her shoulders and back. Finding her daughter's place with her groin. Holding herself there. Nearly shaking from the lightning bolt that passes through.

"Hold your legs back," she says. Taking her daughter by the neck. By the throat. Biting her ear. Listening to her shriek the pain. Feeling her daughter pull her legs back by attrition. By instinct to end the biting agony at her ear.

Unable to control her own body's motion. Unable to cease a sudden, powerful grinding of her hips. Sliding her underwear cloth against her daughter's slid halfway down. Grunting once at the pain coursing through. At the chime ringing her ears and her brain. At the impossible sensations tormenting her body.

Upon her daughter's groin. In the dominance of Amazonian missionary. She presses. She pushes. She grinds her hips powerfully. Until a new motion takes over. To raise her hips up. Then slamming them down again. Raising them up. Slamming them down again. Hearing the whimper in her own voice give her away. Hearing it betray her fear. Her impending loss of sanity.

In the lonely place. The out of the way place. She hears her own voice take over against her will. Choking her daughter without remembrance. Holding her neck. Her throat. Listening to her own voice call the name of God. Claiming him in her hour of death. In the death of her sanity. Hearing her voice begin to wail to the spirits. To wail a siren to the spirits of the prairie. Braving the loss of control. The strikes of lightning throughout every inch of her flesh. Unable to stop the flow of weeping. Feeling the new stress build again in her spirit. Enduring the break of the new tension. Suffering an Armageddon quake in her body. Enduring a seizure sent down into her condemned flesh. Grunting now. Her legs and hips shaking violently. Grunting angrily in her daughter's ear. Holding her roughly by the throat. Holding on, until the Armageddon quake passes through. Until she can breathe again. Until she can see. Until she can think.

Her hand slides away from her daughter's throat on its own. So that the young woman may breathe again. So that the coughs may bring precious air to her lungs again.

The two of them lie still. The mother on top of the daughter. Breathing. Recovering.

She raises up and looks at the girl. Speaking words of ridiculous dominance. Words of such foolish intent.

"You will go downstairs," she says. "And you will cook that *fucking* spaghetti."

The mother slides away from the bed. Gathering the remains of herself from the floor. By way of the cloth of pretense The coverings of hypocrisy in lavender and blue.

The daughter lays there. Quiet. In the lonely place. A place of isolation. A place of grief.

A place of sorrow.

The falling snows have abandoned this part of the timeline for now, to bathe the grieving world in the gray light of false hope for a reprieve. We brave our snowy trip along the interstate highway west to New York, feeling the spirits of eschatology press down harder as we cross over, as though the state of New York were in more trouble than even our beloved Prosperity, and the surrounding cities and counties therein. The snowdrifts seem so much higher here. The filthy, dirty snow piled up to a more mountainous possibility on each side of the highways and busy main roads, until we are reminded why travel is becoming more scarce everywhere, and people are content to wait to die where they are. This ill advised, icy trip plagues the three of us now, having to follow Aunt Cheryl to keep her in desperate company as she travels, west toward where the sun sets behind a layer of gray clouds too thick to fathom. And it seems that the further we go into New York, the darker these strange, permanent snow clouds get, until the hopefulness we felt has begun to freeze again, in preparation for another deadly layer of fallen crystal in the near future.

These clouds are just plain darker. Until it feels like we have driven from a world of bright, false hope to where there is no hope at all. We follow our mistress willingly to the far away, suburban palace of her ex-husband and his new wife, and the estranged daughter slipping further and further away.

I barely remember Lacey Ezman at all. Having played with her a few times an eon ago, in the days when the sky was blue. And I have to admit that yes, I am annoyed by the green, icy mist of jealously formed, as Cheryl so typically, so predictably, acts less committed to us the closer we get to the house in White Mountain. I almost asked her a few minutes back, after we crossed the line into these darkened, New York State clouds, *so why did you drag us along? It's obvious that you don't need us anymore.* But curiously, I noticed that the instant this traitorous, treacherous thought formed in my head, Cheryl turned toward Amanda in the back seat and said *"Are you alright back there Honey? You hungry or thirsty?"* Touching my hand at the same time, patting it innocently and with the fierce commitment of a nurse overcome with compassion.

It was a sign given unto me. A sign to be sure, that what is going on between my sister, me and this beautiful woman is inescapable, and as inevitable as the next great snowfall in summer.

"Did you call Lacey? Does she know when we're coming?"

"You know what? Normally, that might be considered a dumb question. But in keeping with the strangeness of the world around us, with this snowy nightmare around us... no."

"No what?"

"No. They don't know we're coming today."

"Oh my God. Then how do we even know they're here?"

"If they're not, we'll get a hotel. Spend a night here if we have to. I have to see my daughter. I don't trust her father."

"Why?"

"One of the reasons he left me is so he could take my daughter away. He's been slowly turning her against me every since. Every since she was seven years old. I've had to fight to keep her in my life. Every birthday. Every Christmas. Thanksgiving. New Years. I'm there as much as I can be. Begging her to come home."

"Does she come to visit?"

"No."

"How old is she now?"

"She's a year younger than Amanda."

"Fifteen," I say. Remembering the last days of that fateful number in my sister's life.

We roll the icy, snowy streets of this town. Until soon, the ugly, dirt darkened snowdrifts are gradually less darkened, appearing more like white, unspoiled snows along the streets of Prosperity back in Vermont.

And so too, do the houses themselves bear witness to the change in economic scenery, all of them glinting with the same air of self assurance—the same brick and brass fixture prettiness scattered to and fro, until the landscape of this high class neighborhood is in the real world guise of a picture postcard come to life. I feel all that is missing are the horse drawn sleighs and beautiful ladies being pulled along in winter joy and splendor.

Though some of the houses in our neighborhood are mansion-like in size and splendor, there is more of an epic spacing between these homes of privilege, where every sin and secret is more gloriously, and more ingeniously hidden. Across the snow covered spaces of this upscale, upstate suburban neighborhood we travel, where the only trees visible are in the far off distance, to make room for the huge spaces of empty privilege, and the beauty of depravity hidden in the open fields of snow.

These are the homes of privilege. The houses of prosperity. Where corporate success is passed from generation to generation, and divine luck is so oft unaccompanied by morality. Where the depraved choices that are predestined flourish in the shadows, done behind the walls of upper class secret, and the locked doors of what churns beneath cultured civility.

These are the lofty heights of deviance. Where sensibilities are protected by divine assurance, and souls are free to roam the caverns of human darkness born and bred. These are the spaces of the beautiful people. The places carried out and set aside for them. Where the modern mother daughter dynamic is free to give place to the devil. Where there is no Redemption that draweth nigh.

Where the little girl's desire is to her mommy. For love and affection where none will be given. Where the mother sits naked on her little daughter in the night, the pillow in rage pressed hard over her daughter's face. Where the pitiful kicks and the muffled screams happen in the name of discipline, until the Armageddon Orgasm is violently achieved. Big breast sucking in the dark of night, where the earthquaking orgasm is silently achieved. Orgasms repressed in the name of discipline. Over the knee spankings from the mind of Eve. Naked in the bathroom on the edge of Jacuzzi luxury—lust that spanks the daughter's white skin to blood. The power of the hand, moved to the wooden brush from the nightstand. Years of marital resentment poured onto the daughter's fair skin. Discipline done in the fires of lust and sin—these are the hidden signs of the times we're in.

Munchausen by proxy. Daughter's vomited from here to the grave. Buried in a prestige funeral, these are signs of the times we're in. When Candace Newmaker is rebirthed into the arms of the Lord. When the grown teenage daughter endures the pain of the paddling board. When the daughter's 24 year marriage is cut by the mother's mean and meddling swift sword, these are the tragic signs of the times we are in.

When the mother threatens her young cheerleader with the twist of an ear. A secret glass of wine to the little girl or a secret glass of beer. When she holds her daughter down to listen to her scream in fear. This is when the fires of eschatology are near. When the strap-on phallus is pulled on, and the daughter is raped inside her room. When the pregnant teenage daughter is beaten nude, in the daytime dark and gloom. Then taken to the lady doctor, where the child is aborted from her womb. When the daughter commits suicide to escape to the isolation of her tomb. These are the signs of the latter day times we are in.

When the pornographic revelation of the mother daughter exchange club is real. Where the mother lover's society and the secret mother daughter thing have sealed the deal. When mothers and daughters trade orgasms, and every vile and violent emotion that they feel. These are the signs of the Second Coming. The end of the world revealed.

We roll onward through the snow, these three. Haunted by these latter day spirits, the wickedness in high places. The three of us burdened by the weight of the unspeakable, by those things that are too shameful to know. We roll on, in spirits of relaxed and determined surrender, so that the apprehension can pass more easily through. We roll on. Past the houses of upper class and hidden, ill repute, until we drift to the snowy landscape of northeastern prosperity bought and paid for, auburn bricked in picturesque post card perfection.

We disembark our rolling chariot in the spirit of nervous awe, these three, two of us in the fear of the unknown. We step lightly over the snow covered walkway. Past the lawn decorated in perpetual ice and winter, gliding up to the door of this two story mini mansion, where the silver gray markers mock us in Lexus and Mercedes luxury, to tell the three of us that yes, the wealthy inhabitants of this palace are inside, in this summer winter repose, protected from whatever outside forces that might wish to bring them harm.

In the aftermath of knocking. In the wake of a doorbell chime. The three of us stand here. At the door of this northeastern prosperity.

Waiting.

After what seems an eternity in the biting cold, the door to this pristine, suburban mansion opens. To devastate our crystalline expectations with the truth, that there are women who rise above the mundanity of suburban queen, to that of suburban goddess. A Nordic snow bird, she is. With hair as golden as the sun, and eyes as bewitching as blue ice and fire.

In the privilege of beauty alone, she tilts her head in the shock of genuine bewilderment, in absolute, fearless judgment, at Cheryl Ezman's audacity to be standing in her presence in this moment.

"You can't be here," the blonde beauty says, teeth blared in something akin to what happens when a crocodile opens its mouth.

"Is my daughter home?"

The look on the blonde's face is sheer delight.

"I said is my daughter home?"

"Mom?"

I watch the lovely brunette draw in the loudest, deepest breath imaginable. Staring past the blonde witch who guards the door, gazing past her in the awe of first time discovery, as when one sees the beauty of a snow ghost, drifted into corporeal reality.

"Lacey," she says, her hand at her bosom, face anguished in hopeless longing and grief.

"Mom what are you *doing* here?"

Cheryl steps toward the ghostly figure of her memory, somewhere in the background of this desperate plea. But at the moment of truth, the big blonde, this beauty pageant runner up steps in front of her, placing her hand firmly on Cheryl's shoulder. Holding it there with authority.

"You will see her over my dead body."

And suddenly, the shock and awe in Cheryl's gaze is transformed. Burned into the eyes of a snow queen.

"Bitch you better take your fucking hands off me. Or I swear to God and Holy Jesus I'll tear your fucking face off."

But this only serves the blood of this former volleyball princess, who lets her mouth fall open to bare her white bonded bottom teeth in wicked satisfaction.

"Cheryl!" The masculine voice booms in. The voice of divine luck passed through the generations. The voice of a husband come and gone. "Cheryl what are doing here?"

"Michael…Michael I came to see my daughter."

Cheryl tries to get into the house, skillfully blocked by the blonde warrior at the gate. But what battle instincts lie dormant, underneath a mother's love for her daughter? Cheryl finds this natural move of muscle and bone, lifting the blonde's white hands away with a snap, then shoving her hard backwards, slamming her violently against the door, which seems to rattle the woman's bravery into submission.

Cheryl hurries toward the beautiful, raven haired fifteen year old, whose hair falls in full length splendor past her shoulders and down the length of her back.

"Lacey," Cheryl says, suddenly stopped short by her husband's strength in tragic, masculine assurance. "Michael please let me touch her. I haven't seen her in a year…please let me hug her…"

"After what she just told me you're lucky I haven't called the cops."

"Why?"

The boyishly handsome, dark haired real estate king glances at us from his throne. From the security of his empire built. Michael Ezman Properties. Ezman Properties Association. E.P.A. On the eve of a small fortune made.

"I almost feel sorry for you," he says. "Cheryl you need to get help."

"Michael please let me touch her. If you don't let me touch her I'm gonna die. I know I'm gonna die if I can't touch her."

"After what you did to her last summer, touching her is the *last* thing I'm ever going to let you do."

"Why? What did she say?"

"I think you know. It's too disgusting to repeat."

And as if summoned by dark instinct alone, the blonde snow queen, the Heather of Madison Elizabeth Drive steps in full blown audacity, in full protective mode from her place at the door of her early round defeat, to reclaim her place on top in this battle, putting her arms around the beautiful, long haired girl, whose fair features are so delicately touched by an American Indian bride, so far into the branches of the motherline family tree.

In hypocrisy gathered and displayed with determination, she stands with her arms tightly around the beautiful, exotic young girl, as if in full protective possession of her. And this spark flies to the fuel soaked place of the Cheryl Ezman heart and mind, igniting her soul in flame, causing her to burst free from Michael's grip to grab the woman's snow blonde hair with both hands, doubling the woman over, nearly causing her to lose her balance until Michael grabs his ex-wife's hands, straining to pry her fingers away from his new wife's silken blonde hair. Freeing one hand, which manages several blows to the top of the glorious Heather head of hair, before he manages to finally yank the other hand free, along with many strands of blonde hair in the second round desperation with no victory.

"She's a *cunt* licker!" she screams, while her ex-husband pulls her away. "She's a cunt licker Michael, I can *smell* it on her. She wants Lacey to herself…look at her Michael, she wants my daughter all to herself!"

Snow

We stand helplessly nearby, watching Cheryl descend into madness, catching a glimpse of the tight hug between Heather and the young Pocahontas girl, and a look of calm, determined victory in the beauty of her icy expression.

In the haze of a slow motion dream, we watch the lovely brunette be dragged forcefully from the house by masculine anger, against which she has no skill to overcome. In a father's fit of self righteous indignation, he grabs her with all his might, and we watch the beautiful woman go flying off her feet, into the cold of summer ice and snow.

$\mathcal{W}$e brave the aftermath of this trauma as we drive. The three of us lost in the memory of the bizarre scene on Madison Elizabeth, where we watched the epic betrayal of a daughter against her mother, and the proverbial knifing in her back.

These long, dreary moments are punctuated by Cheryl's loud sniffing from the back seat, still laid across my sister's lap after a half hour on this trip back to Vermont. I am unable to escape the strangeness of it all, unable to push it from my spirit, all of it dominated by the presence of the Pocahontas girl herself—who I'll have to admit, might be the most physically beautiful person I have ever imagined could exist in real life, which is truly disturbing for some reason. She was 15 going on 25, every bit as tall as I am, breasts and hips blown up just as wide already, but with a waist even *smaller* than mine, an unnaturally small and deeply curved middle, a shape purely born from her mother, who lies devastated in the back seat in her new daughter's lap.

And I can remember such an air of self-righteous privilege around the girl, as if she were secretly enamored by her own impossible beauty, with hair grown silken and raven black down to nearly the top of her hips, with eyes touched by her ancestral blood, to give her a beauty rare among so-called white girls, to ensure her as the topic of conversation for the rest of her privileged life.

Truthfully, I had always prided myself on my own beauty experience in my little world, having always felt that I was the prettiest girl that walked into any room. But as I keep glancing at my own Aishwarya Rai-ness in this rear view mirror, I am still haunted by the eyes of Lacey Ezman, the Lacey Ezman eyes, and the reality of the end-of-the-world beauty they possess.

A sudden shuffling and louder sniffing calls my attention away from Lacey's eyes for a moment, seeing the teary eyes of her mother, as she raises up in the back seat, appearing so glad that Amanda is with her to cushion the blow, gladly receiving Amanda's incessant cooing and cuddling, as if it is pure nourishment for her soul and spirit. In the mirror, I see the face that is the origin of her daughter's beauty, burdened by a distant, somber look, her mouth slightly hung open so she can breathe more easily. And I can clearly see the workings of what divine luck she possesses with my sister, who raises up from her reclining place at Cheryl's bosom, and presses a firm, enthusiastic kiss to her cheek. I see Cheryl close her eyes, face anguished in such profound gratitude, while Amanda's kiss lingers a moment longer. Then I see Amanda shake her head in 'no' form against Cheryl's cheek, moaning, releasing this kiss with authority, staring at Aunt Cheryl with the determination of an Italian poverty mom kissing her daughter on graduation day.

Then from this authoritative stare, from this post kiss look, I see the sixteen year old daughter whisper in the forty four year old woman's ear with all seriousness, something that makes her look at Amanda in quiet shock and mild disbelief.

"Please," is the quiet sound I hear from Amanda's voice, "I want you to."

"But what would your sister say?"

"She won't care."

"I don't know, Amanda—"

And these words are cut off by another hard kiss to her cheek, then a pressing of the sixteen year old's lips to her ear. And this—followed by a guilty glance of pure shame toward me in the mirror—burns the dyke blood coursing through this woman's veins, and she takes my sister's face by the chin, and lays the energy built up onto her lips, causing the woman in her to groan deeply.

I so desperately want to say, *"God you two, at least let me get you a room first."* But I can imagine what shame and anger this might bring, and my compassion for them begs my discretion. I am indeed, inclined to mind my own business and keep my mouth shut as I drive, unable to keep my awestruck glances away from the mirror, to watch this busty sixteen year old girl kissing this forty something year old woman like she means it.

After their brief eternity in hugging and breathing, I watch Cheryl raise up Amanda's gray sweater and her t-shirt underneath, exposing the huge bra, which still amazes me that under Amanda's loose clothes, it always appears so big every time I see it. A glimpse at Cheryl's face reveals her determination, the almost angry insistence to give in to what must be, as if she were starving and were gazing at glazed strawberries at a desert buffet. And following this look is a mighty squeeze upon one of them, which makes Amanda lose control of her breath on purpose, to announce to every spirit that since the foundation of the world, this was definitely going to happen.

And I must remember to keep my eyes on the snowy, treacherous highways, when the monster trailer truck rolls past me on the left, to remind me that I am not merely a passenger in this, but I am *driving* on this highway, inside this great moving cage we're in.

So I'm not privy to what sights these traveling spirits see, when the woman gathers her nerve of authority, laying her new daughter down flat of her back, pulling one side of her bra down as far as she can, to expose the gargantuan globe, and the nipple already grown to the size of a grape for sucking.

As if driven by a predator's instinct, the woman clamps her lips down on the girl's breast in deep sucking, causing her to groan a gruff *"oh"* into the space of our world, followed by two more of like intensity. I am not privy to what these traveling spirits see, as the other hand of this woman swipes the jeans of this girl in their hottest place; a single, mighty grab and rub abandoned, to concentrate this energy to its proper place, upon the big, wobbling breast of this young girl.

With every stitch of clothes on, and one single breast of the girl exposed, the woman engages herself upon the Virgin's Intercourse, ak.a. the Nun's Intercourse, which is a mighty, determined fellatio of the nipple; a deep, powerful sucking in full, where so much breast flesh is pulled up into the mouth, pulled up and released—a gliding, sliding, pulling motion upon the breast up and down, which drives the message home that there is more to the erotic than what the lower part of the body has to say.

Some can achieve this in various ways, some by kissing, some by massage. And some by what must transpire on these rolling highways where we roam. The girl, fully clothed, big breast exposed, is dominated by the older woman fully clothed, with nary a flash of skin to see, except the lovely, white hand of womanhood, holding the girl's big breast firm and steady. The girl breathes her last breath into the air, understanding from the start what it was she needed from the woman at this moment, and what the woman needed from her.

I am not privy to the sights of what sound I hear, when the girl's breathing suddenly loses its invisibility, and the whispering breezes take form as a voice of triumph, as the 'oh's' return in mightier substance and form, until they flow out as a single, womanly sound, trembled by the powerful shaking of her entire body in the back seat, as the feel of her breast being sucked by her new mother annihilates her soul into oblivion.

It's the sheer size of them, are the words that strike me in the brain, as we disembark our rolling chariot again in the snow. I can never cease to be amazed at the top heaviness of this woman, as it appears in her black turtleneck shirt, which she loves to wear, maybe because it so uncompromisingly delivers the breasty truth to the onlooker. This black turtleneck was her uniform of choice in the car, after removing her gray toggle coat—the turtleneck she was wearing when she and my sister became mother and daughter in the back seat on our way home. The truth of her Amazonian presence is still apparent, even when she is all toggled up in her coat again, the top of it pushed out unbelievably far, to make her seem so much heavier than she really is.

It seems that the heavy breasted history of this woman has followed her down to the present day, along with their extreme sensitivity, to make her a breast goddess in the latter day snow. They give her a look of strength and power, which is apparent to me whenever we are close, and especially when I saw her get mad earlier today, having been made naturally stronger through the years of hefting the things around.

And whereas most women and girls seem to dismiss breasts as just a glorified milk bottle, as just a bra prop to help them when they put on clothes—I am burdened, and always have been, by a secret lust for other women's breasts, even to the point of fetishism, where even as an older child of nine, I can remember laying my face in my mother's 36 C's when I hugged her. Though I try not to give in to it, I am forced to accept that I am obsessed with Aunt Cheryl's body, and the overdeveloped nature of her top half flutters something deep inside my soul.

And it seems that true breast queens, even breast goddesses, are grouped in families few and far between, a condition passed down through the motherline oftentimes, rarely skipping a generation, so that a casual glimpse at the mother's breasts will usually be the prophecy fulfilled later in her daughter. But curiously enough, Cheryl's giant bosomed mother was only her foster mother, who carried a pair of J-cup melons slung inside her bra. Aunt Cheryl told us that her real mother was no breast queen, who died of lung cancer when Cheryl was just a little girl. But her lovely, exotic mother was only half white, born to a white father and a North Carolina

Cherokee breast goddess. A woman shaped like a superhero, I imagine, with bosoms hailed from planet Gigantomastia.

Oddly enough, this same breast anomaly followed the girl Cheryl into her life as a foster child, under the care of Lillian Helder man, the church lady who gave Cheryl a new life, and then took it from her so abundantly.

A beautiful, heavy breasted woman is a gift from God. It is a blessing bestowed to whatever man or woman who is lucky enough to be with her. And a heavy breasted beauty with her own, private breast obsession is as a rare jewel, a precious stone searched for and found in gratitude and thanksgiving. These women have power. Amazonian energy that they can pass into another, to provide them pleasures of the breasts like no other— for a small breasted woman to have her little bosom nursed by a busty tit hound will send her to places she thought she could never go. So that the idea of her husband or boyfriend with their lips anywhere near her breasts will revile her to the core.

My sister and me have borne witness to this. And Amanda was just born again in the back of the car, literally sucked off by a breast goddess, which caused her body to shake like nothing I had ever seen or heard from her before.

My sister's Armageddon Quake torments the theater of my mind, as we stroll the beaten path through the piled up snow on either side of the walkway nearby the house, past the huge bay window, with me walking in front of the two of them who are arm in arm, no longer able to resist whatever new spirit that was descended. Its strong enough to have my sister walk close beside her with both arms wrapped around Cheryl's arm, often looking up into her face, staring at every feature, hoping that Cheryl will look back at her and smile.

And this, she does. A smile of gratitude and deep appreciation tinted with *lust*, like a lezzy wife or girlfriend in the throes of honeymoon energy. Her pleasant, appreciative glances at my sister are laced with a powerful possessiveness—an unspoken need to dominate her, or to have her at her emotional beckon call.

The house has the familiar scent of pumpkin spice inside, a candle left to burn out in the kitchen sink when we were gone, surrounded by water halfway up the glass. Why this, one might wonder, until they remember that our world is plagued by earthquakes great and small, so that whatever shaking this scented candle endures can only shake it to a watery death at best. Either that, or it burns itself down to nothing all day, filling the house with scents best reserved for the advent of true winter in the snow.

In the late afternoon dark, the candle in the kitchen is still lit, to still burn the scent of its calling in the air. Cheryl picks up the hapless, desperate little flame in its little bell jar, taking a deep and busty breath of surrender and memory, then huffing the little flame into a puff of smoke.

I have never felt as compassionate for her as I do at this moment, and I can't help but to just walk into her space and wrap my arms around her, joined quickly by her new spiritual daughter, both of us feeling her sob as completely as we hear it, followed by a trembling strain in her body to resist the pain passing through.

"It's alright Aunt Cheryl," I say. "It's alright. I know it doesn't mean much but we're here with you. We'll help each other."

This beautiful woman takes her cue, turning to me in a full, bosomy hug, in grieving to hide her energy from me has she strains not to weep out loud. Amanda falls slowly but surely in line behind her, to be sure that her mother wife is safe, and sandwiched between us with no escape.

And these perverted spirits that dominate who we are, these spirits in the latter day world we live in—they reach inside her to the core of her being, to acquaint her with the truth about grief, causing her to finally unleash a loud, long siren of pain and bereavement, which is the weeping voice of a full grown and mature woman of means, a sound powerful enough to gather the desire from somewhere deep within.

And in the soft lights of our earthly progression, in our domestic kitchen of dreams, we lead our grieving *mother* to the window of our most tragic fears come to life, sliding open the long, ivory curtain to reveal the landscape of our snow covered world, where there rests the tall and majestic flowering tree, and the final resting place of the woman who gave us life, the three of us, and the white cross that marks the place where she is buried.

"She's watching over us," I say, boldly turning the woman's beautiful, grieving face to mine. She turns away, gazing at Amanda's face to find reassurance, seeing the sixteen year old nod her head in divine assurance, which hardly brings a spark of warmth to the coldness in her heart, mind and body.

"We want you to come to the table."

We guide her mysteriously, enigmatically through her bewilderment and sorrow to the long, yellow oak dining table, guiding her to sit on it with hardly a word from either of us, both of us delighted by her confusion. And strangely enough, the youngest among us is the eldest in this intent, having already suggested this to me, telling me that she saw this substance of it in a vision one morning, somewhere between sleep and awake.

We coax the beautiful, shapely woman to the middle of the table, satisfied that the strangeness of this touches her grieving soul with delight. Amanda and me both take hold of one of the black leather boots she wears high up her calves, unzipping, sliding them off and placing them carefully onto the floor. The look of grief on her face is now calm and questioning, where the sorrow is being pushed aside by curiosity.

"Just relax," I say, pulling the black socks from her feet, rubbing them gently, while Amanda undoes the button, *and* the zipper on her blue jeans.

"Girls, what is this," she says. "Whatever it is, just please don't let it hurt."

"No more pain," Amanda says. Rubbing Cheryl's temples softly, as if she has ever done it even once in her entire life. "No more pain," she says again, leaning down to the beautiful woman, kissing her on the forehead, the nose, then lightly on her lips. Softening Cheryl's look just a bit further, toward acceptance of her Fate.

I take hold of the top of her jeans, sliding them down, further and further away from pretense of modesty, to where the skimpy, black cloth underwear makes vivid account of itself in contrast to her fair skin. As Amanda grabs Cheryl's favorite black turtleneck shirt, and lifts it up and above her pretty head, I notice that even scrunch-faced and anguished, her sensual beauty is untouched, and the spread of her hips on the flat, hardwood table is extraordinary.

What remains is the image of a busty beauty in black underwear cloth, lying on her back, closing her eyes and taking a deep breath, bending one leg up at the knee as she slides her foot flat onto the table. It is a picture for the gods, seen by no human eye but our own, and captured by no electronic eye for hopeless posterity.

With our sweaters and jeans still in place, we commence to what soft rubbing of her skin as we can imagine, sliding my hands from her feet up to her knees and all the way up her thigh, while Amanda slides every ring from her elegant fingers, and even the gold hoop earrings from her ears in tandem. What follows is a brief, sucking kiss to one of her ears that brings one of her legs up again, and a deep, breathy moan from deep inside her.

We wait until every inch of her is caressed and rubbed, until she is relaxed to where her curiosity is conquered by the tranquility of grief again. And as she opens her eyes, to watch us begin to slide out of our sweaters, along with the spirits who watch what we do, I see her mouth relax partially open, as she turns her head back from me to my sister, and I see her throat move from the involuntary swallowing, as her eyes betray the anguish already building in her soul.

And after our t-shirts and pants are done away with, I see her eyes lock onto the places on us that devastate her the most, which is the G cup bra of her youngest spiritual betrothed, and the extra wide spread of my hips down below. I am witness to the premature loss of what dignity she has left, as she takes a deep breath involuntarily, unable to remove her eyes from the curve of my waist, and the spread of it outward down below.

Still in our bras and underwear, we both take a hold of the black bra straps that have held her prisoner, sliding them down past the mountainous cleavage, pulling the cups free from the Olympus Mons, from the Everestian landscape of breast flesh revealed, as these two gargantuan things seem to have swollen up somewhere toward the phantom key of J minor. As for a woman of her size, two of the biggest natural breasts in God's creation.

"Gosh," is the youthful word slipped out of my sister's mouth, as she is unable to close her mouth now, nor hide the shock and awe in her expression. We unlatch the G cup bra, which seems nearly two sizes too small for what it has revealed, tossing it to the floor under the table with the rest of our cloth of hypocrisy, proceeding with the task at hand, which is to each take hold of one of these Vesuvian breasts, and kneed it like so much bread dough, seeing every muscle in her arms and legs tense up, while the words 'oh my God' find their way forward from her in fear.

And while she tenses and breathes this satisfaction, she is unable to keep her own hands from finding their way up, up from the touch of our waists grabbed so firmly, then up to the cloth that holds us in, squeezing both of our bosoms through the breast cloth, causing me to feel as though both my legs will shake by attrition. Amanda is the first to take this final cue, lowering her head to one of the great breasts, which I do at the same time, causing her to voice her body's new worry in a simple "oh, no," shaking her head in denial, as if too much of this power given will start the inevitable inside her body.

Amanda raises up from this beginning, reaching back with such a mischievous delight as I have never seen, unlatching her big bra and sliding it to the floor. I follow suit quickly, unable to look away from the beauty and power of what I see. This sixteen year old plain-pretty, whose face is still touched by a girlish innocence, standing topless down to her tiny pink underwear; big, round breasts so completely wobbled free as to be an unnatural sight, leaning over again to Cheryl's giant floppers, pulling them both up into her mouth one at a time, slurping, popping them mischievously, even holding one in her mouth and bobbing up and down in furious action, literally breast humping the poor woman into a state of near madness and oblivion.

I take hold of the other breast into my mouth, holding it firm inside while Amanda goes crazy on her other one.

"Girls, if I cum like this its gonna kill me," she says, with as much truth as her grieving voice will allow. "I think I'm gonna cum in my tits," she says, as though genuinely amazed at the prospect that the lightning in her body is going to strike first in her breasts alone. And I do what little part I can contribute, concentrating, not distracting myself upon Amanda's natural brilliance, pulling the nipple up and down in slow, determined power, nursing the flesh as though it were nourishment for me, which I find that it is, feeling as though my legs may soon betray me and cause me to stumble.

And to my amazement, I feel the lightning strike my groin from deep inside somewhere I have never felt, which twitches my leg violently enough to lurch me forward involuntarily, which I work hard to try and conceal from the two of them.

"Did you *cum?*" Amanda says, her face washed over with shock and awe, as she stares briefly into my eyes. I can only nod, as I am unable to focus or speak properly, hearing her voice whisper *"oh my God,"* returning to Cheryl's breast with even more enthusiasm, groaning loudly in the effort, causing Cheryl to look back over her head as her body tenses, catching a glimpse of the white cross in the snow.

Upon this vision, upon her new daughter's bouncing, groaning enthusiasm upon her breast, the double pulling at her nipples send suddenly two bolts of lightning to the center of her body, causing her to yell a quick siren into the room, breathing again for dear life, then howling a second wailing siren into the twilight kitchen space around us, descending into madness and weeping, as he entire body spasms, like the last great earthquake over the battlefields of Armageddon.

Part Five

These are the days of the Hahn Dynasty. In the days when the sky was blue.

Li Hahn. And her daughters Debra Lin and Linda Hsu. Sue Hahn. The seventeen year old Asian smart girl. Somewhere in the flow of her eleventh grade year. Older sister to the thirteen year old beauty Debra Lin. The apple of her mother's eye. The sigh in her mother's heart and mind.

The seventeen year old hears her mother's voice. Calling her gently to the back of the house. A voice caressed by sweetness. The sound of forgiveness nurtured and grown.

Linda Sue rises from the academic burden of the day. From whatever subject that carries her into the twilight. Toward the pre-college dreams in the evening day. The small waisted, wide hipped young girl switches down the hall in pre-maturity. In pretty, pre-college girl hope for the future. Headed toward the bedroom of the *"ignorant bitch"* who calls herself her mother.

"Oh, there my big girl daughter," she says. Stretching up to the shelf at the top of her closet. *"I look for letter father write before he die. I think it in this box. You tall enough. Reach up and hand me box."*

The healthy bottomed daughter is overcome with compassion for her mother. This little woman, so burdened with her own secret pain.

In tucked lipped compliance. In a daughter's casual humility toward her mother, she steps inside the small closet space, reaching up for the black shoebox. Suddenly feeling the air rush rapidly around her, and the soft, twilight lamp lighting disappear into darkness.

Her mind slowly processes the rarity of this. That *yes,* the door was just shut in something close to a slam. And the sound of clicking at the knob must surely be her worst nightmare come to life.

"Ma?" is the pathetic, naïve sound she hears in the claustrophobic dark. A sound stifled terribly in what air there is for her to breathe.

"Ma, the door closed," is the next pathetic, naïve sound she hears in the stale, darkened air, lit up so mercifully by the bedroom light that slips through the cracks around the edges, and underneath the old, locked wooden door.

Her hand upon the knob is the painful, second part of the truth. The revelation that no matter what the reason, *yes,* she is locked inside her mother's closet.

"Ma? Ma open the door. Ma open the door I can't breathe..."

This is the last ray of hope she hears from the voice in the space around her. The sound of precious air wasted. The sound of hope slipping away.

And suddenly, she is burdened by devastation. Which is the third part of the truth unfurled, when the precious light of life is snuffed out, and the world around her is suddenly pitch black, to acquaint her with a new sound—that of her own voice. Howling a deep, woman's scream into the dark.

A death scream.

$\mathcal{L}$oneliness spins the flow of time and history. From the tiny House of Hahn, in days when the sky was blue. To the house on the Oklahoma prairie. Where predestiny hath darkened the days of a family in false hope. To burden the hours with grief and fear.

Isolated in the snowy, prairie landscape. Underneath skies of perpetual cold and winter. Jeff Ward braves the sound of eggshells walked. The feel of pins and needles under foot. Having believed the day's calm was a sign. That their friendly trip to the pet store in town was not a mirage. That it had substance and form. That the laughs and smiles his daughter shared when the sunshine yellow, and the royal blue and black colored fish were chosen. Little salt water dreams of a world long since buried in a nightmare. A little project for them to connect with, he thought. A fish the color of hope. The color of life itself.

In his office den hybrid of domestic tranquility, the wealthy Ward hears the voice of warning. The voice of his wife raised in a familiar ire. Screaming at the daughter about the loss of hope. The yellow beauty in their new aquarium, as colorful in death as it was in life. Laying the blame for the fish's lovely death at the feet of her angry daughter.

"I did *exactly* what you told me to do…"

"I knew you'd be too fucking stupid to do it. You've never done anything right in your whole goddamned life!"

"I did not kill this stupid—"

The father is taken aback, by the reality that their sudden silence is more terrifying than their screaming at one another. He is too late to engage the tell-tale shuffling sounds he hears, followed by a crash loud enough to wake every dead soul buried in the snow.

Jeff Ward rushes in something close to pure terror. From his cozy office chair, through the hall, to the livingroom entranceway. Where he stands enraptured. Unable to force another step into being. Unable to take another step. Unable to move into the space of this tragedy, which is the fine and glorious little aquarium, a three foot long masterpiece of saltwater fantasy built—this little aquarium turned over and smashed on the soaking wet floor, under the feet of an angry middle aged beauty and her teenage daughter.

These two women. Locked in a struggle for physical dominance. Both with their arms locked around each other's heads. Bent far over in this struggle. Unable to utter a sound above the heavy breathing.

Jeff Ward can only stand there. Watching the burning of black fire tinted blue. In hopes that this venting. This spilling of truth will serve. Will serve to relieve their suffering. He watches the mother's strength overcome. Flipping the smaller, weaker girl off her feet and landing hard on top of her on the wet floor. *Let them fight*, are the words that burn the core of his brain. Warning him that he is forbidden to move.

From their place of violence on the floor, he perceives a crossing over. The fulfillment of divine prophecy. When iniquity shall abound, and the love of many hath waxed cold in the ice and snow. He watches his wife lay hard and heavy on top of the girl, pounding her on her head, punching her in the face, in her breast and in her ribs. Watching his wife take the last ounce of rage and hatred left out upon his daughter. Knowing that somewhere on the other side of this hell, is the paradise of peace. The dawn of tranquility.

As the mother dominates. As she rests hard and heavy upon her daughter, the quiet in their scene is broken. Is erupted into a chaos of pain displayed. As the mother suddenly begins to scream out in apparent agony. The father watches the daughter flip the mother over onto her back. That he may see the tragedy of human existence. That he may see the mark of Cain being branded. Branded upon the mother's breast through her white collar shirt, as the daughter clamps down upon her breast in biting. Holding her there. Holding her down. Listening to her scream. Holding her down, until her mother's confusion breaks, and she is able to break free and roll away. Standing up quickly. Holding her breast but for a moment. Then dropping her hand away, to cause the husband to cover his mouth in shock. In disbelief at the sheer size of the spot of blood gathering in her white shirt. Growing at the bulge of her breast underneath.

"You fucking *cunt*. I swear to *God…*"

"Touch me again, bitch. And I'll *bite* you again."

"When I touch you again… it'll be the last time."

The mother nods her head in assurance. In assurance of a promise made. Walking slowly. Clumsily past the man at the entrance to the living room. Walking calmly up the stairs. Closing the bedroom door without a slam.

The man gazes at the seventeen year old girl. The seventeen year old woman. Unable to speak as she runs her hand back through her long, earthen brown hair. Breathing a second wind. Strolling in half soaked t shirt and jeans past him. Taking the same current of exhaustion up the stairs. Down the upstairs carpeted hall. Closing the door quietly to her upper room.

The man steps lightly. Upon the sound of phantom eggshells. Upon the pricking of ghostly needles and pins. Drifting to the disaster on the floor. Braving the bizarre, otherworldly devastation. Seeing hope lay dead upon the floor in the field of broken glass and water, amidst the dying echoes of blue life, scattered in pain and beauty throughout.

Cheryl's libido is fueled by the sorrow of the ages. An endless reservoir of pain and misery. A flowing river of deep perversion, siphoned forth by the death of a dream. An end of the world melancholia nurtured and grown, first seeded by the tragic incident in White Mountain, when the full blown truth about humanity was revealed to her. When the last hope she had for a place of family refuge and safety vanished, when the eyes of

Lacey Ezman looked at her. Accompanied by the blonde, blue eyes of her stepmother.

Heather Ezman had moved forward on this opportunity like a corporate shark on a bloody stock tip, wasting no time finding out from her wealthy, connected mother and father what the next step had to be, if the problem of unwanted company is to be solved. Heather's father, judge Wallace Emerick had gone over Heather's memory with the legal fine toothed come, enhancing, embellishing the incident until Cheryl had looked like a crazed child rapist and potential 1st degree murderer, though unfortunately, there were no bruises on Heather's body that could move them to the farthest action.

So, when the police showed up at our home a few days later, tapping on our door with timid authority, they assured us very quickly that no, there would be no handcuffs for the busty suburban beauty, no snowy ride in a police car for the incident in White Mountain. A civil restraining order and a child protective order, two defendants named for two different reasons, both alleging abuse of some tragic kind or another. When the discompassionate, somewhat smarmy lady cop stepped into our home that day, and gleefully read the contents of what sounded like something out of pure fiction, the three of us could not stop looking at one another with our mouths open in total bewilderment, hearing words like *"cunt licker"* and *"pulled my hair"* and *"rubbed my vagina in the shower"* being thrown around like bullets out of a gun. The good cop bad cop routine was on full display; as it is for every pair of policeman on God's earth, as the compassionate male cop—a bald, African American man in full, middle aged mustache broke in and said...

"I've seen this kind of thing before, Ms. Ezman. New wife using the courts to torture the old wife. Worse thing you can do is fight this. Because you can't beat it. And the orders will become permanent anyway, and then they might move forward with criminal charges after that. Best thing to do is stay away. You couldn't' beat these restraining orders with a <u>team</u> of lawyers honey..."

And this was the mercy of God on her, I suppose, which is the death of false hope and delusion. The claims made in the daughter's protective order were from her own mouth, the policeman said, alerting Cheryl to the fact that going anywhere near them would be like opening a tiger cage and throwing rocks at the thing.

But end-of-the-world misery loves end-of-the-world company. And every human vessel through which pain is channeled, needs an exit place for it to go. And every twisted psychology needs an outlet for its perversion. I'm finding it harder to blame our shadowy secrets on Fate, being that Cheryl's perversion has become an integral part of who we are. The breast centered desire she inherited from an Indian grandmother, that was tragically nurtured by a white, southern church foster mother—this breast centered obsession of hers has been fully indoctrinated now, and passed down to the two of us in secret.

Amanda is more accepting. More fully engaged emotionally than I am. Even in public, where she is not the least bit shy when we spend time walking in one of the big superstores that brave this snowy eschatology for the public, grabbing Aunt Cheryl's arm like somebody's girlfriend at a Friday night carnival from days of old, sometimes even kissing her on the cheek without the least bit of shame, which I know lights Aunt Cheryl up somewhere in the center of her body. She will sometimes look around sheepishly while pushing the cart, then glance back at Amanda, and the two of them will laugh a hard, deeply suppressed laugh that doubles them over in the effort to keep it quiet, like two thieves having gotten away with a life altering sum of money they have stolen and hidden away.

And sometimes, I find myself even judging Aunt Cheryl a little. Angry with her for what curse she has brought into our lives, and what dark, twisted and unmentionable thing she has introduced us to. But a part of me knows heartily, and without compromise to cut the pretense, and to not allow myself to fall into this foolishness, being that even the sight of this woman in her giant bra can often cause my mouth to water.

My mind is on fire right now with my sixteen year old sister's newfound orgasmic intensity, which can be brought to fullness by just about anything we do, whether it is breast centered or not. Sadomasochism is the spark that ignites the flame inside her young mind, I think, betrayed by what I saw when Cheryl forced me to put Amanda over my knee, both of us in the nude. Even though the wooden hairbrush bruised and blistered her athletic bubble butt, I can tell that it would have taken more punishment than we had for her to have brought her to tears, as she refused to change her little smart assed attitude no matter how hard I hit her, and no matter how loudly it made her scream.

And when Aunt Cheryl tied one of my mother's sheer black stockings around her ankles, pulled her over her knee and spanked her while sitting on my mother's bed, the loud, growling "oh" sound she made after exactly twenty seven whacks was from a different kind of pain, which made her whole body shake like a paint mixing machine at Sears from just a hand spanking alone.

And I watched, with mild shock and disbelief, as Cheryl had to stand her up and lean her over, Amanda's hands on the bed, pounding herself into Amanda, big J cups hanging free out of the bottom of her bra pulled up, slamming her groin into Amanda until she had one of her patented earthquakes, which always causes her to bellow and grunt like a wild animal.

The two of them are like the mother and daughter versions of the same spirit. The so called sexual soulmates, if there truly is such a thing, where they have a deep and powerful understanding, of what must be done to "get each other off," so to speak. And Cheryl has fully ignited this blue and black flame in both my sister and me, commensurate now upon her breast centered cure for what ails her, in the form of the full blown nursing at Cheryl's breasts morning, noon and night. This, done to activate the hormone, to ring the Chime of the Milkmaids, that will flow an even greater river of pleasure from the reservoir of pain in her mind and body.

$\mathcal{W}$hat happens, when hopeless longing goes unfulfilled? When the third part of the truth is revealed?

The cataclysm of this moment is in the air to be sure. To where I can surely tell that Aunt Cheryl's incessant, persistent laughing and joking with

Amanda is nothing more than a band-aid over a deep cut; a tragically failed and temporary fix to a problem more deeply permanent than what can be accepted or dealt with. Where weeping and melancholia would be the body's better healing—the painful stitching up of an open wound.

But the fear of this otherworldly depression, the terror of it has somehow caused her to retreat. To run in the opposite direction from sadness, until I don't know how even Amanda can stand it anymore. Probably because she is just a kid herself. In the long run, still a teenager. A teenager prone to bouts of unbelievable flights of bubble headed giddiness, in this case, very likely in the same spirit of overcompensation—where truthfully, I know that the two of them are laughing to keep from crying.

But I didn't think much of it when they abandoned me earlier, just after we returned from our icy shopping trip, with a car full of Christmas in summertime. Only one special bag did Aunt Cheryl even bother to take, calling Amanda away from the task at hand, leaving me to the gloomy chore on my own. As the new flakes begin to fall outside, I gather up the last of the many shopping bags, from the big store designed to draw money out of a wallet as much as a winter twister draws condemned souls from their snowbound homes on the prairie.

While I enjoy unbagging all the shoes and shirts and pants not a single one of us is ever going to wear, I am struck by the sudden quiet that overwhelms me, as if the air around me suddenly has life, and chooses to stop breathing for a moment. For some reason, as I lay aside the frilly pink button down blouse Amanda chose to buy, curiosity envelops me like an amoeba, causing me to have to shake my head and try to laugh it off to myself, then finally moving away from our long kitchen table of bagged nothings gathered in exchange for money.

I go up the back staircase, still enveloped by the quiet. Feeling drawn upward by it to wherever it is they are. For some reason, my mind feeds me what I know is a false image, of Amanda on her stomach with her clothes on, her pants down just below her naked bottom with her hands between her legs, with Aunt Cheryl laying flat on Amanda's back with her own breasts out, while Amanda lays there, squeezing and rubbing herself to another growling "oh oh" chorus. This false image burns itself into my mind as I take the soft, padded steps to the upstairs hall, walking slowly, carefully to Amanda's room, quietly opening the door into the gloomy, daytime dark.

Nothing.

But I am more frustrated than relieved that I didn't catch them. Now picturing Aunt Cheryl with her hands *under* Amanda's, while still laying on top of Amanda's back. Feeling Amanda motion her own body into a thundering oblivion.

The theater of my mind powers every quiet step toward discovery. Until I finally get to the door of the room I know they love the most. I quietly turn the knob, slowly pushing the door open into a dark more dreary and gloomy than the first. It is a scene I could not have envisioned if I tried, with my sister fully dressed in her jeans and pale pink button down blouse, laid across Aunt Cheryl's lap on the bed. Cheryl is fully clothed in her favorite black cloth; black pants, black boots, black turtleneck shirt in place, raised up over the *nursing bra* we watched her by—with one single, Olympian breast exposed and hanging down, being pulled so completely into the girl's mouth, with the girl laid across her lap.

My sister is partially curled up, her head comfortably resting on Aunt Cheryl's arm, with her impossibly large breast pulled deeply into

Amanda's mouth in nursing form. And though I step quietly, boldly into the room, I notice Aunt Cheryl have to make no effort to ignore my presence, rubbing Amanda's forehead and hair as lovingly as can be imagined, staring down at the girl in something close to awe and disbelief.

"Our milk came in today," she says, unable to hide the trembling, the rumbling melancholia underneath her voice. "When I woke up this morning, my t shirt was soaking wet."

And though her somber expression does not change, I watch the tears form in both her eyes, to roll a stream of consciousness down her face on one side without a single blink, then down the other side when the blink comes on its own. I stand there, unable to pretend my mind is not blown, even though I am already a prisoner of Aunt Cheryl's depravity. Amanda adjusts herself to a greater, more snuggling comfort, moaning softly once, followed by an epic gulping meant to be heard, as though she had been dying of both hunger and thirst, and was relieved of an end-of-the-world suffering.

To the melody of another soft moan from Amanda, is the rhythm of Cheryl's hand moving to her own breast, holding it firmly, as if trying to push it deeper into the girl's mouth.

"Suck harder baby," she says, barely above a whisper, sliding her legs firm against the side of the bed, boots crossed at the bottom, seeming to lean slightly forward, unable to take her eyes from Amanda's face, from Amanda's closed eyes, from Amanda's mouth at her breast. I see her leg twitch ever so slightly, as the stare on her face grows harder, and her breathing so much more loud and deep.

She shakes her head 'no' once, as through unable to accept the feeling in her body, the rise of a new devastation, the impending fall of barriers unknown. I watch the confusion grow in her beautiful face, as her anguish transforms to frustration, where her breathing and trembling head betray the energy building in her body.

And she is unable to hide the single whimper, struggling to hold her voice in silence and heavy breathing, her mouth hung open in shock and awe, until the tension in her body breaks, exploding power from her single exposed breast to her womb, gripping her, doubling her over with a series of loud, deep grunting sounds, shaking her head 'no' again, as Amanda's sucking sends wave after wave through Cheryl's body, until she begins to groan in long, gruff exclaims of pleasure morphed into the unendurable.

I step over to the poor woman, taking hold of her flailing hand, studying her face, to try and find a false note in this overture played, but seeing only a woman in grief, in grieving to endure the waves of power and passion passing through.

The winds of eschatology continue to blow, gathering into themselves a new snow drifting from the clouds, threatening to bury us alive in this perpetual winter. There is nothing for the world to do but except its fate, and to forget about the foolishness of the outside world, and memories of skies not burdened with clouds of everyday gloom and gray. These are skies pushed to a place beyond weeping, where the expression of their sorrow falls in tears frozen in regret, and lamentation in fluffy white ice and crystal.

And these gloomy skies are often lit up by blue and mysterious white lightning; rivers of energy that often flow gently across the bottom of the clouds themselves, to produce mild and heavy rumblings of booming thunder in the cold. There are times when it is impossible to tell the difference between the thunder, and the rumblings that emanate in anger and warning from the snow covered ground below.

The three of us have settled into these behind closed doors versions of ourselves, still in grieving from the death and burial of our mother, and the best friend Aunt Cheryl ever had. We have all gone to the place where tortured minds go, where the sufferings of living this life become too difficult to bear. But though I know Cheryl often fantasizes about her pills and glass of wine, none of us can bring ourselves to embrace this, and so we take out our frustrations on each other's bodies, trading pains and pleasures ad nauseam, without hesitation and without mercy.

Cheryl has taken to raiding our mother's closet more frequently. Spending more time lost in mother's room, loving to squeeze her top heaviness into my mothers' dresses, looking every bit as graceful in the simple, elegant cloth she finds, whether it is the simplicity of burgundy or navy blue in full length down to below the knee, or the gray business skirts stretched over her hips and black stockings underneath—she loves to dress more and more like my mother did in her classic casual, often sitting with her legs crossed in the livingroom chair, stern faced, hand on her knee while she watches us engage in her new passion, which is to have each of us in full nursing upon one another. Different positions, different levels of dress, from formal wear complete with stockings and high heels, down to the bare skin itself, until each of us have learned what is possible to achieve through breast sucking alone.

These are breast orgasms. Those that seem to start in the breast itself, then flow down to somewhere above the groin, then like a bolt of lightning, causing the whole body to jerk and spasm uncontrollably. It takes me longer than it does the two of them, but what happens to my body is every bit as intense, and always leaves me devastated in the aftermath, and left in shock on the road to recovery.

Even now, as Cheryl watches us on the sofa, lost in the breast sucking yin and yang, where I am on my back with Amanda's breast down in my face, and her face is down onto mine—even now, the both of our bodies are on the blue and *white* fire of this impending lightning, while Cheryl sits so elegantly in the reddest dress my mother owned, with stockings covering her legs in sheer black silk, with a pair of lovely red pumps on her feet. This cloth is married to the ruby of her lips, and of those in the shimmering ruby-diamond earrings that dangle.

Hers is the beauty of the ages. In league with the sorrow that has taken over, as she watches the two of us in the agony of something beyond guilt, while the pain of genuine regret begins to creep in, but not just for what depravities she has burdened us to know. It is for a life lived in the pain of false hope and delusion, the years of longing, becoming as fleeting as a snowflake drifting in the wind, and the realization that under the hidden sun, under the hidden light of this snowy Autumn Moon, there is no longer a reason to have faith in the future, and there is no more pleasure in life to be found under the cold light of this hidden sun.

And as she watches my sister begin the muffled groaning, the writhing of her body and her face buried in my breast below, she knows that there are places in life where the timeline crosses, where the barriers to realization have crumbled and fallen away. And as she watches my body begin to writhe and shake from the current of grieving passing through, she can feel a new and powerful rumbling of herself inside, as that from the clouds and beneath the earth—to warn the heart and mind of having tasted and shared the forbidden fruit, and to bathe the soul and spirit in the fear of impending grief and tragedy.

As the woman in red looks on, at the aftermath of devastation and trauma, she feels with us the epic sound flowing up in doom from beneath the snowy ground, and the flow of it from one end of the snow covered earth to the other.

$\mathcal{T}$he calm and uneasy acceptance of our fates has descended, until we are no longer concerned with the possibility of escape. The pain in Cheryl's life now glows through her expression like a light from behind a curtain, or as the sun has done every so often, from behind a gray cloud veil. Gone is the ridiculous attempt at fungalooga happiness, which can be a weight that is eventually too heavy to carry for some, until they drop the pretense like a hot rock from a cold hand. There is nothing left for us to pretend for. No one in the world left to impress with our ability to be "happy" or "normal."

And so we have allowed ourselves a somber trip through this snowy part of the timeline, until many days have passed where we bear no memory of a laugh or a smile.

The pressures that weigh heavily on Cheryl's mind have pushed deeper into her body, until it has coalesced into something sinister, where the pain she feels must be medicated with a deeper depravity.

And I am a victim and witness to this, while I am laid naked on my back upon my mother's bed, my body roped to my naked sister tied up on top of me face down, roped so that she cannot even roll off of me, her hands tied up behind her back, her brown hair pinned up tightly to her head.

What wicked spirits that have come to life in the room have tickled and tormented me to where I don't know whether to laugh or cry, which is the hallmark of the sadist's beckon call. Roped tightly to my sister laid on top of me, with my arms bound to the sides of my body, I see sadism in my mother's tight gray skirt, with a matching pewter gray turtleneck shirt. Pulling the shirt free from the tight skirt, making quick work of the bra underneath through the witch and wizardry of womanhood. Tossing it away, leaving the shirt covering the new, hanging roundness underneath. Then stepping over to us in her gray cloth and black boots, tearing the white duct tape so skillfully with her teeth, putting the tape so heartlessly over our mouths, to send the spirit of laughter somewhere out into the snow forever.

"I'm not doing this because I want to," she says, her voice soothed in the madness of self delusion. "I'm doing it because I *have* to. I'm doing it because I know it's what your mother would have wanted. And how do I know this? Because she told me."

The types of fear are many. And uniquely distinguished.

Among these is the fear of pain.

And death.

"Your mother came to me in a dream last night," she says. Standing up, looking down at us with a mixture of contempt and pity. The mountains of flesh flopped free under her tight, dark gray turtleneck have gone from intimacy to intimidation.

"Your mother was at the kitchen counter, cutting a cucumber for a salad. She was wearing this skirt. And I said *'Annabelle, I'm going to have a belt across your ass if it's the last thing I ever do.'* You remember how beautiful your mother's hips were."

Upon this note, she crosses her arms, and uncrosses them upon the classic lifting away of her shirt, exposing the gigantic breasts hung down nearly to her waist in bell shaped, bulbous fashion. And with a smile that chills me to the bone, she laughs a little, in genuine recollection of her dream memory.

"And then she said the most curious thing," she says, undoing the zipper along the side of the gray business skirt. Sliding the skirt down her legs past her boots, exposing the magnificent waist curve more extraordinary than my own, breasts swung low and wobbly as she bends over. She slides the skirt down and away, leaving the black leather boots in place, which are married to the scant black underwear cloth stretched across her hips.

From the rear, the upside down heart, teardrop shaped wideness of her hips is remarkable.

"Your mother said, *' What you really need to do, is discipline those two rebellious sluts upstairs. Amanda needs a belt whipping to within an inch of her life. They both do. They need to be tied up and taught a lesson."*

Without as much as a glimpse in our direction, Cheryl steps over to where the black leather belt lies curled in serpentine, in waiting on the dark wood mirrored dresser.

"*What?* I said to your mother. And she said, '*My daughters need the blood striped from their backsides. To keep them from becoming spoiled, prissy little bitches. You have my permission.*' And I said to her, '*you're kidding right?*"

Cheryl picks up the belt. Still looking away. Folding it in classic style.

"Then your mother turned and looked at me. And she said…'*You have to do it.*"

This, Cheryl speaks to us upon this self same turning of the head. Channeling the somber, anguished and determined look she was given by the angel in her dreams.

"I'm going to have to do it," she says. Drifting toward us in a mild, far away bewilderment of expression. "Because she *asked* me to."

And upon this, she looks down at us with a flash of strong disapproval and heavy contempt. With the white tape still over my mouth, I watch Cheryl focus her gaze to Amanda's naked bottom. And I see the leading edge of what threatens the remains of her sanity. Raising the belt up strong and ready in her closed fist, bringing my mother's old, hard black leather belt down onto the bottom of Amanda's buttocks, causing my sister to tense up and grunt loudly through her nose. Then Cheryl does it again immediately, harder this time across the same spot, then a third and fourth time, causing Amanda to have to writhe heavily against me, until the mashing and rolling of her breasts against my own have their inevitable effect on my spirit, while the squeezing of her groin against mine has its undesired impact on my soul.

I brave this ebb and flow of energy in my body, while I watch Cheryl beat Amanda angrily with the belt, my body vibrating with Amanda's muffled screaming, her arms still bound up tightly behind her back in strong, white roped discipline. A glimpse at Amanda's face, the constant writhing of her body tells me that her pain is real, and the flames burning her skin are those of a fire the color of midnight and blue.

Cheryl continues this whipping, across every welt created, building them up, then breaking them down, until I can feel the pain cross over into agony in my sister, as the leather proceeds to cut her white skin to blood. And now, the shaking of her body, the hoarse, muffled screams at my ear, the pounding of the tied up girl's hips up and down against my groin pushes my spirit and soul toward one another, to where the famed irresistible force must collide with the so-called immovable object, to produce the breakdown of Creation itself, and the annihilation of all stability along the flow of time and history in the cosmos.

And Fate chooses the moment of my destruction, when Cheryl brings down the last blow I am able to see through clear vision, her beautiful teeth clenched in a grimace, her dark areolaed breasts wobbling mightily from the blow, splitting the skin on my sister's buttocks in a new place, causing my sister to writhe and fight to be free, which makes my eyes roll back and close on their own, unable to resist the collision of worlds inside my body, and the flow of the muffled sound of a siren, born from the place where I felt my soul and my spirit collide.

$\mathcal{T}$he weeks coalesce into the four winter winds, merging together above us high and low, to fall in whirling from skies of ashen gray regret. We rest accursed from the Sun's daily rise and fall, perceiving nothing of the earth's turning from one evening day to the next. With the rest of the world we lie hidden, under this blanket of eschatology, where the Sun has turned to darkness in the gray, and where the Moon no longer gives her light. Of what morning or evening star there was or shall ever be, the world lies in mourning to remember, having only the picture and video images to recall, of the light that ruled the twilight and breaking dawn, where mankind's last hope of Redemption draweth nigh.

Underneath these old and new clouds of grieving, we travel our path through these winter Winds of Time, unable to distinguish the passing weeks from the days that have birthed and made them. Under the rolling gray, in the days and weeks beyond my sister's 16th birthday, Cheryl Ezman hath delighted herself in her god, which is the exploration of our teenage sensuality, and the explosions of unendurable pleasures in each of our minds and bodies. She has given herself over to this reprobate mind, to laugh and curse away all boundaries and pretense with aggression, until Amanda and I understand the nature of screams, and whether or not they are caused by pleasure or pain.

I stand blindfolded between them. In our mother's softly lit bedroom, where the spirits of what Cheryl must live and breathe have the most life, where we are the most hotly consumed by her blue and black fire. Of these flames I must see only in my mind, as I feel them burning red across my face, as my sister slaps me with angry intent, while Cheryl holds me tightly by the arms, before using what Amazonian strength her body hath formed, to tear the white tank t-shirt I wear down the front of my body, to expose both my breasts in a powerful jerk and wiggling. In my mind's eye, in the soul of what has become of me, I see and feel the tearing of my white tank t-shirt, in harmony with the music of my loud, grunting voice heavy with lust and apprehension, perceiving the cool air in my mother's room tickle the nipples of both my breasts.

Look at them, Amanda, Cheryl says. *Are you sister's breasts not perfect? Touch them, cup them and squeeze them. Both of them. Now let them go. See how perfectly they sit. How perfectly high and rounded they are...* and at this moment, from my blind and unseeing eyes, I feel her rough and firm touch at the front of them, feeling the lighting strike from two points of origin, to spasm my entire body from their strike. She takes firmer hold of both nipples, twisting them to the point of pain, firmly telling me to put my arms down, which I cannot obey, evoking the loudest, firmest voice we have heard from her thus far... *put your arms down!* she orders, in a tone just beneath a yell, punctuated by the hardest slap from my sister, which shocks me into a deep grunt, where I hear *hold still*, spoken firmly in my ear. Amanda angrily tears the rest of my white t-shirt away, until I am as completely nude as the two of them are, except for the wearing of their blue and black fires hanging down.

As to Cheryl's thin member gathered and chosen, so mercifully lubricated for what must be done, I feel her fingers at the center of my bottom, spreading me open while she trembles with desire, perceiving the sliding inward of the worm that dieth not, until I rest at the edge of crying out to God for mercy. *Hold her by her breasts, Amanda... hold her still for me... can you feel my cock in your ass Belinda... do you feel my cock growing inside you?* And the pressure is such that I cannot answer so easily, which brings the turning of the screws again, to send the lightning of pure pain from my nipples to my voice. *Yes!* is the sound I hear from somewhere in the room, as the rest of herself is pushed past the Gates of Sodom, and she holds herself still and tight up inside me.

Her breathing is loud in my brain, from the warm breath at my ear, where I perceive the trembling in her body that already threatens to be born. In my mind's eye, I see Amanda's young, newly sixteen year old lips apart, her expression relaxed in quiet awe at what she sees and what she feels in her body. She watches Cheryl spank the front of my breasts without mercy, seeing her grab my ear with her teeth, to better see me descend toward helplessness and fear. *Take her by the nipples Amanda... take a good hold of them,* which Amanda does with youthful over-enthusiasm, which I can feel in uncompromising flame. *Twist them good Amanda, she can take it, she's a big girl, she's almost a grown woman, pull and twist them like you mean it...* and this command, unfortunate for me, brings an agony I have not yet felt before, causing me to shriek and pull against them both, until Cheryl grabs my ear again. I know I must stand here and cry out, while my sister's expression darkens to something beyond cruelty, where the sensations are the most severe inside the tormentor, until these energies coalesce into one. In my mind's eye, I see, I feel my sister's body begin to shake where she stands, a single, mighty shuddering that leaves her confused, having been called and chosen by the spirit of Sadism at its most unmerciful.

Yes, the voice breathes in my ear... *Oh God, yes. Did you feel your sister cum? Did you feel it?* And then I hear Amanda swallow then grunt from the energy left over passing through. *Hug your sister Amanda... lay up against her... put your lips to hers...* and in the dark, in my blinded eyes I see, and I feel my sister's kiss firmly against my lips without shame, feeling the breath from her nose on my lips and face, knowing that she perceives this new power of hers, this graduation from what was to what must now and forever be. She hugs me closer, and I hear her breath on one side of me, and the breath of our captor on the other.

And from behind me, I feel Cheryl's hands slide down to the front of me, fully aroused to where I can feel the electric touch of her hand. *Now, nurse your sister Amanda, yes, go down to her nipples, take one into your mouth...yes... suck the milk... suck the milk from your sister's breasts, gently, but deeply, take it deep into your mouth, stay on this nipple, stay until your sister cums... "* And I feel the dim light in the room enter my mind through seeing eyes, as Cheryl pulls off the blindfold and tosses it away, so I can see the manner of my impending death and destruction. *Watch her, Belinda, watch her take the milk from your breasts... watch your sister take the milk from your tits...* and this sends a knowing, natural moan through Amanda—who takes such a firm and expert hand and mouth to my breast, her pretty young face anguished over in post trauma, and the phantom pain of new desire.

The sight of my sister at my breast, the feel of her lips and tongue at my nipple, the warmth of Cheryl's breath at my ear, the cushion of her gigantic breasts on my back, the magic of her touch down below, all come together above the smooth, deep and moaning bass of the fire inside my bowel, until I can no longer control the breath in my lungs, and I hear it gathering strength and getting away from me on its own. *I want you to cum... I want to feel you cum on my cock...* the words of which react to haze my vision, and I can only hear myself begin to scream, though without the slightest control or purpose of intent, as the voice of depravity seeks the path of least resistance from my soul, through my lungs, from my mouth and into the chill of my mother's room. And the rubbing down below continues ad nauseam, pushing me beyond pleasure to what cannot be borne, making Cheryl roughly tell me to *hold still! Let it pass through, let it out through your voice,* which I do, but this time with full will and purpose, to scream to the heavens of the nature of deviance, and of what churns beneath cultured civility.

And somewhere in the mist of this scream, I feel an electric trembling against my body, and I hear a pitiful, plaintiff moan escape from Cheryl's spirit, as she suffers the quaking of her entire body, which trembles her voice to quivering, which I can feel flowing from the depths of her tortured soul and into my own.

*W*inds weep and howl in misery, in grieving for what they know, for what pain they hear when the snows fly, the weeping sorrow of every human soul—and foreknowledge of what traumas are coming upon the earth. And they mourn with every traveling flake of snow, for the judgment of souls, for the punishment of the wicked populace, and their reward for every secret thing. These secrets are called forth from the heart of man, to bring the necessary evils into the world, transformed by human sensibilities into pleasure by divine right, rather than perversion and sin.

We stand as a billion others around the world in the ignorance of our calling, hidden under the roofs from the freshly fallen snow, comfortably private and privileged in our mother's bedroom, where it is that Cheryl knew this latest and greatest work hath ought to be achieved. For us, perhaps it is a welcomed diversion; a simple, hidden pleasure of youth, the warm embrace of her love and attention, to replace that which we had lost, and had so casually, so uncasually buried in the snow.

In our dead mother's room, the spirits of eschatology rise and fall, to lend us the proper minds for these violently vitriolic acts, the acts of abomination to our Lord and Savior, these acts of obsession to the earthly ties that bind. In the name of God, we give ourselves to what sins we are called to perform, with the knowledge that even the wicked sword is touched by God in battle, so that his will doth come and go, that the plane flies into the tower, that the children are corrupted in their appointed hour, that they explode in atomic power, by the fervent and sovereign will of God.

Somewhere outside of conscious thought, away from rational accessibility, this drives the three of us deeper and harder into each other, which I see so clearly but cannot perceive, as I watch my 16 year old sister with Cheryl's heavy, overdeveloped breasts in her hands—standing in front of Aunt Cheryl, who is unclothed down to her underwear bottoms—Amanda pushing up Cheryl's breasts like two great floppy pillows and letting them flop repeatedly back into place. Somewhere inside her human spirit lies this need as a pure hunger, acknowledged by a deep breath in her, and a groaning, low pitched sigh. What privilege is this, to watch so gigantic a pair of breasts in the nude on a such a beautiful woman of 40 be pushed, squeezed and flopped by a sixteen year old girl?

And this sixteen year old girl is suddenly ripe with knowledge, as she begins to suck Aunt Cheryl's breasts like two great milk bottles, evoking a very loud, deliberate moan from her as she looks down at what her niece is doing. She watches the young girl suck with knowledge and determined, focused precision, gazing up into Cheryl's eyes for approval with each hard and loud sucking pull. Amanda's sucking is hard enough to redden the white skin around Cheryl's areolas, which I know is exactly what she requires today. *That's it,* she says, *try to get that milk you know is there— you know you want that milk, don't you? Let your sister have some, Baby.* And I know to take one into my hands, which I do so gladly with such nervous tension and desire, and I proceed to drink this phantom milk, wanting to taste it and let it run in gulps down my throat.

Is this the milk of kindness the world once talked of and smiled about under sunny skies? Is this the milk of compassion? What compels me to drink so hungrily at the breast of my mother's best friend? Right beside my ear, my sister's loud kissing and smacking inspires me to look over, then kiss her on the cheek while she pulls a nipple into her mouth. *Oh, God* says Cheryl, a pitiful, involuntary sound born from an inner awakening, from a love even deeper than where she thought she had gone. *Kiss her again, Baby—kiss her again—taste the nipple with your sister—*now, Amanda and I are both dueling lip and tongue across Cheryl's nipple, which makes her body twitch once upon a hazardous breath in her lungs. *Put your tongues together—kiss your sister's tongue,* and before we know it, my sister and me are fumbling through our first real kiss—breathing, sucking each other's lips softly, pushing our tongues together in lush, wet kisses.

Snow

Amanda! Where have you gone! Where is the younger sister I knew, the girl of my sweetest hopes and dreams! Where have you been kidnapped from by us, and where in the world is it that you have gone! This is the knowledge of good and evil we taste, the fruit of that fateful tree, which brings with it a curse that cannot be broken, except by the shattered bond of life itself, and the blood and pain of death. As the condemned souls we are, we kiss in obsession, possessed now by the madness of pure lust, even while Cheryl gets down to her knees to stroke in spit the eight and ten inch members we wear.

I have pity for my sister still, who hardly remembers the walking, escorting motion to the bed, which has her laid horizontal in a fog of burning in her young body. It does to her, I suppose, what it does to me, to see the beautiful middle aged woman on her knees, choking on the cock of her dreams deep throated, with her two gigantic breasts hanging down, then straddling Amanda, her hands down between her legs, face anguished as she guides the head of a rocket to its destination. The look on her face is determination and agony, this, the pain of realization and completion when the deepest, darkest desire is brought into being, to ride the sixteen year old girl's penis into ecstasy. After every inch times ten is strived toward the woman's womb, she rests there, fully loaded over Amanda, one hand on my breast and the other hand on Amanda's. *I feel every inch of your cock*

Amanda—can you feel your cock up inside me? Amanda hardly knows how to answer, but gives the affirmative anyway, unafraid—determined to survive this final and greatest initiation to perversity.

Push up a little Honey, Cheryl says—*push it up into me—fuck me like I wanted to fuck your Momma, I loved your Momma and I wanted to fuck her—does that shock you—look at me Amanda, does that shock you?* But Amanda is not intimidated, shaking her head no in bravery, having already burned in the hell of rape. What is the other side of Hell, but Paradise*? Now take hold of my breasts—hold them there while your sister fucks me in the ass—that's right Belinda, get behind me—*

Although Cheryl and Amanda are calm, committed to what they must do—in my heart there is a reticence—the hesitation of guilt, the glitch that comes when innocence makes one last gasp and claw before death. I get behind my mother's best friend, and by her command, spit down into her exposed anus. Then I take my cock into my hands, the eight inch blue and black fire, and I slide it into Cheryl's backside, listening to her bellow out like a she-demon—which causes me to reposition myself in dominance—in she-doggy style over her back. *That's it Belinda—push it in, push it in for your Momma. Your Momma is watching, she needs for you to push your cock all the way up my ass*—the mention of my mother activates a fear and dread in my body, sparing no energy from my groin, to where I am suddenly at one with the member that pushes into the woman from behind—causing me to push past a barrier inside that blocks the member loosely. I push past it carefully, but with force, amazed without mercy when Cheryl cries out one last time—*Yes, it's in, your cock is in me Belinda. Do you feel your sister's cock too? Huh? Do you feel your two cocks together inside me...* I feel nothing of my sister inside her, but I am one with this end-of-the-world diversion, my arms wrapped tight around Cheryl's waist, my teeth clamped down on her naked white shoulder. What does it do to Amanda's young body, to see the middle aged woman wrapped up and bitten by her older sister? Why does it inspire her to writhe her groin? *Don't move too much Amanda, please, I don't want to cum yet—*

What madness is this I see! Are we as others, or how unique are we! *Amanda don't move—lie still—yes, that's it, now Belinda, I want you to fuck me slowly, yes that's it...no, don't take it out, just squeeze it in slowly, yes, that's right, deep up into my ass—yes, keep squeezing—keep pushing—you'll push me over the edge—I'm going to the die from this orgasm—yes, fuck me to death Belinda—my nipples are calling to my mind—telling me not to move, to wait for it—I can feel it in my tits—its starting in my tits Belinda—I'm going to cum in my tits—don't move— don't move—let it come through my tits and my ass—*I don't know what this is, this bewitching insanity I see, but she is clearly out of her mind with a unique and powerful lust—that has caused her to ramble *I'm going to cum in my tits* and her movements are now involuntary at her groin, pushing herself back against me in a painfully slow, deliberate rhythm until she is locked still, while her voice rises to the Moon's high and fervent pitch, and then she falls over this cliff as I am witness to what I have never seen before; a grown woman straddled between two young girls, lost in a howling wail of defeat, which falls down upon a mighty jerk backwards… on both our blue and black fires deep inside.

Part Six

*I*t is the breakdown of cultured civility. Here at the end of the age, in the days before, during and after the years of snowfall.

The busty, brunette beauty drives the cold, snowy highways in icy determination. In the pain of a psychology crossed over. Feelings and sensibilities frozen in time. When pain has gathered itself to a place beyond durability.

The brunette beauty drives these apocalyptic highways of new falling snow, comfortable in her new hiding ride. A Tundra as black as night. Bought and paid for by privilege. For whatever end of the of the world task there is at hand. Braving these summer winter streets in cold resolve. Gathered and pulled along upon the wave of inevitability. Unable to push the blonde snow bird from the theater of her mind. The blonde now imprinted upon her soul.

The brunette beauty is unable to push the blonde beauty away from her spirit, nor the things she knows she does in private. The things she does to the fifteen year old exotic. To one of the most beautiful girls on the face of the earth. The Pocahontas Girl, with the almond shaped eyes and smooth, fair skin. The Pocahontas Girl, whose hair flows a midnight river of silken loveliness down the length of her back. Whose breasts sit perfect in their early C major key already, above the tiny waist, and young hips bubbled and spread to youthful infinity.

The brunette beauty drives on. Burdened by the light of these two burning her mind, knowing in her heart what has already begun. What has already transpired between them. The brunette beauty rolls on. Tormented by the sight of the naked blonde, standing close to the naked Pocahontas Girl, holding the girl's head with both her big, white hands. A tongue kiss so deep. A probing so committed that it causes the young girl to gag twice in the effort. Moving over to the bed, to begin the spit in every slit, and ice cream licks from tit to clit. Obeying the blonde headed, behind closed doors calling of her privileged life, which is to taste every inch of this girl, from the top of her forehead to the bottom of her feet.

The brunette beauty drives on. Suffering the heat of these images displayed in the car windshield before her eyes, as the older woman she sees is unable to restrain herself upon the fifteen year old beauty.

Employing her patented, big tongued ice cream licks to the girl's face like a dog in heat. Nearly slurping her way down to the girl's neck and shoulders. Moving onto the bed, the two of them stark naked. The strong, athletic blonde's muscles tensed in readiness from head to toe, her body firm in natural athletic prowess. Breasts flattened by cruel predestiny. Huge nipples made more huge, more sensitive under the young girl's willing lips and tongue.

The brunette beauty drives on. Unable to push away this slit licking snow queen. Unable to close her mind from the woman on top of the young girl. Watching her hold the young girl down in roughness, pulling the young girl's breasts up deeply into her mouth. Holding it there, pulled high up. Face deeply anguished, cheeks dimpled in the sucking effort. Achieving this, until she knows her body cannot take another. Moving on from her breasts down to the girl's waist. Wet licking the girl's naval in determination. Loving the girl's twitch and shudder from the effort.

The brunette beauty looks on as she drives, gazing the theater of her mind, as the blonde snow cat licks the prize that she herself was denied. Watching her place her mouth at the young girl's chastity. Holding it there. Uncompromising. Watching the young girl's face anguish over in beauty. Satisfied, that the fruit shared between them is forbidden. Pinching both the girl's nipples. Licking her chastity to devastation and ruin. Licking. Sucking. Having to breathe the scent of innocence corrupted through her nose. The perfumed scent of the natural order. The taste of innocence sweetened by knowledge. The taste of forbidden fruit in the soul.

The blonde beauty stays there. Her tongue flicked at the swollen clit pulled inside her mouth. Determined to make this kill. Sworn to watch the death of cultured civility.

The blonde flicks this licking upon the girl. Between the girl's legs held open. Holding both the girl's nipples in authority. Hearing the arrival of warning. The change in breathing rhythm. The tensing of the girl's muscles. The flow of a new voice over the whispering breath from her open mouth.

The blonde holds her there. Face buried in the birth of womanhood. Sucking the life. Sucking the life of the little girl lost.

What trembling is this she feels? This, the trembling, the rumbling from deep within every muscle and bone? The trembling that gathers itself up in the girl's voice, to produce the requisite *oh my God*, and two high pitched soprano shrieks for the ages. Her body shaking the Armageddon Quake. Attempting to push and pull away. Wondering why she has to scream again. Why the pleasure has morphed into something beyond pain. Into something she cannot endure.

The blonde knows when to give mercy. When to raise up, and stare at the swollen, pink tapestry of her handiwork. Sliding lickety split back up the girl's body. Past the naval. Past the nipple for now. Back to where the tongues from twain shall meet. Where the girl can taste the sweet corruption. The taste of forbidden fruit on the woman's tongue.

The brunette beauty arrives at her destination. At the palatial house in White Mountain. Committed to sitting there. Committed to letting the snow bury her in this icy tomb. Her heart and mind still burning with the remains of a secret. Of a secret shared with no one. No one except her own tragic self, and what the cruel, uncompromising spirits have allowed her to see. Allowed her to feel. Sitting down the road just a bit. Still able to feel the blonde laid atop the young girl, in the aftermath of trauma. The lust in her body at its peak. Holding the girl down, her lips clamped over the girl's breasts again. Full circle. With as much of the girl's soft, spongy breasts pulled into her big mouth as she can hold. Unable to release the sucking hold even once. Noticing that she need not move her groin. That the sucking at the girl's nipple is all it takes. The pressing of her groin upon the girl's leg in perfect stillness is all it takes. Knowing the powers that be are plugged in. Feeling something happen to her body that she never thought possible. Hearing her voice moan of its own volition. Hearing it tremble, as her body begins to shake. Riding the wave of trembling for many long seconds into her condemned future. Barely able to breathe. Barely able to see. Hearing the moan become gruff and hoarse. Finally having to unsuckle the girl's breast so she can breathe. So she can come to life again. Staring down at the dark areola. Fascinated by the stark contrast to the girl's fair skin around it. Staring at this nipple in awe. Reading it. Listening. Struggling to hear what message it entails. What encouragement. What admonishment. What warning.

The big blonde twitches again. Still staring at the breast of the young girl. Feeling the wet on the sheets. Feeling her body recover from the swooning. Resurrected from a touch of dying.

The brunette beauty looks on. Released by the spirits from the knowledge of secrets unknown. Released so that she can think. So she can reason.

Every muscle in her body tenses, when the tall, Nordic blonde steps out of the house. White jeans, white coat in place. A vision in full, snow bunny casual. Soon followed by the end-of-the-world eyes. Eyes of apocalyptic beauty. Eyes of eschatology.

The brunette watches the two of them come together in the snow. Walking leisurely together, down the snow covered concrete walkway to silver SUV luxury. The snow queen and the Pocahontas Girl. Together. Committed to one another in the snow.

The black Tundra comes to life down the road. Moving quickly across the icy space of what is meant to be. Rolling fast into the driveway behind the silver SUV. Blocking it in.

In the haze of a slow motion dream. The brunette beauty disembarks her rolling chariot in black. Every inch of herself enshrouded in this selfsame cloak of night. Every inch of her in black cloth from head to toe. Vesuvian breasts bound up for battle. Black turtleneck, black jeans, black high heel boots firmly in place, in league with the hair as black as pitch, eyes bewitched as gray as winter.

She steps in infinite knowledge. In complete purpose of being to the silver SUV, standing at the driver's side window. Watching the snow queen turn her head away from the Pocahontas Girl, to stare in self-important, judgmental disbelief. Her mind blown by the audacity of what she sees.

The brunette warrior watches the blonde's expression change, when she raises the *pistol* fashioned in black. Pointing it at the eyes of beauty.

Moving her finger upon the trigger, sliding it backward as across an eternity of waiting. Feeling the pistol jump in her hand. Seeing the window of the future break, as the blonde's head snaps backwards, then slumps over toward the steering wheel. A rhythm decorated by the cause of blood splattered, and the melody of a young girl screaming in terror.

From inside this hell, the young girl screams with the blood of her blonde queen splattered all over her face and white coat. Staring at the figure dressed in black, as it glides around the front of the SUV. Moving towards the passenger side window.

These are screams of clarity. Screams powered by the greatest fear known to man, as she watches the figure stop at her window and raise the pistol, pointing it at her face. At her eyes.

The brunette warrior feels the pistol jump in her hand again. Seeing another window to the future shattered and gone. Watching the girl's eyes take a turn to the grotesque, both gazing inward at the hole appeared in her forehead. Leaning back against the seat, her head slumping to the slide, blood splattered upon the snow queens matching white coat and hair.

The brunette beauty lowers the pistol. Gazing in the warriors satisfaction. Studying the canvas of her handiwork. Turning away, tossing the gun into the deep snow in the lawn. Knowing that it would likely never be found. Not caring one way or another.

The brunette beauty returns to her rolling chariot in black. Cranking it to life. Gliding it from the mansion driveway on Madison Elizabeth. Rolling casually through the streets of this town. Leaving the streets of White Mountain to be buried. To be frozen in a new field of falling ice and drifting snow.

Snow

These are the days of Noah, before the coming of the Son of Man.

As the snows come alive time and again, they drift down and around the hopeless and the dispossessed, grieving to give warning, but in mourning where none shall be given. The snows fall mightily on the Oklahoma prairie, to witness the Ward Dominique, when the itching in her brain catches fire—and every evil, every foul moment in her life coalesces into one need, and she coaxes her loving daughter from the safety of the father, to the middle of the open prairie on a walk, and she brandishes the blade under the new fallen snow, and she stabs Veronica in the shrieks and screaming of old and new, until her daughter lays dead on the white prairie floor. The snows witness her trembling, stumbling return to the only place of safety there exists—to the arms of her understanding, loving husband— who crumbles under the weight of blood and *"no,"* refusing to accept the blood on his wife's hands and the lifetime of guilt and blood on his own. He runs from the prairie house, by way of his wife's snowy footprints— following, howling them over the open ground, to where the still and bloody form of his beloved daughter lays. His mind sparks the image of his beautiful, short haired blonde wife in the pain of Insanity's Rage, unable to stop the turn of the blade, and its driving forward and back again. He lifts his daughter from the cold, and he takes her down the path of footprints in the snow, until the wife can bear witness to the sign—her husband on the floor in howling, masculine suffering, holding the body of the girl who cried for love, but received the shining blade of hatred and steel.

These are the Days of Noah, before the coming of the Son of Man.

Here, in the Seventh Year, since the days when the sky was blue, I see the snow drift to the grave of Linda Sue Hahn, in agony for a life passed so gingerly through, then so violently and tragically away. This, the soul and body of goodness, who flew to the far north country where we live, to bring happiness to our Prosperity, Vermont—and to the school where I was ten. Is there memory in every snowflake, that crosses the barriers through space and time? Is the farthest corner of Man's folly, buried in the genetics of every flake of snow, the record of every fool's errand, and every sin and evil that must come? Do these buried flakes of snow, at the Cemetery of the Southern Pine, do they likewise carry the record of what the tiny flurries from seven years ago saw and heard, whether the Asian teacher was taken to the suburban home of her lady principal, and paddled to bruises and blood? Is this memory engrained in these falling flakes of snow, of the phonecall placed to May Hahn in such broken weeping, and utterly devastated desperation, to beg forgiveness to her mother for every wrongdoing, to beg permission to return home to the loving arms of warmth and motherhood? Do these flakes of snow, seven years hence, cry for what was seen and heard, when May Hahn spoke the words:

"You had it coming... for what is deserved by a daughter who disobeys her mother... I told you that your steps are a curse, because you chose to leave, when I told you to stay—and now you cry to me, when the spirits punish you for what you asked them for? Deborah Lynn is my daughter now. You are not my daughter. You are a disgrace..."

Do the snows remember, as the tragic calm of uneasy acceptance washes over Linda Hahn's face, and she goes to the gunshop and buys the revolver? Do these snows remember me, when I sat in my 5th grade classroom, and watched the beautiful Asian woman drift in red Asian cloth, and put the revolver against her head and pull the trigger? Is the thunderous bang of the gun recorded in the piles of white ice and snow, that seek to cover the body of May Hahn over her daughter's grave—the cold, black steel in her hand, and the bloodstained headstone of Linda Sue Hahn?

These are the Days of Noah, before the coming of the Son of Man.

In the Seventh Year, these snows bear witness to the Woman of Straw—the big breasted beauty who was the devoted friend and wishful lover to Annabelle, who curiously rides the snowmobile alone—the one forged in blue and black fire—riding it to the front of her own palace seeking pills and a glass of wine. But she knows that for what she is, for what it is that she has done, there cannot be a peaceful sleeping away, so that the curse of it can be broken, and that maybe, her two living victims will have a small chance in the world. The snows bear witness to crimes and misdemeanors, to friends and lovers, to the high minded and the simple, to those who seek to know their path along this journey.

They see the Woman of Snow ride the machine down the main road in, through the gate and beyond, toward where the interstate highway lays waiting. She rides onto the highway overpass, to watch the cars and the trucks go by. And she leaves the machine abandoned, looking to the clouds in that Great Looking Away, seeing so far beyond this earthly plane, to the mind and presence of the Almighty God. In eyes of winter beauty, hair as the Raven's Fan, the Woman of Beauty walks slowly from the overpass, making her way past the snowy trees, to the busy highway below. And then she waits for the space to clear, the space between life and death. From the end of this cleared space on the highway, traffic renews again, led by the speeding, black 18 wheeled truck. She suppresses the smile, so appropriate, a smile so easily suppressed by fear. She waits. Hearing the black monster's roar grow louder. Staring at its eyes that shine—that have sought her out in the thousands of miles they have traveled, to devour her body in cold and blood. Cheryl senses the Reaper, feeling the skeleton image in her soul, counting herself lucky that the flames of Hell are not requisite, and she braves the warm tears in her eyes and upon her lovely face—then she steps onto the highway of lost hope at the moment of truth, turning into the blaring sound of screaming tires, which is Death, and the blaring of the horn, which is the Trump of God. Her body is slammed and whipped downward, pulled into the screaming path of rubber, down the length of their heavy, sliding and rolling until there is left of her body a limp, broken mass of bones and flesh on the highway, defiled time and time again by even the passing cars and the horrified drivers and passengers within, until one big white SUV goes screeching to the side to start the chain reaction, sending cars slip sliding, squalling and slamming into each other for a mile, then slowing and stopping traffic behind for seven miles more.

These are the Days of Noah, before the coming of the Son of Man.

As it is written, the evening day is deep twilight, nearby the edge of night. Somewhere beyond these clouds of grieving, there is still a sun that sets in the west, rolling beneath the western gate, in grieving for what tragedies have befallen the world underneath the clouds, and for those that are still yet to come.

Amanda and I languish at the barrier between day and night, on the edge of an apprehension difficult to bear. We have braved the strangeness of this particular day— through the chiming of every hour, from the morning where Cheryl's ghost haunted us with her bizarre absence, through the afternoon and into this snowy twilight. Hardly a half hour has gone by, where Amanda has not been pushing buttons on her phone, trying to find out where in the world it is that her new mother could have gone.

And I hesitate to include myself in this mysterious new psychology, which is truly the modern mother daughter dynamic unrestrained, where the maternal instinct here is born of a lustful craving, accompanied by an inexhaustible flow of grief and sorrow. In my heart, I know that what Cheryl has done to us is merely a fulfillment of prophecy; that there are no tragedies bestowed that are not common to man, and throughout this latter day earthen landscape, there is truly nothing new under the sun.

Belinda...

> *Had some unfinished business to take care of today. Hug and kiss your sister for me. I love you both with all my heart.*

> > *Cheryl*

And the ironic tragedy of this ridiculous note is that if it was intended to ease our minds, it only served to have the opposite effect, which has kept us both uneasy all day. Both of us cooking and eating since this morning, trying to shove the pain of Cheryl's unnatural absence down our throats with every swallow. We had even considered a trip around the neighborhood in the black and pink snowmobile, noticing that the blue one was missing since early this morning. If this 'unfinished business' of hers was just a ride around the neighborhood, then where is she now? She couldn't have gone far, could she? We were supposed to all take a ride to her house, then go for a drive in her new Tundra. In our driveway, her black SUV is as snowed in as it ever was, which we noticed this morning when we woke up. So she must be coming back soon, right?

And this is what we have told ourselves over and over all day, to try to escape the onset of fear and dread, which lurk in the shadows of every corner, threatening to reach out and grab us, and send terror through our blood like crystalline flakes of snow.

But in keeping with the spirit of latter day doom, we have lost the ability to feign happiness over Cheryl's odd disappearance, and we can only sit in front of a movie on television, with Amanda resting her head in my lap on the gray sofa, both of us enraptured by the brunette woman on the hill, strolling up behind her little brunette daughter at the well. And the two of us brave this apocalyptic shock, when the brunette woman wraps a black plastic bag over her daughter's head, suffocates her, and throws her daughter's body into the well of darkness down below.

In the wake of this endtime revelation, of the enmity placed between a mother and her daughter at the end of the age, we hear the doorbell chime, accompanied by the fearful knocking. Why is it so eternally true, that there is so much to fear, from a fateful knocking at the door?

Upon this current of relief and dread, we hurry to the door, wondering why Aunt Cheryl is bothering to knock, and why she has come back to us so close to the edge of night. She must have left the snowmobile at her house, is the thought that forms in the air around me, so she could walk through the drifting snowfall, and deal with the pain of her life's tragedy. I open the door, prepared to engage this snowy, bosomy hug even before Amanda, and kiss her full on the mouth, and thank the merciful God in Heaven for bringing her back to Amanda and me.

But when I open the door, I am greeted by the somber eyes of revelation. Those that concern the third part of the truth, which is cataclysm. These eyes of the municipal man in blue, that brown skinned, middle aged mustache man of compassion sent to us by Fate alone, steps inside our home, and relates the truth of what tragedies there are in the snow, and of what souls have been chosen to leave the suffering of this earthly plane behind, to find peace at the shores of Paradise, and a stroll through the meadows and flowering fields of Heaven.

Cheryl Ezman! Woman of straw! Mother of pain! Daughter of Fate! Thine was a soul of grief bestowed. A tragic reminder to all the spirits who gaze in judgment and sorrow, that the tragedy of human existence is Fate, and thine is a heart born east of Eden, of sins passed down from the mother of all living. Of these powers and principalities that tormented your mind and body, of what effect could you have against them? This was a mountain too high for thee, dear Cheryl, a valley where the shadows took hold of thee, and would not allow you to escape the pain of this life, nor the clawing hand of dark predestiny. Yours was a soul of goodness corrupted, my dearest Cheryl, where the seeds of innocence were planted in thy youth, but were choked by the weeds of depravity, born from the wickedness of those around you, who sought to destroy the purity of your childhood, and bury you in a coffin of deviance and sin. How could you fight these demonic spirits, Cheryl Ezman, that laid you awake at night in the agony of craving, to press upon you a hunger unfathomable—until you were as an addict in need of her fix, to poison you with this selfsame motherline drug passed down, until you knew before God of your dark calling! Of what commission you were given by birth! Thine was a soul of tragedy, dear Cheryl, a wayward spirit on a path chosen a thousand years before you were born, making you have to tremble and weep in prayer, until you understood that no, dear Cheryl, these prayers will *not* be answered for thee. And yes, my dear Cheryl, you *will* obey these dark spirits sent to torment thy flesh, until the mind of Eve is passed to a new generation, and the darkness which is man and womankind is sent to the end of the world.

Now rest, my new mother. Rest in the bosom of thy reward. To compensate thee for the pain you lived from birth, and for the pain that took your mind and body in death. Rest now, dearest Cheryl. Take hands with the one whose Star once shined in the skies above the evening, where our latter day Redemption draweth nigh. Rest easy now, dear Cheryl, in the paradise of knowing, that your new daughters will see you again in their fondest dreams, and know in their hearts where it is that their beloved mother could have gone.

I hold my sister tight, feeling her body shake from the energy of sobs and weeping. Unable to stop the onset of my own haze of vision, and the falling of a single tear from a soul of grief, and a well of eternal pain and sorrow.

Icy winds bear witness to the dying trees of November, when the Forest Moon remains hidden by the clouds, unable to see me turn eighteen years old, in the seventh year of snow. Earthquakes rumble the earth far and wide, and the snow blows day and night without ceasing, until whole neighborhoods have already been lost, and the delusional rest in uneasy hope and despair.

When I see through the huge bay window—and I see the rose Amanda stumbling behind the electric snow blowing machine, falling tiredly so flat on her face, I know that the ghosts that haunt us are too wide and deep in their power, and the future of Prosperity is delusion, despair and death.

We are lifted as snowflakes in the wind. Carried miles and years away from the Death of Prosperity. Vermont has faded into our fervent memories, from the hidden Forest Moon, and a Thanksgiving twenty years ago. The house in Prosperity stands empty now, barren, nearly buried. Frozen dark and lonely in the cold.

We pride ourselves among the fortunate—those who were called and chosen to live and regret, when the November quakes of that time became so severe as to begin knocking us off our feet, and rattling our mansion home to its foundation, as the winds did not cease to blow. I don't know if it was Faith or Fear, but every part of me understood that Vermont and all places North East were about to be made an example of, to reveal once and for all that these are the last days, before the coming of our Lord and Savior. As we departed our mother's earthly heaven, that had so soundly killed her heart in fear, we learned that we had missed by only a day, the surest sign of His coming. There was an earthquake, such as had never before been witnessed by the Northeast, shaking the Empire State to its foundations rural and urban, which so few heeded as the final warning, splitting from the frozen Great Lake Plains to icy Long Island Sound. Even while we escaped the highways south, there arose such a mighty wind, that a winter Dust Bowl descended from the clouds, gathering the powder from hundreds of miles across, to send walls of snow from Montreal to Montpelier, from Ottawa to Ohio, until parts of the whole North East above West Virginia looked like an Alaskan snowfield, with the occasional house and lonely forest grove visible, where millions were frozen inside a tomb sent by God.

These icy winds blow so far above and away from our flight to Egypt, from our trip through dawn and twilight, searching for Tomorrow's Home. It is here that we rest, twenty years and twenty five miles down east, away from the death of the woman of ice, and the ghost that haunts the buried Cross of Snow. This is our new paradise, our new November's retreat. The small house in Martin County, North Carolina my father never sold, in a place called Williamston. Down east, where the land was once colored by the trees and cropfields, now all gently covered in the Field of White. These twenty years, these many miles have faded much of the pain we knew and understood, so that it hardly plagues the theater of our minds anymore. Pain buried somewhere north, somewhere in the heart of memory, in the place where our beloved mother has come and gone.

Our little southern Thanksgiving feast is prepared, and it awaits our rendezvous in the kitchen. But now, we stand in the front yard of our new home beneath the Autumn skies of gray—and we hold hands as we stare at the power of Almighty God, glowing through a small break in the clouds, shining a ray of hope for us to see, and a beam of light that climbs from Earth to Heaven.

ABOUT THE AUTHOR

Jonathan Michael Lovejoy is a graduate of the University of North Carolina at Greensboro, with a B.A. in Religious Studies, and a graduate of Liberty University with an M.A. in Theological Studies. He currently lives in Winston Salem, North Carolina.

For more info on the author's life and career, visit jonathanlovejoy.com